"AWAY BOARDERS"

"AWAY BOARDERS"

by Daniel V. Gallery

W · W · NORTON & COMPANY · INC · New York

To
Career Sailormen

Contents

"AWAY BOARDERS"

Fatso

IN THE crew's quarters of LCU 1124, at sea in the Mediterranean, an acey-deucy game was in progress. Acey-deucy is the Navy version of backgammon and has been a popular game aboard ship since the days of sail. It is about 90 percent luck and 10 percent skill. Tradition says that John Paul Jones was the first all-Navy champ at it, and that he claimed his opponents were all shot full of luck, whereas he played a scientific game. Every sailor since Jones's time has claimed the all-Navy title at one time or another and has made similar statements about his own and his opponents' games.

This game was between Jughaid Jordan and Izzy Ginsberg. It was the final game of a tourney for the ship's championship and was being watched with interest by the rest of the crew, including John Patrick Gioninni, BM 1c, skipper of LCU 1124. A good-sized pot of money depended on this game, as well as many side bets by kibitzers. The game had reached the stage where the next two or three rolls would decide it.

Jughaid surveyed the board, rattled the dice box, spoke to the bones, and threw them out on the table. Up popped an ace and a deuce.

"Acey-deucy! . . . the name of the game!" exclaimed Jughaid.

This roll entitled him to move one square with one man, two with another, to take any pair of doubles he wanted, and to get another roll. It practically put the game on ice for him.

"*Shit*," observed Ginsberg.

"Watch your language, kid," said Cap'n Fatso. "There's sailors present."

The sailors present were an improbable crew of fugitives from the draft. They could have served with distinction under Captain Kidd. First of all there was the skipper, Gioninni, known throughout the Sixth Fleet as Fatso. Fatso, a veteran of World War II and Korea, was nearing the end of a long and more or less faithful naval career. It had been very faithful indeed whenever bombs and torpedoes were exploding around him, but no more faithful than necessary in peacetime. He had swum away from three ships that got sunk under him in World War II, and had won two Navy Crosses. He figured he was now living on borrowed time and proposed to live the full life until the loan was called.

Fatso was one of those all-round old-time sailor men who are fast disappearing from the modern mechanized Navy. If you needed somebody to run the fo'c'sle while making a flying moor on a battleship, or to secure the hanger deck for heavy weather, or to lower a boat in a rough sea, Fatso was your man. He was thoroughly familiar with all the tricks of wind and wave, in calms and in storms, and all the younger members of his crew figured he must have served as an apprentice boy with Noah in the ark.

Fatso was thoroughly familiar with the U.S. Navy regulations and observed them meticulously, whenever his conduct came under the direct scrutiny of the high command. But he knew, of course, that the regulations were written for the guidance of those unfortunates who wouldn't know what to do if it wasn't all written down for them in a book. They were not intended to be taken literally by old-timers like himself. As far as Fatso was concerned, the regulations required him to be ready at all times to defend the United States at sea, and to do whatever the tactical situation in the heat of battle demanded, in his best judgment, to assist the United States and embarrass the enemy. But outside of that they were very flexible and depended on the exact situation which prevailed at the time.

Fatso's interpretation of the regulations was sometimes questioned by narrow-minded junior officers who lived by the letter rather than the spirit of the book. But, whenever this happened and he was called to account by higher authority, Fatso would simply put on his dress blues with four rows of campaign ribbons and two Navy Crosses on his chest. The Admiral would always find it hard to believe his accusers.

As Jughaid was trying to make up his mind what doubles he wanted to take for his acey-deucy roll, a hail came down over the voice tube from the bridge: "Sail ho!"

"Where away?" called Fatso back up the tube.

"Broad on the port bow," came the reply.

"Can you make her out?" called Fatso, following the time-honored ritual for answering a lookout's hail.

"It's a Russian cruiser," was the reply.

"Well—here we go again," said Fatso. "We'll probably have another chicken game with this guy." He got up from the table and went out to the bridge.

There was a Russian cruiser, her upper works just coming over the horizon broad on the port bow, crossing his course at right angles. The chicken game that Fatso referred to results from the fact that in a crossing situation the Russians pay no attention whatever to the rules of the road. When the Russian has the right of way, this presents no problem. You simply maneuver to keep out of his way and pass astern of him. But, when you have the right of way, it can result in a sticky situation. The rules of the road say that the ship having the right of way *must* hold its course and speed unless danger of collision "becomes imminent."

So, if you have the right of way and the other fellow does not maneuver to avoid collision, it puts you on the spot. You are required to hold on until danger of collision becomes imminent. If you change course or speed too soon and a collision results, the court will hold you to blame. If you wait a little too long and get sunk, it will be small consolation to have the court find you were not to blame. This results in a situation where the ship that does not have the right of way can play a chicken game with the ship that does by just holding its course and speed until the last possible minute. From experience, Fatso knew that the Russians played this game with our ships all the time. In this case, he had the Russian on his port hand. So he was required to hold his course and speed and let the Russian go astern of him.

Fatso watched the Russian for several minutes while her superstructure and hull came up over the horizon. Her bearing from him did not change, showing that if both held their present course and speed there would be a collision.

"I'm going to see how far this guy will go this time," said Fatso to Satchmo, who had the wheel. "If we have to, we can always turn sharp enough to make him miss us, even when it's too late for him to do it."

"Aye aye, Cap'n," said Satchmo.

The Russian was loafing along at twelve knots, the same speed as LCU 1124.

"Look at all them radar antennas they got topside," observed Satchmo. "I've never seen so many on one ship before."

"Yeah," said Fatso. "Those are their missile-guidance radars. They got anti-aircraft missiles that are damned good. They're giving us a bad time with them out in Vietnam. You can see their missile mounts now, one forward and one aft."

"Are those like our Polaris missiles, Cap'n?" asked Satchmo.

"No. These are anti-aircraft missiles. They got a target-seeking gismo that homes them right in on a plane. That's what they used to knock down our U-2 plane over Siberia a few of years ago—remember?"

"Yes sir," said Satchmo. "That was Garry Powers' plane."

When the Russian got in to about a mile Fatso said, "Give him a blast on your whistle. One long blast."

Satchmo pulled the whistle cord and let out a blast. This signal indicates that the ship making it intends to hold her course and speed and cross ahead. The other ship is supposed to answer with one blast, meaning she understands and will pass astern. No reply from the Russian.

When the range got down to half a mile, Fatso had Satch sound another blast. Still no answer. Fatso took station at the pelorus on the port wing of the bridge, watching the bearing of the Russian carefully. It was not changing.

"All right, Satch," said Fatso. "I've got the conn now. Steady as you go. Be ready to work fast if I tell you to."

"Aye aye, Cap'n," said Satchmo. "Steady on course 180."

They were rapidly approaching a situation now where one or the other had to do something or there would be a collision. Fatso could afford to hold on a little longer than the Russian because his ship was smaller, handier, and could turn shorter. This advantage was, however, somewhat outweighed by the fact that if he held on too long he would probably get sunk, whereas the Russian would wind up with a small dent in his bow.

Fatso held on as long as he dared. He was just about to order Satch to put his rudder hard right when puffs of steam came out of the Russian's whistle as it issued a series of sharp blasts. This is the danger signal under the international rules of the road and means that the ship making it is taking emergency action. Fatso glanced quickly at her stern and saw the water being churned into great white swirls as her screws began going full astern. The Russian's bearing began drawing aft very slowly. Fatso held his course and speed.

By now the Russian was beginning to tower over LCU 1124. Black smoke was pouring out of both her stacks as the engineers threw the astern throttles wide open and the fire rooms struggled to keep up the steam pressure. Fatso still had time to throw his rudder hard over and make the ships miss. If he didn't—it would be mighty close.

But Fatso had his pelorus on the Russian's bow and decided it was going to miss his stern by about six feet. He held on. Several heads popped out on the level below him, looking up at the Russian in grave concern.

"Pay no attention to that guy," yelled Fatso at the spectators. "Just go on about your business as if nothing was happening."

The flare of the cruiser's bow now came between Fatso and the cruiser's bridge. "He can't see us now," declared Fatso to Satch. "So far as he knows, he's going to hit us."

"Yassah, Cap'n," said the wide-eyed Satch, who evidently agreed with the Russian.

The cruiser's bow, visibly shaking from the engines going full astern, swept past Fatso and missed the stern by about ten feet. Fatso still insists that he passed under the jack staff on the cruiser's clipper bow. LCU 1124 continued on course south, speed 12, as if she had the whole ocean to herself.

As LCU 1124 emerged to view from the cruiser's bridge on the port side, the commotion back at the stern around the screws stopped, a light started blinking on the bridge, and her yardarm suddenly was full of signal flags. Jughaid jumped to the signal light to answer the Russian but Fatso yelled at him, 'Pay no attention to him—just ignore the son of a bitch."

In a few minutes the Russian stopped blinking, kicked his engines ahead, and proceeded on his way. As he was dropping over the horizon, Fatso remarked to the boys on deck, "I'll bet that Russian skipper is down in his cabin now, putting on a clean pair of drawers."

LCU 1124 was a unique craft of the Sixth Fleet. Although presently on detached duty, she was not actually a commissioned ship of the U.S. Navy. She was a ship's boat, belonging to a landing ship dock, the USS *Alamo*. But she was the granddaddy of all ships' boats, a bargelike craft, 110 feet long, with a 25-foot beam, and displacing 200 tons.

Ordinarily she was carried around inside the well deck of the *Alamo*, which housed a number of smaller amphibious craft. For landing, the *Alamo* would flood her well deck, open the huge stern gate, and these smaller craft would swim out and take the marines and their gear in to the beach. All of these craft run right up on the beach and lower ramps over which the marines swarm ashore.

LCU 1124 was designed to carry the larger pieces of equipment that the marines like to take along when they go ashore to spread peace and good will, such as halftracks, tanks, and artillery pieces. She was a flat-bottomed craft powered by twin diesel engines. The whole forward part of the craft was storage space, with a ramp in the bow which was let down after beaching. The crew's quarters, engine room, and pilot house were in a structure aft. The crew's quarters consisted of the messroom, bunkroom, lounge, and galley. These were all in one compartment aft, running across the whole beam of the ship. The pilot house was on the level above this, and the engine room on the deck below. There were folding bunks along the sides of the crew's quarters, a mess table in the center, and the galley at one end. At the other end were the radio and TV sets and the Captain's cabin. This latter facility was just an oversized swab locker with a bunk, washstand, and small desk. But it did provide Fatso with the privacy which is traditional for the captain of a combat ship. Outside on the well deck were the head and washroom.

Although LCU 1124 belonged to the *Alamo*, which carried her pay accounts and records, she actually spent little time on board the larger ship. Except when engaged in landing exercises she spent most of her time on detached duty, hauling odd bits of freight around the Med and delivering it to the ships of the Sixth Fleet and outlying shore stations. She was practically an independent command on detached duty, which was the reason why Fatso had gone to considerable lengths to get assigned to her. It had always been his ambition to command a Navy ship. Command of a commissioned ship is of course beyond the reach of an enlisted man. But command of LCU 1124 was the next thing to it.

Fatso's second in command, and the only other old-timer aboard, was Scuttlebutt Grogan, Machinist's Mate 1c. He and Fatso had been shipmates in the war against the Japs and also in various wars with the MP's and Shore Patrol on all the waterfronts of the world. Scuttlebutt was chief engineer of this craft, and was one of those engineers who can tell what his machinery is doing just as well while sitting in the messroom as he can down below looking at the gauges. Any change in the rhythm of vibrations from his engines alerted him, just as a little squiggle on a seismometer tells a scientist all about a small earthquake taking place a thousand miles away. Between him and Fatso they had all the skills necessary to take a ship anywhere in the world in fair weather or in foul. That is, they did until the Navy started filling up the ships with computers and black boxes.

To take care of the electronics equipment on board they had "Professor" Henry Cabot Worthington. The Professor was a spoiled brat from a prominent New England family. He was a dropout from school—from the second year of a post-graduate course in atomic physics at MIT, where he had been a brilliant student. But he had got into a hassle with his old man about a chorus gal they were both chasing and had simply walked out and joined the Navy. The Professor handled all scientific questions that came up on LCU 1124.

Another college dropout in the crew was "Judge" Frawley. The Judge had been a student at Columbia Law School and one of the leaders of his class. However, when certain of his extra curricular activities had come to light, he decided to drop out—or more accurately, to bug out, hotly pursued by the faculty and the cops —and join the Navy. Naturally the Judge was the legal officer on board LCU 1124.

Jughaid Jordan was a dropout from an earlier stage of the educational system. A hillbilly from Tennessee, he had dropped out of the sixth grade to help his pappy run his still. When the revenooers cracked down and put his pappy in jail, Jughaid lied a little bit about his age and joined the Navy.

Webfoot Foley was their ordnance expert. He had been kicked out of the paratroopers and the Underwater Demolition Team because they claimed he took unnecessary chances. Webfoot claimed, with some justification, that anyone who joined either one of those outfits was taking an unnecessary chance. But Webfoot was an expert frogman who could handle all forms of explosives with great skill. His shipmates claimed that he had acquired this skill by working as an apprentice safecracker before joining the Navy. Webfoot denied this.

Izzy Ginsberg was a former newspaper photographer from Brooklyn. Izzy had the distinction of being the only man ever kicked out of the photographers union for violating professional ethics. By various outrageous subterfuges he had managed to get a lot of sensational, exclusive pictures. This made the other photographers look bad, so they had him kicked out of the union and he joined the Navy. Izzy was the expert commentator on board on the Arab-Israeli conflict.

The final member of the crew was Satchmo Page, Stewards Mate 2c, and the only one aboard outside of Fatso and Scuttlebutt who was on his second cruise. Satchmo was one of our disadvantaged citizens. On a dark night he would loom up in a blacked-out clothes closet as a dark spot. Satchmo blew a hot trumpet and could easily have made a good living on the outside playing in a name band, or as a chef at the Waldorf, for that matter. But Satch liked the Navy, would soon be making first class, and was figuring on making a career of it.

All these men, despite their widely different backgrounds, had one thing in common. They were all adventurous spirits whose outlook on life was the same as Fatso's. They could all engage in enterprises which can be severely punished under military law and at the same time give the outward appearance of being Boy Scouts who are helping old ladies to cross the street. Men who possess the initiative and strength of character to do this naturally gravitate to positions of responsibility and trust in the military service, and these men were being well fitted for such positions by service under Fatso's command.

After dinner that evening, the boys gathered around the radio to listen to the news of the world. At this time, early in 1970, peace and good will reigned throughout the world, except in Vietnam, most parts of Africa, the Russo-Chinese border, and on the college campuses of the U.S.A. In the U.S. we maintained law and order by allowing the students to take over the college administration buildings, beat up the deans, run the Marine recruiters off the campus, and burn down the ROTC buildings. Elsewhere in the world, whenever an international crisis arose, the UN promptly passed a resolution urging both sides to be calm, and then went back to its main job of trying to wangle enough dough out of the U.S. to pay its bills.

Of course the Arabs and Israelis were not getting along very well together, either. Every day, each side made commando raids into the other's territory in retaliation for what the other side had done the day before, and Cairo and Jerusalem issued abusive statements about each other.

Presently the radio news came on: "Cairo: Egypt announced today that two hundred innocent women and children were killed yesterday by Israeli bombs dropped on the outskirts of Cairo. President Nasser said the attack was unprovoked and that retaliation would be swift and deadly."

"Holy cow," said the Judge. "It looks like the Arab-Israeli War is about to heat up again."

"It's a damn lie," said Ginsberg. "The Israelis only attack military objectives. They probably shot up an Arab airfield."

"How the hell can you mistake a suburban area for an airfield?" demanded the Judge. "It was probably some trigger-happy fly boy like the ones who shot up the *Liberty*."

The radio continued: "Switzerland: A jet airliner bound for Israel exploded and crashed shortly after take-off today. All eighty-five on board were killed. Arab saboteurs in Berne claimed they had planted a bomb on board the stricken plane."

"There," said Ginsberg. "You see what kind of sneaking animals these Arabs are?"

"But they only killed eighty-five," observed the Judge. "The Israelis killed two hundred."

"Nuts," said Ginsberg. "Them Arabs are all pigs. We're going to have to wipe 'em out—every one of them."

"Vietnam. U.S. forces advancing in Cambodia captured a huge enemy base yesterday with vast quantities of arms, ammunition, and food. The U.S. high command announced that the Cambodian operation is a huge success so far and is proceeding on schedule."

"Maybe that will shut some of the doves up for a while," observed Fatso.

"Washington, D.C.," continued the radio. "A group of five thousand agitators marched down Pennsylvania Avenue to protest extending the war into Cambodia. They carried Viet Cong flags, tore down and burned the U.S. flag at the State Department, hurled rocks and stink bombs into the offices, and shouted obscenities at the police. The police exercised great restraint but finally had to use tear gas to prevent the demonstrators from storming the building. Ten policemen were hospitalized, three in serious condition. The mayor issued a statement afterward praising the conduct of the police and saying that their expert handling of the demonstration prevented it from becoming a major disorder. Five of the demonstrators were arrested and charged with loitering."

"Good Gawd Almighty," said Fatso.

"Five of 'em charged with loitering," observed Scuttlebutt. "I'll bet that will be a lesson to them."

"In Vietnam we shoot anybody with a Viet Cong flag," observed Webfoot.

"They tore down our flag and burned it," said Jughaid. "If anybody's got a constitutional right to do that, then you can have the Constitution, so far as I'm concerned."

"Pretty soon we'll be getting those kind of people aboard ship," observed the Judge. "I see where they got underground groups of protestors in the Army now. They grow long hair, publish dirty newspapers, and they're even claiming the right to organize a soldiers and sailors union, now."

"Boy, won't that be something," said Scuttlebutt. "The skipper says, 'No liberty tomorrow,' so the crew goes on a sitdown strike and pickets his cabin."

"I'd just like to see one of those dirty longhairs come aboard here," observed Fatso. "I'll give him something to protest about."

CHAPTER TWO

Malta

NEXT MORNING LCU 1124 entered the harbor of Valletta, Malta, where the U.S. had a small supply base. Making their way past the medieval entrance forts, they wended their way through the fishing boats of the harbor and up to the dock assigned them by the signal station at the entrance. As they approached the dock, Fatso said to Jughaid, who had the wheel, "Okay, Jughaid. She's all yours. Take her alongside."

Jughaid idled his engines and looked the situation over. It was going to be tricky tying up in the spot assigned to them. They had to squeeze into a space about 115 feet long between the stern of a British cruiser and the bow of a big oil tanker. This might take a little backing and filling, because LCU 1124 was 110 feet long.

"How do you want me to make it, Cap'n," asked Jughaid, "port side to or starboard?"

"Suit yourself," said Fatso.

Jughaid kicked her ahead slowly, pulled up alongside his berth about fifty yards offshore, and then swung in and headed directly for the dock. He came in just missing the bow of the tanker on his starboard side with about ninety feet of open water between his port side and the stern of the cruiser. He stopped his engines and coasted in till his bow almost touched the dock at right angles to it. Then he yelled at Satchmo up in the bow, "Okay, Satch—get your bowline out."

Satchmo tossed a heaving line to two British sailors on the dock. They took in the heaving line hand over hand with the bowline attached to it and threw the bowline over a ballard on the dock. Scuttlebutt took a strain with the forward winch till the bow was touching the dock. There was about a two-knot tide running, which swung the stern to port and carried LCU 1124 right in toward her berth. With a little help from the engines at the last, Jughaid warped the ship right into her assigned spot, port side to, about two and a half feet to spare, bow and stern.

During this maneuver, Fatso had been leaning on the rail apparently paying no attention to what was going on and saying nothing. As the last line went ashore Jughaid called over to him, "All tied up, Cap'n. Permission to secure the engines?"

"Okay," said Fatso. "Nice landing," and went below.

This was indeed high praise from Fatso, who belonged to the Ernie King school. His theory was: Don't expect a medal for doing a good job. That's what you get paid for. So just those two words coming from Fatso, "Nice landing," were very high praise indeed.

Shortly after tying up, Fatso went ashore to check in with the chief in the supply office. Fatso and the chief were old friends from way back. As the chief busied himself at the coffee urn Fatso asked, "Well, what's been going on around here since the last time we were in?"

"Apt-solutely nothing," said the chief. "Not a gahdamn thing."

"Well, it all counts on twenty," said Fatso. "Just the same as if you were on the firing line at Yankee Station. What have you got for me this time?"

"A couple of shipments of diplomats' liquor," said the chief. "One goes to Tel Aviv and the other to Athens."

"Okay," said Fatso. "We'll take care of it."

"We're transferring a man to you, too," said the chief. "He's a new kid we haven't any place for here. Maybe you can use him."

"Okay," said Fatso. "We'll put him to work."

While Fatso was ashore, a queer-looking figure came trudging down the dock with a sea bag over its shoulder and a guitar under its arm. It looked like an American sailor, except it had shoulder-length hair and a heavy black beard. The figure boarded LCU 1124 and found its way aft to the messroom, where an acey-deucy game was in progress.

The Professor was about to roll the dice when the figure entered the messroom, set his sea bag down on deck and took off his hat.

The Professor stopped rattling the dice box, his jaw dropped, and finally he said, "Jeezus Keeriste."

"It looks a little bit like Him, at that," said the Judge. "But I don't think it really is."

"Hi ya, fellas," said the figure.

All hands gaped at the newcomer in astonishment and no one replied to the greeting. Finally the Professor said, "Are you looking for somebody on here?"

"I guess so," said the figure. "Or maybe you're looking for me. I got orders to report to this bucket for duty."

All hands focused their attention on the newcomer and for a moment no one spoke. Finally Ginsberg said, "Hell—it's got to be a gag. He's wearing a wig and a false beard."

"Well, who do I report to?" demanded the figure. "I got a set of orders here that says proceed and report to LCU 1124 for duty."

This was the first time a situation like this had come up. Usually LCU 1124 got its personnel from the crew of the mother ship, the USS *Alamo*. They were all hand-picked by Fatso and there was always a quite a list of young hopefuls waiting for a vacancy to occur.

"Lemme see those orders," said Scuttlebutt. He studied the paper for a moment, noted it was signed by the CO of the naval station, Malta, and then said, "You'll have to see the skipper about this. He's ashore now. But he'll be back pretty soon. . . . Have a seat."

The newcomer took a seat at the table and the others all studied him in open-mouthed amazement. Finally one of them said, "What's your pitch, sailor?"

"How do you mean?" asked the newcomer.

"I mean you must be for—or against—something. What is it?"

"Well, I'm against the Establishment, naturally," said the newcomer.

"Whaddya mean, the Establishment?" demanded the Judge.

"I mean the 'ins'—you know. The military-industrial complex and the international bankers. The politicians and, you know, the cops."

"How about the college professors?" asked the Judge.

"Some of them belong to the Establishment, too. But most of them are on our side."

"Whaddya mean, *our* side?" demanded Scuttlebutt.

"I mean the oppressed minority, you know, like you and me. People whose constitutional rights are denied them by the Establishment, you know."

"How the hell did you get in the Navy?" demanded Scuttlebutt.

"Oh, I volunteered," said the figure.

"Volunteered for gawd's sake," said Izzy incredulously. "You must of been higher than a kite on pot—or maybe having a bad trip on LSD—when you did that."

"No. They tried to draft me for the Army. But I outsmarted them, and joined the Navy."

"The guy does have some sense at that," conceded Scuttlebutt.

"How come you let your hair grow that way?" asked Jughaid. "Don't they have no personnel inspections up here at Malta?"

"Yeah. They have them. They kept telling me to get my hair cut. But I didn't want to."

"They must run a funny Navy here at Malta," observed Scuttlebutt. "You better get a haircut before our skipper sees you."

"Oh—he'll get used to it," said the newcomer.

Soon after this, Fatso returned aboard. As he sat down at the head of the table and called for a cup of coffee, his glance fell on the newcomer. He did a double take and his jaw dropped. Finally he turned to Scuttlebutt and said, "Who's your long-haired friend?"

"New man. Just reported aboard for duty, Cap'n," said Scuttlebutt, handing Fatso the orders.

Fatso studied the orders and noted they were in proper form and duly signed by the skipper of the naval base. "Well," he said, "it looks like we'll have to move over and make room for Seaman Adams here. We've got a spare bunk and locker, haven't we?" he asked of Scuttlebutt.

"Yes sir, Cap'n," said Scuttlebutt. "No trouble about a bunk and locker."

"How long you been in this Navy, son?" asked Fatso.

"Six months, skipper," replied Adams. "Three months in boot camp and three here at Malta."

"When was the last time you had a haircut?" asked Fatso.

"Back in boot camp," said Adams.

"Hunh!" said Fatso. "Didn't they ever tell you to get one in Malta?"

"Well, yes, they did. But I didn't think I needed it."

"Oh, I see," said Fatso. "Well, you need one now."

"Uh huh," said Adams, dubiously.

"Are your clippers working okay, Webfoot?" asked Fatso.

Webfoot, among his other duties, was ship's barber. "Yes sir, Cap'n," said Webfoot. "They sure are."

"Then break them out," said Fatso, "and trim Seaman Adams' hair a bit."

"Aye aye, Cap'n. Can do," said Webfoot. He went over to his locker, got out an electric hair clipper, plugged it in and said to Adams, "How long do you want it on top?"

Adams squirmed uncomfortably and said, "Buzz off, mister. I don't want a haircut."

"Oh, yes you do," said Webfoot, as four of the boys got up from the table and took station, two on each side of Adams.

As Webfoot approached with his clippers, Adams started to get up, but was seized and restrained by the four.

"Hey, what the hell's coming off?" yelled Adams, as he struggled to get loose.

"Some of them flowing locks of yours are coming off, pal," said Ginsberg, as Adams found himself unable to move. He struggled briefly, saw that he was helpless, and then yelled at Fatso, "You mean to say you're going to give me a haircut whether I want it or not? You mean to say I got nothing to say about this?"

"No indeed," said Fatso, "you got a constitutional right to free speech. You can say any damn thing you want to. But you'll get your hair cut just the same."

Webfoot began to apply the clippers and cut a swatch across the top of his head clear down to the scalp. Adams struggled a bit at first, but soon found it was useless, stopped struggling, and submitted. In a short space of time his flowing locks were shorn and his head was as bare as a billiard ball.

"How about his whiskers, Cap'n?" asked Webfoot, brandishing the clippers.

"No-o-o," said Fatso. "Let him keep them for a while."

Adams ran his hand over his bald pate and looked ruefully at his shorn locks lying on deck. "You got no right to do that," he said to Fatso.

"We gotta do it," said Fatso. "We got a ship's order, put out by the Captain of this bucket, saying that hair shall be neatly trimmed. So there isn't a thing we can do about it."

"It's illegal," declared Adams. "You got no right to put out such an order. That was assault and battery, what they just did."

"Judge Frawley here is our legal expert," said Fatso. "How about it, Judge? What do you say about that?"

"It's what we lawyers call a moot point," said the Judge. "The Supreme Court hasn't ruled on it yet. So, until they do, you gotta get a haircut. But you got a right to complain about it."

"Yeah," said Webfoot. "Just as soon as we get to Naples, you can go around and see the senior chaplain there. He'll give you a sympathy chit and the key to the weep locker."

"That's a hell of a way to run a Navy in a democratic country," declared Adams.

"Well, lemme explain to you how we run this ship," said Fatso. "Whenever any question comes up about what we're going to do, we take a vote on it. Everybody has one vote—one man, one vote, just like the Supreme Court says. That is, all except the Captain have one vote. He has one more vote than all the rest. So that way there can never be a tie vote, and we always know what to do."

Adams continued to feel his head, and said nothing.

"So-o-o," said Fatso to Scuttlebutt, "you assign Seaman Adams a bunk and a locker, and put him on the watch list." Fatso got up from the table and went to his cabin.

Next morning just before they got underway from Malta, a civilian technician came aboard with half a dozen big black suitcases. "Jenkins," he said, reporting to Fatso. "I'm with the CIA. I've got some special gear here to deliver to the *America*."

"Okay," said Fatso. "We can take care of it for you. Any special instructions about it?"

"No," said Jenkins. "It's electronic equipment—and I'm going along with it."

"Oh. Okay," said Fatso. "This ain't exactly a luxury liner we got here. It will be some time before we join up with *America*. But we can give you a bunk and a place at the table."

"That's all I want," said Jenkins. "And a place to put these suitcases out of the weather."

"Bring 'em right in here," said Fatso, "and stick 'em up over there in the corner."

⚓ CHAPTER THREE

USS *America*

WHILE THESE THINGS were going on on board LCU 1124, the rest
of the Sixth Fleet was about its business of maintaining control
of the seas and spreading peace and good will throughout the
Mediterranean. To do this, the fleet is organized into task forces.
The spearhead of the fleet is the Striking Force, which consists of
several carriers, cruisers, and a couple of dozen destroyers. This
group ranges through the Med from Gib to Istanbul, conducting
exercises at sea and visiting places where the sight of its ships
in the harbor may stiffen the backbones of our NATO allies. This
is the arm of the fleet which makes our foreign policy effective
and adds weight to the words of our diplomats. Its carriers have
planes which can deliver atom bombs to a range of two thousand
miles and blast a large city off the face of the earth.

Another major element of the fleet is the Amphibious Force, to
which LCU 1124 belonged. This element consists of a marine bat-
talion embarked in various ships which carry an array of smaller
landing craft capable of beaching themselves. In case any small
countries around the Med take any ill-advised action, these leather-
necks are always ready to appear offshore, land, beat the hell out
of the local inhabitants, and restore peace and good will.

The third element of the fleet is the Service Force. This consists of oilers, supply ships, and ammunition carriers. It has peri-
odic rendezvous at sea with the striking and amphibious forces
and supplies them with beans, bullets, oil, antistink lotion, and
everything else required to keep the peace.

The Sixth Fleet has no fixed base in the Med. The Service Force,
which shuttles back and forth from the U.S., provides the fleet

with a mobile base whose status cannot be jeopardized by local upheavals and revolutions, which are S.O.P. these days, especially in North Africa.

Command of this fleet was vested in Vice Admiral Hughes, who flew his flag in the cruiser *Milwaukee*. A high-powered radio network including satellite relays kept him in constant touch with the Commander in Chief of U.S. Naval Forces, Europe, in London, and C. in C. Allied Forces Southern Europe in Naples. By means of satellite relays, the Pentagon could bypass the normal chain of command and issue orders to him by scrambler phones, which upset carefully arranged military applecarts throughout his bailiwick.

The Striking Force was currently at sea just west of Malta. On board the attack carrier *America*, Rear Admiral Mason was being briefed. Seated in front of a large vertical chart of the Med in Flag Plot were the Admiral, his chief of staff, and operations officers. On the bulkheads around them were displays showing the state of readiness of all their ships and planes and the ships of all other navies in the Med, the current weather map, and many other items of interest. In the rear of the compartment was the coffee urn, presided over by the Admiral's messboy.

An aide, pointer in hand, was filling the Admiral in on the latest flashes from hot spots around the Med. "The Israeli government has just announced that the bombing of Cairo in which those civilians were killed was a mistake due to a mechanical failure in one of their aircraft. To show their good faith in this matter, they have just advised the Egyptian government that among the bombs dropped was one five-hundred pounder with a twenty-four hour delay fuse. They have advised the Egyptians that this bomb should be defused immediately."

"Well—that's very thoughtful and neighborly of them," commented the Admiral.

"Cairo has announced," continued the aide, "that Russian SAM missiles are now being installed around Cairo and at nearby airfields. Russian technicians are advising the Egyptians on these installations and are assisting in training missile crews."

"Those are the same missiles that have been knocking down our planes in Vietnam, aren't they?" asked the Admiral.

"Yes sir. And several of the latest Russian ships to arrive in the Med have them, too."

"What do we know about these missiles?" asked the Admiral.

"They are radar-controlled beam riders," said the aide. "They have about a forty-mile range and follow a radar beam until they get about ten miles from the target. Then they send out their own radar signals and home on them. They have an influence fuse and are a very effective anti-aircraft weapon."

At this point another aide interrupted and held out a telephone on an extension cord to the Admiral. "We've got a call via satellite on the scrambler phone from the Pentagon, Admiral," he said. "Assistant Under Secretary for Defense Morgan wants to speak to you."

"Well, here we go again on some goddamn crackpot project," said the Admiral, as he took the phone. "Admiral Mason speaking," he said.

"Good morning, Admiral," said a voice. "This is Under Secretary of Defense Morgan calling."

"Yes sir," said the Admiral.

"How are things going out there, Admiral?" asked the Under Secretary.

"The situation is under control, sir. Everything is just about normal," said the Admiral.

"Admiral," said the Under Secretary, "I'm calling about a reconnaissance flight we would like to have you make over Cairo."

"Er . . . yessir," said the Admiral.

"We want you to fly at forty-five thousand feet over the city and get us some high-definition photographs. We are interested in their air defenses around the city."

"They've got Russian SAM missiles there now, you know, Mr. Secretary," said the Admiral. "They have shot down several of our planes at forty thousand feet in Korea with them."

"Yes. I know that. But we don't think their missiles are operational yet," said the Under Secretary.

"Well, Mr. Secretary," said the Admiral, "we can do it if we have to. I assume you will take this up through the regular chain of command and that I'll get orders for this from my boss, Commander Sixth Fleet?"

"Well, I hadn't figured on doing it that way. I thought this phone call would be enough. But I can do it that way if that's what you want," said the Secretary.

"Yes sir, Mr. Secretary," said the Admiral. "I prefer it that way."

"Okay. Over and out," said the Secretary.

The Admiral handed the phone back to his aide and said to the chief of staff, "Every Under Secretary of Defense seems to think he is a commander in chief. That's the third time this month I've had to tell one what the chain of command in this fleet is."

"What did he want, sir?" asked the COS.

"Just a photo flight over Cairo," said the Admiral. "A fine chance to get a plane knocked down and have a nasty international incident on our hands. Those goddamn bureaucrats are a menace to the national defense. . . . Now—where were we when we were interrupted?"

"We were talking about the SAM's around Cairo," said the aide. "Russian technicians are installing them and will train the Egyptians in how to use them."

"Meantime, didn't we get good pictures of them installed on that new cruiser that just came out of the Black Sea? Much better than you can get from forty thousand feet?"

"Yes sir," said the aide. "One of our destroyers got real good closeups of them the other day. We've sent them to Washington."

"Anything else?" asked the Admiral.

"No sir."

"Okay," said the Admiral. "I believe we'll be landing in about fifteen minutes. I'm going up on the bridge to watch it."

On the flag bridge, the Admiral cast a critical eye over the formation of ships. Three miles out from the flagship there was a circular screen of a dozen destroyers to protect the big ships from submarines. They do this by constantly pinging in the water with their sonars and listening for answering echoes returning from the depths. This may seem like a waste of time in peacetime. But the Russians had submarines in the Med now—and the Russians are completely unpredictable.

Inside the screen on each beam of the flagship about a mile away were two heavy cruisers. Each had a powerful battery of guns and also had target-seeking missiles like the Russian SAM's.

About a mile ahead of the *America* and on the same course for the time being was a Russian destroyer. This snooper accompanied the task group wherever it went, hanging around the big ships, taking pictures, getting in the way, and making a general nuisance of herself. Ordinary sea manners require a single ship to keep clear of a formation. But this Russian had the manners of a Marseilles tugboat skipper. He barged about through the formation at will, forcing big ships to change course to avoid collision, and generally managed to get in the way whenever the carrier turned into the wind to launch or land aircraft.

In the center of the formation was the attack carrier *America*, sixty thousand tons, carrying an air group of one hundred jet planes and with her magazines full of atomic bombs. This was a very powerful force indeed, capable of wreaking more havoc in this world than all the bombs dropped by both sides in World War II. True, it could be wiped out by one accurately placed atom bomb, or half a dozen submarine torpedoes. But the *America* was well able to defend itself against either form of attack, and its mobility made it impossible to pinpoint. It could be west of Malta today and near Suez tomorrow, with planes that could reach out to the other side of the Urals.

On the flight deck, preparations for the next launch were in progress. The thousand-foot, four-acre flight deck was a beehive of activity. On the port side, the canted deck landing area was kept clear at all times, ready to land any plane in the air that had to come down. Flight operations are around the clock these days, day and night whenever the carriers are at sea. On the starboard side, fifty fighters and bombers were parked in the after section with wings folded, while mechanics readied them for flight.

A flight-deck crew in action is a colorful spectacle. They all wear different-colored shirts to show what their jobs are. Arresting-gear men wear brown, gas crews and ammo handlers red, tractor drivers and taxi directors yellow, plane captains blue, and fire fighters green. All wear helmets and the key men have earphones, so the Air Officer in his cubbyhole above the flight deck up in the island can talk to them by walkie-talkie over the roar of jet engines, which, of course, when they are lit off, drown out even the powerful bullhorns.

At this point, tractors were hauling planes for the next launch forward and spotting them near the catapults, of which there are four. When they have those expensive airplanes in tow, tractor drivers proceed as carefully as an old lady parking a brand-new car. But they are all frustrated hot rods, and when they haven't got a plane in tow, they roar around the flight deck wide open, skimming the edge of open elevators in a way that would scare the grit out of an astronaut.

As the tractors dragged the planes up, each catapult crew spotted the first plane for the launch on its cat. A dozen sailors eased it carefully into position, where the breaking link was hooked into the tail. Then the heavy tow bridle was attached to the landing gear and thrown over the catapult shuttle. This latter is a towing hook which sticks up through a slot several hundred feet long running down the deck and is propelled by a steam jet controlled in the catapult room just below the flight deck. It boosts the plane from a dead stop to 140 mph in little more than a second. With the bridle in place, the shuttle is eased forward to take a strain and put tension on the breaking link that holds the tail.

Presently the pilots came trotting out of the island in their flight gear, kicked the tires, and climbed into the cockpits. Then began the starting ritual. The Air Officer pressed the button on the bullhorn and his voice boomed over the flight deck, "Now check all loose gear about the decks."

Plane captains took a quick look around for buckets, wing lines, swabs, or cockpit covers adrift near their planes.

"Check wheel chocks and wing lines," continued the bullhorn.

Plane captains checked wheel chocks in place and wing lines taut.

"Stand clear of jet exhausts and intakes," boomed the bullhorn.

The penalty for disregarding this warning is severe and messy. Everybody who hasn't got a job on deck drops off into the gallery walkways.

"Stand b-y-y-y-y to start engines. *Start Engines!*"

The flight deck explodes with a great *whoom* as the jet engines light off, run up to full power, and throttle back.

The catapult crews run through a quick final check of the bridles, hold-back pins and wing locks as the pilot is carefully checking each item on his take-off list. As he completes the list, the pilot holds his right hand out with thumb up to the catapult officer, and slides his canopy shut.

Meantime, things are happening on the flag bridge. The staff duty officer has figured out a course that will put the wind seven degrees on the port bow, smack up and down the center line of the canted deck. If the Admiral is on the bridge, he goes through the formality of asking permission to turn into the wind, gets a curt nod in reply, and then yells over the wing of the bridge at the chief signalman, "Signals! Course pennant zero two zero."

The chief barks the order to his signal floosies and they bend on the flags and haul them out of the bag and up to the yardarm as if the Old Nick himself were urging them on with a red-hot marlin spike. Throughout the fleet, the other ships have their spyglasses on the flagship, the signal forces spring into action, and on each ship the signal "Corpen zero two zero" is bent on and hauled halfway up to the yardarm, indicating "Signal received, we are looking up its meaning."

Everybody knows the meaning of simple corpen signals so almost immediately the signal is two-blocked, meaning, "Signal is understood; we are ready to execute."

The chief signalman on the flag bridge yells up to the staff duty officer, "All ships acknowledge." After a final look around, the duty officer yells, "Execute."

Down come the flags on the flagship, followed immediately by those of the other ships.

On the bridge of each ship, the OOD says, "Right standard rudder," the helmsman spins his wheel, and the task group begins turning into the wind, leaving great creamy white wakes behind them. They are ready to launch.

A whirlybird tuning up on deck revs up, flutters off, and stations itself at masthead height a little on the starboard bow. This is the plane guard. If anybody goes in the water, it is his job to get over there, drop frogmen, and get the people out of the plane and into the sling which the hovering whirlybird lowers. The average time from splash to back on board the *America* is about two minutes.

Down at the catapults they have run up the blast shields while the ship has been turning into the wind. These are large sheets of metal which lie flat on deck ten feet aft of the planes until launching time. Then they are raised on edge to deflect the blast from the afterburners up in the air and away from the planes behind on deck.

The cat officer holds his right fist over his head with one finger up and the pilot shoves his throttle all the way against the stop. When his jet hits top speed he nods his head to the cat officer, who puts up another finger. The pilot hits his afterburner, which lights off with a noise like thunder, drowning out all the other jets. The pilot then braces himself, salutes, grabs the stick again, and waits patiently for about a second. The cat officer takes a quick look down the deck to make sure it is all clear, still holding his fist over his head with two fingers extended, and then sweeps his arm down, pointing to the bow.

Down in the cat room a light flashes from amber to green and the chief pulls a lever admitting high-pressure steam to the catapult piston. The tow bridle stiffens as the shuttle urges it forward, the hold-back link breaks, and away she goes, accelerating in little over a second to flying speed before she reaches the bow. At the bow a doohickey snatches the bridle off as it flashes by and whips it under the overhang of the flight deck. The pilot hauls back on his stick, flips his wheels up, and away he goes, into the wild blue yonder.

Meanwhile the planes of the previous flight have been returning and circling high overhead, getting ready to land. They can land during the launch, if necessary, but usually they wait till the last plane is off before coming in. As the last planes are being taxied to the catapult, word goes out from CIC, "Land airplanes. Fighters are first to land."

A group of four Phantom fighters have been circling the ship, throttled back to two hundred knots at five thousand feet. The leader immediately gives the breakup signal, wiggles his wings, and dives out of the formation, pulling up ahead of the ship on the starboard bow at about five hundred feet. He squirms out of his chute harness, opens his plastic cockpit cover, runs down the checkoff list, dropping his hook and wheels, and starts a slow turn to the left. He rolls out of his turn still at two hundred feet a little on the starboard quarter of the ship, throttles down to final glide speed, and looks at the deck ahead for the meatball. Meantime, the landing signal officer on his platform at the stern checks to make sure his wheels and hook are down.

The meatball is a spot of light from a gyro-stabilized projector on deck set to shine a narrow beam at the exact glide angle down which the plane must come. There is a horizontal line of lights on deck, and when the pilot is coming down the beam exactly right this line bisects the meatball. If he gets too high the meatball goes above the line—too low, it goes below. The pilot fiddles with his stick and throttle till he has the meatball centered, and then all he has to do is just keep it there till he hits the deck. The instant he touches the deck, he jams his throttle all the way forward. If his hook catches a wire, he yanks the throttle off and the arresting gear snubs him to a stop in short order. He picks up his hook, drops the wire, and taxis out of the landing area to starboard. If his hook jumps the wires, he's got full power on, and the canted deck gives him a clear runway ahead. He then becomes a "bolter" and roars down the deck and into the air to go around and try it again.

This is quite different from the way it used to be in World War

II, before the canted deck and the meatball landing system came along. In those days you landed on a straight deck, heading right at the planes that had landed ahead of you. Halfway up the deck were the barriers. These were three heavy cables stretched across the deck at propeller hub height.

There was no meatball in those days. You got in the groove astern of the ship and then followed the directions of the landing signal officer, who stood on a platform at the stern and controlled your approach with hand-held flags. He would signal too high, too low, too fast, too slow, or just right—hold it. As you neared the ramp he gave you either a cut or a wave-off. On a wave-off you gave her the gun, pulled off to port, and went round again. On a cut you whacked off the throttle and settled on deck. The number one rule then was "never touch your throttle again after a cut." If your hook jumped the wires you had to just sit there and take it when your plane went into the barriers. This brought you to a sudden stop. But it usually didn't do any more than bust a prop and shake the pilot up a little bit. If you gave her the gun trying to go round again and didn't make it, you would plow into a mess of parked airplanes on the forward part of the deck. There would be blood, guts, and feathers all over the place (but no brains).

As the last planes to land taxi out of the gear, the bullhorn booms, "Secure from flight quarters." The plane captains and gas and armament crews get busy readying the planes for the next flight. There is no rest for the weary when a big carrier is on a round-the-clock schedule. The only time those crews have to themselves is when their planes are in the air.

CHAPTER FOUR

Plane Shot Down

DOWN IN CIC the boys settled down for what they hoped would be an uneventful watch. CIC (Combat Information Center) is the brain of the ship. It is in voice communication with all planes in the air and has an array of radar scopes which keep track of all of our own and any other planes and ships which come within range. The radar can see things at night and in fog just as well as in the daytime. In the old days whenever things started to happen the captain used to head for the bridge. But nowadays most captains head for CIC to get the hot dope.

In the center of the compartment is a big vertical plastic plotting board on which all targets held by any radar scope are plotted. Seamen plotters with various-colored grease pencils stand behind this board wearing phones to the various radar operators. When an operator spots a blip, he phones the dope to the seaman, who marks it at the proper bearing and distance from the ship, which is always at the center of the board. These seamen have to learn to write backward on the board so those on the other side can read correctly.

Shortly after all planes of the new flight had completed their radar and radio checks and started on their missions a blip appeared on the edge of the big vertical board two hundred miles to the east. Five minutes later it was forty miles closer, coming directly toward the *America*. The CIC officer got down off his stool and walked over to the long-range-search radar scope. He watched over the operator's shoulder while the antenna made a couple of sweeps around the horizon, noted that the blip continued to come straight in, and then said to the operator, "What do you make of that blip, son?"

"I dunno, sir," said the lad on the scope. "It's a good solid blip, coming in pretty fast. We picked him up at two hundred miles, so he must be flying high, about forty thousand feet. It's probably some airliner."

"Maybe," said the CIC officer. "But we're not on any regular air route here. . . . I'm going to intercept him."

He went back to his stool, picked up his mike, and called the leader of the combat air patrol, which consisted of four armed fighters circling at thirty thousand feet over the ship.

"Tom Cat One. Tom Cat One," he said. "We have bogy approaching from zero nine zero. Estimated altitude forty thousand. Ground speed about three hundred knots. Intercept and identify. Over."

"*America*, this is Tom Cat One. Roger," came the answer. "Understand bogy bearing zero nine zero at forty thousand, ground speed 300. Intercept and identify. I am on my way."

On the big board a blip identified as four fighters started out from the center of the board to meet the incoming bogy.

Five minutes later, Tom Cat One called in and reported, "We have bogy on our intercept radars." A minute later he called, "Tallyho—bogy is in sight—altitude forty-two thousand feet. Closing to identify."

Two minutes later, Tom Cat One came in again: "*America*, this is Tom Cat One. Bogy is a Russian Pushkovik. We have him surrounded and are flying formation on him. I am directly astern at fifty yards. He is not carrying any bombs on his wings. Over."

"Okay, Tom Cat—good work," said the CIC officer. Then, throwing a couple of switches to the bridge and flag plot, he said, "Report to the Captain and Admiral that a Russian Pushkovik is coming in at forty-two thousand feet. We have intercepted him with four fighters. He has no external bombs. He will be over ship in fifteen minutes."

Soon the Captain was down on the flag bridge, consulting with the Admiral. "Do you want me to launch any more fighters?" he asked.

"No," said the Admiral. "I see you've got four on the catapults ready to launch. That's enough for the time being."

"Any special instructions for Tom Cat One?" asked the Captain.

"No-o-o," said the Admiral. "I think our regular rules of engagement cover the case adequately. So long as he doesn't molest us, we simply give him close escort and keep our guns ready. If he opens his bomb bay near the fleet—we shoot him down."

"Yes sir," said the Captain. "My boys understand that."

A few minutes later, Tom Cat called in. "We have fleet in sight, on the horizon. Russian has throttled down and is descending."

Soon a formation of five planes appeared dead ahead, heading right at the fleet at an altitude of three thousand feet. They circled the *America* several times, one fighter just a wing span behind each wing tip of the Russian and two drawing a bead on him from directly astern. Then the Russian descended to mast-head height and made several passes around the *America* at close range. Finally he flew past the starboard wing of the bridge close aboard, gave a friendly salute, waggled his wings as he passed the bridge, and flew off to the east.

"Well," observed the Admiral to the Captain as he disappeared over the horizon, "he ought to bring home some pretty good pictures from this trip. Send that flight leader of yours up to flag plot when he lands. I want to have a word with him."

"Aye aye, sir," said the Captain.

Later the Admiral was talking to Tom Cat One on the flag bridge. "What did that chap do when you intercepted him?" he asked.

"He just waved—and shook hands with himself," said the pilot.

"Was there anything unusual about his behavior?"

"No sir. He just went on about his business as if he had just as much right up there as we had. He didn't seem at all concerned when we closed in on him."

"Did he man his guns?"

"No sir. He didn't have any guns. He had photographers in both his turrets, and they got a lot of close-up pictures of us."

"Yes—and they got some good ones of this ship—and we got some of him, too."

"Incidentally, there's a Russian task group out there about 150 miles east of us," said Tom Cat. "Two heavy cruisers and six destroyers."

"Hmmmm," observed the Admiral.

That evening after sunset, pilots were being briefed for the next flight scheduled to take off in half an hour. The pilots, wearing their G suits, sat in the ready room, sipping coffee and facing the briefing officer with the moving visual tape from CIC behind him.

"The weather is CAVU," said the briefer, "and predicted to remain so. Moonrise is at 2100, three-quarters full. There will be a four-plane combat patrol stationed at forty thousand feet over the ship. All planes will carry a full load of ammunition, plus two sidewinder missiles. If you make any intercepts, the rules of engagement are close escort with two directly astern. If plane is definitely identified as Russian or Egyptian and if he opens his bomb bay in vicinity of our ships, shoot him down. Any questions?"

"Yeah," said the flight leader. "How can you tell if he opens his bomb bay at night?"

"You'll have almost a full moon tonight. You shouldn't have any trouble seeing his bomb-bay doors."

"Hmph," said the leader.

"In addition to the combat air patrol," continued the briefer, "we are sending out one reconnaissance flight. That's you, Wigglesworth. You are to fly at forty-five thousand feet and cover a sector fifty miles on each side out to two hundred miles to the east. The Russian task group was out there this morning, and you may run across them this evening. Flying at forty-five thousand you'll be on our radar screen at all times. Your plane is equipped with an infra-red camera which is all programmed for this flight. All you gotta do is fly out on course 080 to two hundred miles, fly south for fifty miles, and come back in on course 280. Any questions?"

"Yeah," said Wigglesworth. "What ships have the Russians got in that group?"

"Two heavy cruisers and six destroyers. They will stick out like a sore thumb on your radar scope."

Presently word came over the squawk box, "Pilots, man your planes." The pilots slipped into their Mae Wests, gathered up their hard helmets, and trotted up to the flight deck.

It was a dark night and the moon hadn't come up yet. But the flight deck was lit up like the playing field at Yankee Stadium by large batteries of floodlights shining down from the island.

The four planes of the combat air patrol were already parked on the catapults and went off first. As the fourth one roared down the deck, the taxi director pointed his lighted wands at Wigglesworth and crossed them, meaning, "Hold your brakes." Then he swept his wands down from side to side, telling the plane captain to pull his chocks. The plane captain crouched underneath the plane, yanked out the chocks, and scrambled into the gallery walkway with them.

Then the taxi director, walking backward, made beckoning motions with his wands. Willy released his brakes and taxied slowly up the deck. Pointing at one wheel with his wand and then another for Willy to hold his brakes, the taxi director maneuvered him up to the catapult. The crew swarmed around him, lined him up, hooked up the breaking link, and adjusted the tow bridle. Meanwhile, Willy ran down the final items in the checkoff list and shifted his gaze to the cat officer.

As the various members of the cat crew finished their jobs, they gave a thumbs-up signal to the cat officer and scrambled clear. As the last one dropped into the gallery walkway, the cat officer faced Willy, held one lighted wand overhead, and made vigorous stirring motions with it. Willy shoved his throttle against the stop, his jet roared up to full power, and he stuck his fist out, thumb up

The cat officer raised his other wand and Willy hit the afterburner. It lit off with a great roar, and his plane strained against the breaking link and trembled. Willy braced himself, saluted, and went hurtling down the catapult and off into the darkness. As he felt his wheels leave the deck, he hauled back on the stick, flipped the wheel-retract lever, and concentrated on his gauges in the cockpit, holding his wings level and his nose up.

The first five hundred feet are the hardest on a night launch. The penalty for making small mistakes close to the water is severe. After you pass five hundred feet, it's just a milk run. As his altimeter wound past 500, Willy throttled back a little, relaxed, and got ready to deliver the milk.

He climbed to forty-five thousand feet, circling the task group, throttled back to cruising speed, squared away on course 080 and checked out with CIC. "Tom Cat 5 at forty-five thousand starting outbound on course 080," he said.

A matter of fact "Roger" came back from CIC.

It was a clear, dark night as aerology had promised, with a brilliant array of stars overhead and the glow from the impending moonrise lighting up the eastern horizon. With his plane on auto pilot and his gauges all reading normal, there wasn't much for Willy to do but sit there and admire the sky. "It's an easy way to make a living," he observed to himself, as he cruised along.

Two hundred miles out he turned south and called in, "*America*, this is Tom Cat 5 at forty-five thousand feet—turning to south leg."

"Tom Cat 5, Roger," replied *America*.

Shortly after turning south, Willy was singing softly to himself when he noted a group of small blips just coming onto the edge of his radar scope dead ahead.

"That will be the Russian task group," he observed to himself. "I'll be passing right over them. I'll wait till I get a little closer before I report 'em."

A few minutes later, he was singing:

> "Now flying's a dangerous game, so they tell;
> A few flipper turns and you're headed for hell;
> The saddest of sights is a young aeronaut
> Attempting to pilot a plane when he's taut;
> So we'll hoist a few cases, we'll . . ."

At this point there was a blinding flash, the plane shuddered as if it had hit a brick wall, and Willy was knocked cold.

Half a minute later, Willy came to. His plastic cockpit hood was shattered and he was obviously spinning violently. The cockpit was dark and the only sound was the wind whistling through his shattered windshield. There was no vibration and no engine noise. His engine was dead. He moved his stick and kicked the rudder, but there was no response. The controls were slack.

S.O.P. in the jet jockey trade when you find yourself in a situation like this is to consider that your contract with the government to fly that airplane has expired, and to bail out. He reached up to pull the face curtain down in front of his face before bailing out, but it wasn't there. He hit the eject button and the explosive charge propelled him out into the night, seat and all.

After a couple of end-over-end somersaults, the seat flew apart and left Willy still tumbling with no visible means of support. Willy thought fast. He had no idea how long he had been knocked out or how much altitude he had lost during the blackout. He fumbled for the ring of his chute and was about to pull it when he got a glimpse of the moon just beginning to peek over the horizon and realized he was still pretty high. If you pull your chute at too high an altitude, you are apt to freeze in the subzero weather as you float down. And if your emergency oxygen bottle doesn't work, you can die from lack of oxygen in the thin air. Willy's chute had a barometric element in it that was supposed to trip it at fifteen thousand feet. So Willy decided to wait a little while.

Soon he stopped tumbling and was falling at terminal velocity in spread-eagle fashion, face down. Below him he saw a ball of fire descending, leaving a trail of sparks behind it—evidently the wreckage of his plane.

He was beginning to think that maybe his automatic chute opener was stuck when it suddenly pulled the pins on his seat pack. Out came the pilot chute, dragging his main chute behind it, which opened with a crack like a five-inch gun. Willy was suddenly jerked upright, decelerated, and left swinging there at fifteen thousand feet.

It takes almost fifteen minutes to come down in a chute from fifteen thousand feet. During this descent, Willy had time to reflect on his state. He had checked in with the ship when he turned south only about ten minutes before his plane came apart. At forty-five thousand feet he should have been clearly visible on their big search scope, so they should have a reasonably good idea of where he went down. He had a one-man life raft with a lot of special equipment attached to the seat pack of his chute. As soon as he hit the water he would have to get that out, inflate it, and scramble aboard. They would probably find him by 10 A.M. next morning. Things could be a lot worse, he thought, as he floated down.

By the time he hit the water the moon was well up over the horizon. He unbuckled his harness as he neared the water and squirmed out of it as he hit, hanging on to it with one hand so his rubber boat couldn't get away. Soon he had it inflated and scrambled aboard. In the process of doing so he lost overboard the little radio transmitter with which it was equipped. "Well," he thought, "what the hell. I don't have to tell them I'm down. They probably know it by now, anyway. They can find me tomorrow without the transmitter."

Meanwhile, back on the *America*, the operator was watching Tom Cat 5 on his scope shortly after the report that he had turned south when suddenly the blip disappeared from his scope. He steadied his beam on the last spot where he had seen the blip, turned up the gain, and still got no return.

"Tom Cat 5 has gone off my scope," he reported to the CIC officer.

"At what range," asked the officer.

"At two hundred miles," said the operator.

"Hmmm," said the officer. "He was flying at forty-five thousand. We should get a good solid blip on him at that range. Keep searching that bearing."

Then, picking up his mike, he said, "Tom Cat 5, Tom Cat 5, *America* calling. Over."

No answer. He called again several times. No answer and still no blip on the radar scope. He called the bridge and reported, "Tom Cat 5 has disappeared from our scopes and does not answer calls."

Soon the Admiral and Captain had their heads together. "I suggest we run east all night at thirty knots, sir," said the Captain. "That will put us right in the area where he went down by sunrise. We can give the area a thorough combing, starting at daylight."

"Okay," said the Admiral. "That's what we'll do. Have you any idea what may have happened to him?"

"No sir, we don't. He checked in with us by radio about eight minutes before and everything was normal. Then suddenly he just disappeared off the screen. No mayday—and no answer to our calls."

"Obviously whatever it was happened suddenly," said the Admiral. "The place where he disappeared is where the Russian task group was this morning."

"Yes sir," said the Captain. "It's quite possible the Russians shot him down with one of the SAM's they got on those new cruisers."

"In which case the odds are that he didn't survive, so we'll never know what happened," observed the Admiral.

Next morning the task group combed the area with the whole air group. You might think that with fifteen ships and one hundred planes over the area all day they couldn't help finding Willy. But a one-man life raft is a very small object and the sea is big. Three or four planes passed nearly over Willy, and several times during the day he had the upper works of ships visible on the horizon. But they didn't see him.

The searchers did find an oil slick. But that could have been caused by many things. They found no wreckage. By the end of the day they were convinced that Willy had disappeared without trace, and abandoned the search.

CHAPTER FIVE

Leave Malta

BACK ON LCU 1124 they were getting ready to get underway from Malta. Fatso and Scuttlebutt were standing on the starboard wing of the bridge and Adams was at the wheel. Presently the Professor yelled up from the well deck, "All ready for getting underway, Cap'n."

Fatso said casually to Adams, "You think you can take her out?"

"Sure," said Adams.

"Okay. You've got her," said Fatso.

Adams walked over to the port wing and yelled down at the well deck, "Cast off aft. Hold the bowline."

Then he went back to the wheel, put his rudder hard over to the left and kicked his starboard engine ahead. The ship took a strain on the bowline and the stern began to swing out. As it cleared the cruiser astern, Adams kicked both engines astern and yelled down on deck, "Cast off in the bow."

The bowline came in and the ship backed out into the harbor. As he started to swing toward the entrance, a tug with a barge in tow came out of a ship ahead of them. Adams reached up for the whistle cord, gave it two yanks, cut under the stern of the barge, and headed for the entrance.

"By gawd," observed Fatso to Scuttlebutt, "the guy does know how to handle a boat. Even knows the rules of the road. Maybe we can make something of this guy."

"Humph," observed Scuttlebutt.

As they cleared the entrance they came to course 090 and squared away heading for Iraklion in Crete.

At lunch that day they were listening to the radio news from home. "Washington: The President announced that efforts to control inflation are succeeding. The cost of living only rose one per-cent last month. There are signs that the economy is cooling off but the administration does not foresee a depression. The stock market took another plunge yesterday and hit the lowest point in the past six years."

"New York: The New York post office is swamped by the flood of mail piling up on account of the postal strike. The garbage men, railroads, and air controllers are also on strike, all demanding higher wages on account of the increase in the cost of living. The President announced plans to call out the National Guard to move the mails."

"How the hell are you going to stop inflation when everybody strikes for higher pay?" demanded Scuttlebutt.

"When the cost of living goes up, you gotta have more pay, don't you?" observed the Judge.

"Does the cost of living go up because they get more pay or do they want more pay because the cost of living went up? Which comes first, the hen or the egg?" demanded Scuttlebutt.

"Well, they're going to hafta do something to stop these strikes," said the Professor. "They go on strike and get a raise in pay, so the cost of living goes up and nobody is any better off than they were in the first place."

"The only way you can stop them is with wage and price controls," said the Judge. "And that goes against our whole free-enter-prise system."

"Well, all the big corporations keep on making more money, so the workers are entitled to more pay too, aren't they?" demanded Webfoot.

Adams, who had just come off wheel watch, was just finishing his lunch. "I heard a story once that explains this strike business," he said. "It seems that back in the days before the AF of L and the CIO got together, there were these two Italian boys. One of them belonged to the AFL and one to the CIO, and they were arguing about the respective merits of their two unions.

" 'AF of L—she's a no good,' said the guy who belonged to the CIO.

" 'Whatsa mat AF of L?' says the other one.

" 'Ah-h-h—AF of L you gotta too many ums.'

" 'Whaddya mean—too many ums?' says the AF of L guy.

" 'AF of L you gotta the maximum, you gotta the minimum,

you gotta the optimum, you gotta the *ulti-matum*. That's a too many ums. CIO we only gotta one um . . . *fuck 'um.'* "

The radio news continued: "Naples: Sixth Fleet announced today that one of its fighter planes disappeared last night on a flight over the eastern Mediterranean. A large-scale search operation is in progress today."

"That's the first plane they've lost in some time," observed Scuttlebutt.

"We'll be in that area tomorrow," said Fatso. "So all you guys keep your eyes open for flyers paddling around in rubber boats."

That evening the boys were sitting around on the well deck under the stars listening to Fatso and Scuttlebutt swap yarns about how they had won the war.

"I was on the *Bonne Homme Richard*," said Scuttlebutt. "She was a hell of a fine ship. Had the best flight-deck crew of anybody in the Third Fleet. One day we took a kamikaze on the flight deck. He hit just forward of the elevator and started a hell of a fire among the planes they were loading for the next flight. I was playing acey-deucy in the flight-deck ready room with old Geezer Hawkins. He was the luckiest guy I ever saw. Didn't know nothing about the finer points of the game, but was always coming up with acey-deucy when it was the only thing that would save his neck. I just about had him beat when he rolled an acey-deucy this day and we heard a hell of a crash outside. The fire alarm went and Geezer says to me, 'It's my move when we come back.'

"We damn near lost the *Bonne Homme* that time. The whole forward end of the flight deck was ablaze, and pretty soon the bombs on the planes began cooking off and there was hell to pay. A two-hundred-pounder went off and took old Geezer's right leg off right at the knee. I drug him away just before a thousand-pounder on another plane went off that would of blown him to kingdom come.

"I went down to sick bay to see him after we got the fire out and the first thing he said to me was, 'You lucky son of a bitch. I had you beat cold in that game if that goddamn Jap hadn't hit us. . . .' Never did say a word to me about saving his life."

"I saved a guy's life once during the war, too," said Fatso. "When the *Lexington* got sunk. It was early in the war at the Battle of the Coral Sea. The Japs put a couple of torpedoes into us, blew two big holes in our bottom, and shook us up pretty bad. But we would of come out of it okay except that they started leaks in our gas tanks. This was before we learned how to control gas fumes, and pretty soon there was gas fumes all over the lower decks. Then the explosions started that tore us apart inside. We might have been able to get her back to port even then. But the Japs were right on top of us and the other ships had to get out. So we abandoned ship, and one of our own tin cans finished the old gal off with torpedoes. I was still on board when she rolled over and sunk. When I surfaced after getting off there was a young aviator in the water alongside me with no life jacket. He had been hurt fighting fires and was just about to go down when I got to him. I swum around holding him up for about an hour until a tin can picked us up. . . . Admiral Halsey gave me a medal for it—old Halsey just loved to hand out medals."

"Yeah," said Scuttlebutt. "Now tell them who this guy was."

"It was an ensign named Hughes, just out of Pensacola," said Fatso.

"And tell them what he's doing now," said Scuttlebutt.

"He's a vice admiral now," said Fatso. "Commander of the Sixth Fleet."

"Gee," observed Adams. "This gives you an in right at the top. You must be able to get away with murder with a drag like that."

"Whaddya mean?" demanded Fatso. "I don't need no drag," he added piously. "I just do my duty like everybody else, and keep my nose clean . . . but of course if I happened to get into a jam, the chances are the Admiral would listen to my side of the story."

Next morning Fatso came on deck just before sunrise. It was a clear, cloudless morning and a few stars were still dimly visible in the west. There was a sharp horizon to the east, brilliantly lighted by the oncoming day sweeping across the world from the east. "Have you ever seen the green flash?" asked Scuttlebutt of Satchmo, who had the wheel.

"You mean at sunset?" asked Satchmo. "Yes sah. I've seen it several times."

"Ever seen it in the morning?" asked Fatso.

"No-o-o," said Satch. "It only happens at sunset."

"No. It happens in the morning, too," said Fatso. "But it's harder to see in the morning. At night you're watching the sun as it goes down, so you're looking right at it when it turns green. In the morning you're not looking right smack where the sun comes up usually, it only lasts about a second, and so you don't see it."

"What causes the green flash, Cap'n?" asked Satchmo.

At this point the Professor came on deck and Fatso said, "Maybe the Professor can explain it better than I can. How about it, Professor? We're talking about the green flash. Can you explain it to us?"

"Well, yeah," said the Professor. "I've never seen it, but I've heard about it. And I've talked to people who claimed they had seen it. It doesn't happen every day. You've got to have very clear air with no haze and a sharp sea horizon. When you get exactly the right atmosphere, the air acts like a prism and it splits the sunlight up into the colors of the rainbow. When the sun is above the horizon, the colors from one edge of it mix with the colors from the other, so you don't see the rainbow colors. It comes out as plain white sunlight. But as the sun goes down, you see less and less of it until finally there is just a little sliver left—almost a point source of light. That's when you see the green flash for about a second, just before it disappears. Actually, the last color in the spectrum is blue, but you don't see that because it blends with the color of the sky."

"Uh huh," said Fatso. "Well, you can see it in the morning, too, if you're looking in exactly the right place when the sun pops over the horizon."

"Well—yes. I suppose you can," said the Professor. "The same process occurs as at sunset, except in reverse."

"The sun will be coming up any minute now," said Fatso. "I'll bet we see it this morning."

The three of them concentrated their gaze on the eastern horizon. Presently the edge of the sun peeked over it just as green as grass. It only lasted for a little over a second, but it was unmistakable.

Soon after sunrise they were cruising along at ten knots with a light breeze blowing when suddenly Satchmo, who had been looking out on the port bow with his binoculars, sang out, "Sail ho."

"Where away?" demanded Fatso.

"About two points on the port bow," replied Satch, holding out the glasses. Fatso took the glasses and aimed them at the spot Satch indicated.

"Yeah," he said. "There's something out there all right. Right on the horizon. But I can't make out what it is."

"I think it's a man's head," said Satch.

"Maybe so," said Fatso. "Head for it and we'll see."

As they approached the rest of the figure came over the horizon, and it soon became apparent that it was a man in a small rubber raft. "By gawd, that must be the pilot of the plane that went down the day before yesterday," observed Fatso. And that's what it turned out to be.

All hands were on deck by the time they reached Willy, and eager hands reached out to help him aboard.

"Ain't this something," remarked Willy, as he scrambled aboard. "The whole damn fleet was all around me here yesterday and couldn't find me. Now you guys come along and pick me up after they give up."

"You're the missing pilot we heard about on the radio, I guess," said Fatso.

"That's right. Lieutenant (JG) William Wigglesworth from VF 124. My plane blew up on me the other night and I had to bail out. I been paddling around in this rubber boat here for about thirty-six hours."

"Well, come on down to the messroom," said Fatso. "We'll give you a square meal and frame a dispatch to the *America*."

Soon a dispatch went out to the *America*: "Have recovered Lieutenant Wigglesworth in good condition Lat 34-30 Long 19-50. He says his plane blew up and he bailed out. Request instructions."

After they got the dispatch off Fatso said to Willy, "Any idea what happened?"

"No," said Willy. "I was just flying along at forty-five thousand feet, everything normal, and all of a sudden there was a hell of an explosion. Knocked me cold. When I came to I was spinning, my controls were slack, my engine was gone, so I bailed out. I couldn't see well enough to tell how much was left of the plane. But I did see a big fireball go into the ocean."

"Were there any other ships around you when this happened?" asked Jenkins.

"Yeah. I had just picked up the Russian task group on my radar. I was about fifteen miles from them; two cruisers and six destroyers. But I never saw them."

"Hmmm," said Jenkins. "Maybe they knocked you down with one of those SAM's we've been hearing about."

"Could be," said Willy. "All I know is there was a hell of a flash; it felt like I had hit a brick wall, and I went out like a light. I was damned lucky I came to in time to bail out."

"I think it was a SAM that got you," said Jenkins. "There's nothing can happen to make a plane suddenly blow up like that."

"I been thinking about that too," said Willy, "ever since I been in the water, and I've just about come to the same conclusion, too!"

"Well, I've got some gear here that will enable us to find out about these SAM's and bitch them up," said Jenkins, pointing to his black boxes stowed in the corner.

"What's that?" demanded Willy.

"A lot of special electronics gear to go in your planes. There's a radar search receiver that will tell you whenever a radar beam hits your plane and what direction it came from. If the beam zeroes in on you and stays on you, this will alert you that it is probably the guidance beam for the SAM. We've got another black box that searches for the homing beam put out by the missile. As soon as you pick that up, you flip a switch and put out a beam of your own that buggers up the SAM and turns the missile away from you."

"Hmmm," said Willy. "Sounds like a tough way to make a living to me."

"Why?" asked Jenkins. "All you gotta do is flip a few switches."

"Yeah," said Willy. "But if any one of your black boxes doesn't work, you've had it. These guys play rough. I've had one of these things burst right in my face, and that's enough. I'll let somebody else fly your black boxes around and see if they work."

"Would you care for a little snifter, Lieutenant?" asked Fatso.

"Yeah—I don't mind if I do," said Willy.

Fatso went to his cabin and came back with half a tumbler of Old Grand-Dad. Willy tossed it off with gusto.

"How about some bacon and eggs, Lieutenant?" asked Satchmo.

"Yeah—I could use that, too," said Willy.

As Willy was finishing his bacon and eggs a half hour later, a whirlybird came fluttering over the horizon and circled the ship a couple of times. "Well—that's pretty fast service," observed Fatso.

"Except they should of picked me up yesterday," said Willy.

Fatso headed into the wind and slowed to four knots. The whirlybird fluttered over, hovered at thirty feet for a while looking things over, and then set down on the well deck forward.

"I'll bet that's an all-time first for this type of craft," observed Fatso.

"Well—so long, skipper," said Willy. "Thanks for picking me

up. I'll have something to say to the Admiral about that when I get back."

"Don't mention it," said Fatso. "Always glad to pick up shipwrecked fly boys."

Jenkins tried to talk the whirlybird pilot into taking him and his boxes along too, but had no luck. The pilot said he didn't have room for all that stuff.

⚓ CHAPTER SIX

Balloon Trick

LATER THAT DAY he, Fatso, Jenkins, and the Professor were seated in the mess room having a cup of coffee.

"You know," said the Professor, "I can sympathize with that flyer for not wanting to rely on your black boxes to protect him from SAM's. You gotta depend on a half a dozen of them, and if any one of 'em doesn't work, the penalty is very severe."

"It may sound kind of hairy," said Jenkins, "but it isn't; as soon as you get the signal from the Sam's homing radar, you just flip your transmitter button and send out a signal that turns the SAM away."

"Do we know enough about their radar frequencies and the frequency band of the SAM homers to do that?" asked the Professor.

"Well, no. We don't know their frequencies," said Jenkins. "That's why it takes so many black boxes. But we put enough equipment in the plane to cover the whole range of frequencies. So we'll pick it up, all right."

"If all that stuff works," said the Professor. "If it doesn't—then another poor fly boy has had it."

"I been thinking about that angle of it, too," said Fatso. "The only way you can find out the frequency of that missile homer is to be within range of it when it's working. And if it works the way it's supposed to work, the only guy within range of it gets shot down, so he can't tell us what the frequency is."

"That's right. Except we've got search receivers that cover the whole spectrum. And they'll find it in time for us to bugger it."

"Yeah," said Fatso. "But wouldn't it be nice if we knew ahead of time what their homing frequency is?"

"Sure. It would eliminate a lot of search equipment and make things a lot simpler," said Jenkins.

"Well, maybe I've got an idea for finding out their search radar frequency," said Fatso. "During the war, the German subs used to pull a stunt on us with an aerology balloon. When they came up at night to charge batteries, they would have an aerology balloon on deck anchored to a small float with about ten feet of line and a big handful of tinfoil attached to the balloon. If any of our destroyers came along while they were charging batteries, they would drop this balloon overboard and submerge. The gob of tinfoil hanging on the balloon gave exactly the same kind of a blip on a destroyer's radar that a submarine's periscope did. Nobody likes to close in on a guy at night when they figure he is looking right down their throat with his periscope. So the destroyers would circle around the blip all night at a respectful distance, figuring they would nail the guy next time he had to surface again for air or to charge his battery. Meantime, the sub would go deep and buzz off. Come sunrise and the destroyers would find a silly goddamn balloon grinning at them and the sub would be long gone."

"Yeah, I read about that in a book about the Battle of the Atlantic," said Jenkins. "Half the time, the destroyers' skippers wouldn't even report it because it made them look silly."

"That's right," said Fatso. "Now I think maybe we can work a similar gag on the Russians to find out about their SAM frequencies."

"How do we do that?" asked Jenkins.

"Well," said Fatso, "suppose we get about twenty miles upwind of the Russians at night, and then turn loose an aerology balloon with a lot of tinfoil hanging on it. The balloon will go up to about thirty thousand feet and drift over the Russian ships. They'll get a good echo off the tinfoil with their radars, and maybe they'll launch a SAM at it. You could have all your black boxes set up on here to pick up and analyze their radar signals. We wouldn't interfere with their SAM homer, so it would take the missile right on in to the balloon and bust it. The Russians would assume they had shot down another one of our planes."

"Hmmm," said Jenkins. "Maybe you've got something there."

"I think it would depend on how sharp their radar operators are," said the Professor. "The speed of the balloon would be much too slow for a plane."

"Sure. But they'd get a real good echo off of it. And it could be a whirlybird. They haven't got a bunch of college professors on watch on their radar. They are evidently a pretty trigger-happy bunch, and they shoot down anything that comes near them at night. They had no way of knowing our plane was a fighter the other night. It could just as well have been an airliner."

"It's worth trying, anyway," said Jenkins. "After all, we've got nothing to lose."

"The Russians are in this area," said Fatso. "And we may run across them. Why don't you break out your black boxes and set 'em up so we can monitor their frequencies if we do run across them?"

"Okay," said Jenkins. "Can do."

"I'll help you," said the Professor. "I know a thing or two about electronics."

Late that afternoon they sighted the Russian task force dead ahead.

"Hah!" said Fatso. "How lucky can you get? Have you got your gear set up yet?" he asked of Jenkins.

"Pretty near," said Jenkins. "It will be ready by dark."

The wind was out of the northwest, so Fatso maneuvered to get upwind of the Russians, keeping their upper works visible just over the horizon. At sunset Jenkins reported, "All set, Cap'n. What time does the balloon go up?"

"As soon as it gets dark. About an hour from now," said Fatso.

An hour later, Jenkins and the Professor were seated at the table in the darkened messroom. In front of them was an array of black boxes with various dials and indicators. Once a minute a blip appeared on the radar scope attached to one of the boxes. "That's his air search radar," observed Jenkins. "It takes just a little over a minute to make its full sweep all around the horizon. I've got a good reading on it now, and have all the dope on its pulse repetition rate, frequency, and wave shape."

"Will his homing signal be the same?" asked the Professor.

"No," said Jenkins, "we don't know what its frequency is. That's why we need so much equipment to be sure we pick it up when it comes on."

"How about it down there?" yelled Fatso down the voice tube from the bridge. "You guys all ready?"

"All set any time," replied Jenkins.

Out on the well deck, the Judge and Jughaid were standing by with an erology balloon blown up to its full five-foot diameter.

Suspended beneath it on a short line was a double handful of tin-foil with long streamers hanging down from it.

"Okay, on deck—let the balloon go up," yelled Fatso.

Up went the balloon, rising at two thousand feet a minute and propelled by a brisk breeze toward the Russian fleet.

For several minutes after it went up, nothing happened. The Russian radar continued to sweep once around the horizon every minute, making a pronounced blip on the scope every time it swept past. Then the blip, instead of flashing on and off as the beam swept by, stopped and held steady.

"Hah!" said Jenkins. "They've spotted our balloon."

"They sure have," agreed the Professor.

For several minutes the blip held steady. Jenkins and the Professor scanned the dials of their black boxes carefully for signs of any new radar activity.

"They're making up their minds now," observed Jenkins. "Another minute or so will tell the tale."

A few minutes later, he let out a whoop and said, "Hah! They fell for it! His homing signal just came on. A SAM is on its way up to our balloon now." He grabbed a pencil and scribbled down the frequency and pulse repetition rate of the new signal. "Bridge!" he yelled up the voice tube. "Watch the sky to the south—you may see an explosion in the air." He tuned another black box on the new signal to analyze its wave shape.

Pretty soon there was a yell from the watchers outside and Fatso's voice came down the tube. "We just saw a hell of a big flash in the sky about ten miles south of us, up around ten thousand feet."

"Yeah," replied Jenkins. "And we just lost our radar signals down here. That was their SAM—exploded by the balloon."

A few minutes later there was a jubilant conference in the mess-room. "We gotta get this dope to the fleet right away," said Jenkins. "This could save us from losing some more planes."

"Okay," said Fatso. "Write up a dispatch and we'll send it. Be careful what you say, because we can't code it and the Russians may read it."

A few minutes later a dispatch went out to the *America*. It said, "Have info of vital importance to you. Suggest you send helicopter and pick up technician plus five hundred pounds of gear. Lieutenant Wigglesworth can amplify."

"You wouldn't think they'd fall for a simple trick like that," observed Scuttlebutt. "Wasting a SAM on a silly goddamn balloon."

"Well, the SAM couldn't tell from the echo it was getting whether it was from a balloon or a fighter plane," said Jenkins.

"No. But you'd think they would notice this thing was only making thirty knots. It couldn't be a plane."

"Sure," said Fatso. "But you gotta remember we caught them by surprise with this thing. All of a sudden their radar shows a blip coming over them. They probably had some young lieutenant on watch in CIC, and he was on the make to show how smart he is. The other night, as soon as they saw the blip from our plane coming over, they let go at it. They did the same thing this time. The SAM homed in and blew up the balloon without a trace, just the same as it did the plane. So now some young Russian lieutenant on watch in CIC will probably get a medal for shooting down another one of our planes. . . . It just goes to show that sometimes you can dust off an old trick and use it over again. Even with all the black boxes we've got these days, people have to run 'em and you can sometimes fool people."

Next morning the whirlybird from the *America* fluttered down on the well deck and took off Jenkins and his gear. On the *America* he was immediately ushered in to flag plot, where the Admiral and Captain were waiting for him.

When the introductions were over, the Admiral said, "Well, what have you got, Jenkins?"

Jenkins related the tale of the balloon. Soon after he got started, the Admiral interrupted and said, "Hell, yes. I remember the Germans pulling that stunt. Fooled a hell of a lot of very smart people with it, too."

When Jenkins finished, the Admiral said, "Those trigger-happy bastards. Apparently they shoot down anything that comes over them at night, and no questions asked. This clinches what happened to our plane a couple of nights ago. They shot it down."

"They sure did," said the Captain. "So what do we do about it?"

"We just report it to Washington and let them handle it," said the Admiral. "And of course they won't do a damn thing about it because they'll say we've got no conclusive proof. But meantime we don't fly over those guys at night any more."

"You don't have to stop flying over them now, sir," said Jenkins, pulling a notebook out of his pocket. "I've got here all the technical information we need about their search radars and guidance beam, and also the homing signals of the SAM. I've got a couple of black boxes you can put in your plane that will tell the pilot when they fire a SAM at him and will enable him to jam their homing signal and divert the SAM so it won't come close enough to bother him."

"Well, that's fine," said the Admiral. "But for the time being anyway we don't fly any planes over those guys."

Next day the *America* got a dispatch from Com Sixth Fleet saying, "Request you fly high-altitude photo flight over Cairo."

When the Admiral saw this he said, "Well, the goddamn whiz kids are going to have their way after all. Get that electronics expert Jenkins up here."

When Jenkins came into flag plot the Admiral said, "Just how sure are you that this gear you've got will perform as advertised?"

"I'm certain of it," said Jenkins. "We got the proof of it the other night with that balloon."

"The hell you say," said the Admiral. "All you got was proof that their homer and fuse work. You didn't get any check on your jamming equipment."

"Well, yes. You're right about that, sir. But we know how their homer works. And we checked our jammer against our own missiles with the same homers in them. It works like a charm."

"All right," said the Admiral. "I've got to send a flight over Cairo. I want it equipped with your gear."

"Aye aye, sir," said Jenkins. "Can do."

At the preflight briefing the next day the briefer said, "This will be a photo reconnaissance flight. Fly at forty-five thousand feet. All you have to do is turn your cameras on fifty miles from Cairo and fly directly over the city. As soon as you reach a point directly over the city, turn around and come back. You can outrun any MIG's they send up to intercept you, and we don't think their SAM's are operational yet. However, in case they are, your plane is equipped with detectors and jammers. . . . You've been checked out on them, haven't you?"

"Yeah," said the pilot. "I spent all yesterday afternoon with Jenkins."

"Okay. So you know what indications you'll get on your radar scopes. As soon as you get the homing signal from the SAM, you just turn on your jammer and that's all there is to it."

"Yeah," said the pilot. "And what's my story in case I *do* get shot down?"

"You got lost. That's all. You didn't know where you were and you had no intention whatever of flying over Egypt."

"Okay," said the pilot.

The flight went off as briefed. Fifty miles from Cairo, the pilot switched his cameras on and they took pictures at ten-second intervals, showing the terrain below in fantastic detail. A woman carrying a jar on her head was clearly visible in those photos, taken from nine miles up. The SAM missile sites were unmistakable. Shortly after he switched his cameras on, the pilot began getting a blip on one of Jenkins' black boxes as the Cairo search radar beam swept past him. After about five blips, the beam steadied on him. The pilot poised his hand over the jamming button and mentally ran through his bail-out procedure. Soon his homing detector flashed on and the pilot shoved his jammer button.

Looking ahead and down, he soon saw the SAM coming up at him and leaving a trail of white smoke behind it. Presently it began steering an erratic course and veering off to the right. It passed below him and about a mile abeam and went on its way harmlessly. This performance was repeated by two other missiles before he turned back over Cairo and by one other as he retired. A group of six MIG's took off after him but couldn't catch him.

Back on the ship after the plane returned the Admiral had Jenkins up to see him again. "Young man, I congratulate you," said the Admiral. "Your black boxes worked like a charm. They shot four SAM's at our lad and he diverted them all. None of them even came close."

"Yes sir," said Jenkins. "The gear worked fine. Of course, one thing that made it easy was knowing the exact frequency and pulse repetition rate of their radars. We got that from that balloon business the other night. Without that it would have been much more difficult. But we still could have done it."

"I believe you said that balloon stunt was the idea of some sailor on that LCU, didn't you?" asked the Admiral.

"Yes sir," said Jenkins. "It was the skipper's idea. Boatswain's Mate First Class Gioninni. He's a real sharp character."

"Okay," said the Admiral. "I'm going to send him a letter of commendation."

CHAPTER SEVEN

Egyptian Gunboat

MEANWHILE AT THE Newport News Shipbuilding Company yard in Portsmouth, Virginia, construction of a small ship of war was nearing completion. She was a two-hundred-foot gunboat, diesel powered, that would make thirty knots. No armament was being installed at Portsmouth, but mounting rings were built in the ship for four 40-mm guns and two SAM launchers. An Arab crew of eight men were in Portsmouth supervising construction, ready to take over and sail the ship to Egypt when she was finished.

A conference was in progress between the chief constructor and the Egyptian skipper.

"You have not put air conditioner in my cabin yet," said the skipper.

"But I told you last week, the plans don't call for that," said the constructor.

"But I want it," said the skipper, "and you've got to put it in."

"Sorry," said the constructor.

"The trials are coming off in about a week," said the skipper. "It will be a lot easier for you on the trials if I get it."

"Look," said the shipbuilder. "The cost of this craft has already gone beyond the contract price, and this is a fixed-price contract. This isn't like a U.S. contract, where you have changes and overruns and the final price can be two or three times the original one. We've just got to take our loss on this one."

"Couldn't you charge my air conditioner to that big U.S. carrier you're building?" asked the Egyptian. "No one would ever know the difference."

"No," said the constructor.

"You're apt to have trouble on the trials if I don't get it," said the Egyptian.

"Well—we'll cross that bridge when we come to it," said the constructor. "I'm sorry, but you just can't have an air conditioner."

Soon the skipper was in the office of the executive vice president.

"Well—good morning," said the V.P. "How is that fine ship of yours coming along?"

"Very well, sir," said the Egyptian. "Except we've found one small oversight in the plans which must be corrected."

"What's that?" asked the V.P.

"There's no air conditioning in the ship. It gets very hot in the Red Sea and we've got to have air conditioning in all living quarters."

"Well," said the V.P., "this would involve a change of contract which would take at least six weeks, and we have a delivery date to meet with penalities for being late just two weeks from now."

"I won't accept the ship without it," said the Arab.

This was an alarming development. This contract had been a pain in the neck to the shipbuilders right from the start. The Egyptians had demanded a lot of changes; the company was losing money on the contract and was anxious to get the ship out of the yard and off their hands. "We have to deliver two weeks from today," said the V.P. "You can install air conditioning later, after you get to Egypt."

"We'd never get it in Egypt," said the skipper. "It's got to be done here."

"Well, the only way we can do it here is to negotiate a change in the contract—and you know how long that would take—at least a couple of months."

"Well, look," said the Arab. "I don't want to be unreasonable. Maybe it would take you six weeks to air condition the whole ship. But you could air condition my cabin in a day. If you do that, I'll wait for the rest until we get to Egypt."

The V.P. wanted no part of any contract negotiations for air conditioning the whole ship. He knew from sad experience that such negotiations with the Egyptians were long-winded affairs. He wanted to get rid of this craft as soon as possible. So he said, "All right, Captain—we'll put air conditioning in your cabin for you."

This was all the Arab had set out to get that morning, anyway. So he left the V.P.'s office well satisfied with himself.

While this was going on in Portsmouth, there was a formal meeting in the Secretary of State's office in Washington. The Israeli ambassador was calling to present a note from his government. The note protested the sale of the ship being built in Portsmouth for the Egyptians.

"Mr. Secretary," said the ambassador as he presented the note, "This is a very serious matter to my government. My government has a small Navy intended primarily for harbor defense. If the Egyptians acquire this ship it will change the whole balance of power at sea at a time when peace in the Near East is balanced on a knife edge. Your government has refused to sell us fighter planes and the Russians are supplying MIG's to the Egyptians. My government strongly protests this sale and urges yours to stop it."

"But, Mr. Ambassador," said the Secretary, "the contract for this ship was let over a year ago. There was nothing secret about it, and you've had a whole year to object before the ship was built. The shipbuilders now have considerable investment in it. If we prevent the sale now, they will have to swallow a big loss."

"Which is more important, Mr. Secretary—the peace of the Near East or a small loss to the shipbuilding company? After all, you have barred the sale of fighter planes to Israel, but you are supplying them to Libya. Those planes will go right to the Egyptians, and you know it. This will upset the balance in the air. The Russians are building up the Egyptian Army. There are twenty big Russian transport planes per day landing in Cairo with all sorts of arms and technical advisors. We are not just going to sit back and watch while the Egyptians build up their forces to the point where they can overwhelm us. Pretty soon, if this keeps up, we will have to strike before it is too late. This ship is meant for one purpose only—to attack us. I most urgently request that you stop delivery of it to Egypt."

"Very well, Mr. Ambassador," said the Secretary. "I'll make your views known to my government. But I can't make any commitment to you right now as to what action we will take."

Next day there was a meeting of the National Security Council in the White House. In addition to the usual members present, the Chief of Naval Operations and Chief of Staff of the Air Force were also there at the request of the President. The first item on the agenda that morning was the note from Israel. It was the lead story in most of the morning papers across the country that day, nearly all of them expressing sympathy with the Israeli position.

"Why are they making a federal case over one lousy little gunboat?" asked the Air Force COS of the CNO.

"They're just setting the stage for something else," said CNO. "This gunboat doesn't amount to a hill of beans."

"I see by the papers," said the COS innocently, "that you have run into an overrun of two hundred forty million dollars on the nuclear carrier."

"Um—er—yes," said the CNO. "I also see where you have had to ground all your TFX's."

"Harrrrumph," observed the COS.

When the President entered, all hands stood up respectfully. The President gave them a curt nod, sat down, and tossed a copy of the *New York Times* on the table.

"The first item of business," said the Secretary, "is the Israeli note received yesterday afternoon."

"Before we take it up," said the President, fixing his eye on the Secretary of State, "I'd like to know why the first time I hear about a thing of this kind is when I read it on the AP news ticker. Don't you people have the phone number of the White House?"

"I apologize for that, Mr. President," said the Secretary. "I thought the news would keep overnight. But it seems there was a leak."

"Can't you control security in your own shop any better than that?" demanded the President. "I'll swear that about half the time the way I find out what this government is doing is when somebody leaks it to the newspapers."

"In this case I'm pretty sure the leak was the Israeli ambassador," said the Secretary.

"I wouldn't be surprised," said the President. "He's thick as thieves with most of the press. He sure got a front-page splurge out of it," he added, pointing to the headlines in the *New York Times*. "Well—let's consider what we're going to do."

"I'd like to have the CNO comment on this first," said the Secretary of State.

"Well," said the CNO, "I think they are making a mountain out of a mole hill. This one small ship really won't upset the balance of naval power in the eastern Med. The Russians have quite a fleet there now, based on Alexandria. They are the ones who can swing the balance of power in the Med either by direct intervention or by turning over several of their ships to the Egyptians. The Israelis know that. I think they are just paving the way for another protest about selling those planes to Libya."

"I agree," said the COS of the Air Force. "Naval power is of no significance between the Israelis and the Egyptians. Whichever side has control of the air can wipe out the other side's naval craft any time they want to. Right now the Israelis have control, and this new craft would be a sitting duck for them. I agree that this thing is probably just laying the ground for a further protest about the sale of those fighters to Libya. This could really upset the balance of power if they wind up in the hands of the Egyptians."

"I won't say I agree that naval forces are just sitting ducks," said the CNO. "But if the Egyptians get those planes from the Libyans, and if they learn to fly them—it will make a difference, all right."

"Yes. They do have a training problem," conceded the COS. "They lost all their best flyers in the six-day war. Even they weren't very good."

"One thing you may want to consider," said the CNO, "is that Newport News is our mainstay in the shipbuilding industry right now. They are building a nuclear carrier, four destroyers, and two Polaris submarines for us. This little bucket isn't good for anything else. If we stop this sale we will be saddling them with about a five-million-dollar loss."

"They will probably charge it off as an overrun on the carrier," observed the Vice President to the Secretary of Defense, seated alongside him.

"Harrumph," said the Secretary of Defense.

"I agree," said the President, "that this thing is probably just a ploy leading up to something else. But they're making a big thing of it and they'll have most of the liberal press and all of the TV networks on their side. And we've got to remember that the Jews have a lot more votes in this country than the Arabs do." ("Strike that from the record," he said in an aside to the soldier who was running the tape recorder.) "'See me after this meeting," he continued to the Secretary of State. "We'll work out some sort of an answer for the Israelis."

In the executive office after the meeting, the President said to the Secretary of State, "Well, what do you think? How should we answer the Israelis?"

"If we stop the sale now, the Egyptians will raise hell about it," said the Secretary.

"They will—and with good reason," said the President. "But they'll get their money back. And the Arabs don't pack the political clout in this country that the other side does. I want to stop the sale of that ship."

"We really have no legal grounds on which to do it, Mr. President," said the Secretary.

"Have your legal experts get busy and find legal grounds," said the President. "Your lawyers can justify anything if they put their minds to it."

"Okay, Mr. President," said the Secretary. "I'll frame an answer to the Israelis telling them what we're doing. We'll get a blast from the Egyptians about it—but we can cross that bridge when we come to it."

Most of the newspapers in the country had editorials that day supporting the Israeli protest. All the TV networks joined in the clamor for stopping the sale. When our answer to the Israelis was announced next day, approval by the media was practically unanimous.

There was not a word of protest out of Cairo about this. In the office of the shipbuilding company a few days after the decision was announced, the president of the company was conferring with his board of directors.

"This is an unfortunate and unpredictable setback," he said. "We have to refund five million dollars to the Egyptians, and we're stuck with a hull that is of no use to us. We can salvage something out of the diesel engines. The hull is a total loss. But we can weather this. After all, the U.S. Navy can't afford to let us get hurt too bad. We've got seven ships on the ways for them now, and more in the design stage. We can charge this off as overhead on some of our future contracts. Make out a check for five million dollars to the Egyptian government," he added to the treasurer.

A couple of days later there was a development which put things in a different light. Newport News got a feeler from the Ecuadorian government for the purchase of the Egyptian craft. This was a great break for the shipbuilding company. They immediately checked with the State Department to see if there was any objection to the deal.

The State Department said, "Okay, if the offer is legitimate. Let us check it with the Ecuadorian embassy."

The embassy replied that the firm involved in the deal was an Ecuadorian fishing firm which wanted the craft as the flagship of its tuna fleet, and the deal was perfectly legitimate. So Newport News opened negotiations for the sale of the craft.

The bid for it was three million, which was two million less than the company had invested in it. But it was three million more than they had expected to get out of it, so the deal was closed.

A crew of swarthy Spanish-speaking characters checked into the shipyard and took over the craft. Next week they ran her through the trials and accepted her without a hitch. The company got a check on a Swiss bank for three million dollars, and next day she sailed. She proceeded down Chesapeake Bay to the Virginia Capes, sailed out, and then, instead of heading south for Ecuador, headed east across the Atlantic.

The day she sailed there was a revolution in Ecuador and a group of young colonels took over the government. Among the many crimes which they charged to the previous government was conniving with the Egyptian government to buy the ship from Newport News. It seems there was no Ecuadorian fishing company involved. The previous government had made a deal with the Russians for five million dollars to buy the ship, furnish a crew, and sail it to Egypt. The ousted government had pocketed two million on the deal, and the ship was now on her way to Egypt, with orders to report in to the Russians and then be transferred to Egypt.

This caused a big splurge in the press and on TV. All the many friends of Israel had a field day accusing the State Department and the military-industrial complex of collusion with the Egyptians. Pundits pontificated about the credibility gap, and proposed that the Sixth Fleet be ordered to intercept and seize the craft when she got to the Med. Newport News Shipbuilding Company was termed a gang of merchants of death and protesters carrying Viet Cong and Israeli flags picketed the shipyard hurling insults at the workers. Eventually a group of hardhats from the shipyard charged into the pickets, beat them up, and put them to flight.

There were riots on several college campuses protesting this deception of the American people. Students invaded the dean's office at Harvard, beat up members of the faculty, and used the office as a privy. The President of Harvard refused to call the police and issued a statement calling on the students to be calm. The Israelis sent an indignant note to the State Department demanding that we intercept this craft. This generated another meeting of the National Security Council.

At this meeting when the Secretary of State finished reading the Israelis' note, the President said, "Well, I can't say that I blame them for complaining."

"Well, I do," said the Secretary. "I think they've got a lot of crust to complain about this. After all, this is just exactly what they did to the French about a year ago—except they did it with six motor torpedo boats that they claimed were going to a Swedish fishing firm."

"Well, yes. You're right about that," conceded the President. "Apparently it makes a difference when the shoe is on the other foot. So what are we going to do about this?"

"What *can* we do, sir?" asked the Secretary. "A legal deal was made, in good faith on our part. The craft is on the high seas now. I don't think we can do a thing."

"How about it, Admiral?" the President asked the CNO. "Couldn't you have the Sixth Fleet intercept her when she gets to the Med and bring her into port?"

"Well, of course, if you say so we can do it, sir," said the CNO. "But I don't know what the international lawyers would say about it."

"It would be flagrantly illegal—piracy on the high seas," said the Secretary of State. "We wouldn't have a leg to stand on."

"Now just a minute," said the Secretary of Defense. "International law is a very fuzzy code. Actually it's whatever the strong nations choose to say it is. It's only the small nations that are bound by it. If we intercept and seize the ship, I'm sure our international lawyers can dig up precedents to justify it. I recommend that we tell the Sixth Fleet to find it, commandeer it, and bring it in to port."

"It isn't a small nation we're dealing with here," said the Secretary. "It's Russia. They're the ones who bought it."

The President tapped the table thoughtfully for a moment and then said, "I think you're right about international law, Mel—it's whatever the big nations say it is. But I'm not going to get into any argument with Russia about it in this case." Turning to the Secretary of State he said, "Send the Israelis an official note saying, 'Nuts.' Have your boys expand that to about a page and a half of diplomatic language and send it off."

"All right sir," said the Secretary of State. "Matter of fact, I was reading their reply to the French when they pulled their stunt about a year ago and the French complained. I can quote a lot of their stuff verbatim, right back at them."

On board the Egyptian ship, the news of the revolution when they were a day out in the Atlantic caused grave concern among the crew. In the messroom there was a discussion in progress as to what they ought to do. "I think we should go to Ecuador," said one sailor. "There is a new government there now. They don't want this ship to go to Egypt."

"We can't do that," said another. "Our contract is with the Russians. They are going to pay us well. If we go to Ecuador, we won't get paid at all, and we were working for the old government. The new one may put us all in jail."

"Well, then, we should go back to the United States," said the first.

"We can't do that either. We wouldn't get paid and the U.S. has recognized the new government. They would probably turn us over to them. We have orders to report to the Russians when we get to the Mediterranean. They are the ones who will pay us, and the only way we can get our money is to turn the ship over to them."

Later the skipper came down from his air-conditioned cabin and had a talk with the crew. He confirmed that the Russians were paying them and that there was no chance of getting their money out of the new government. He said, "The Russians are expecting us and will send us instructions shortly after we get to the Mediterranean. We will be flying the Russian flag and they will escort us when we get close to Alexandria. No one will dare to molest us, and the Russians will pay us as soon as we get to Alexandria."

So they proceeded eastward, flying the Russian flag.

CHAPTER EIGHT

Iraklion

BACK ON LCU 1124 the night after the balloon incident when Adams went to bed, Webfoot said to the others, "Let's pull the belt trick on this guy." They agreed. So after Adams was asleep they removed the belt from his pants and shortened the end that was attached to the buckle about a quarter of an inch. Webfoot was quite handy at this and could do it in such a way that it would not be noticed. Of course the other end of the belt with the buckle holes in it was not affected.

The idea is to do this each night for about two weeks. Each day the victim's belt is a little tighter and after three or four days, he has to let it out a notch. After he has done this about three times, he begins to get worried about his weight. Meantime, the boys are also fiddling with the only scale on board, and adjusting it each day so that it weighs things about two pounds heavier than it did the day before. Before long, the victim of the belt trick is convinced that he is blowing up like a balloon.

The first notch didn't bother Adams. The second one did, especially when the scales told him he had put on five pounds. He began taking setting-up exercises and cutting down on his chow.

A couple of days later they sighted Crete, and passed the entrance to Suda Bay close aboard. As they passed the eastern shore of the bay the rusting hulk of a large cruiser was visible on the beach. "That's HMS *York*," said Fatso to the boys who were gathered on deck to look at the scenery.

"What happened to *her?*" asked Jughaid.

"Eyetalian frogmen got her," said Fatso. "There was a big

British fleet in here before the Germans captured the place. One night four Eyetalian PT boats slipped in through the nets. These were boats you had to ram right into the ship to fire the torpedo. The idea was to sneak in slow, get in as close as you could, and then aim your boat right at the ship, give her the gun, and jump overboard. They got four British ships that night, and one of them was that one there—the *York*. The British were able to get her underway and run her up on the beach before she sank. So she sat there on an even keel with all her upper works out of the water for the whole war, right where you see her now. The Luftwaffe would come over and see her sitting there and their fly boys didn't see anything strange about a cruiser sitting right up on the beach. They thought she was a perfectly good ship, and they bombed the hell out of her about a dozen times. Wasted tons and tons of bombs on her. The British didn't want the Eyetalians to know how good their frogmen were, so they finally announced she had been sunk by the Luftwaffe. And that's the way it is in the history books today. Just goes to show that you can't always believe everything you read, even in the official history of the war."

"You know," said the Professor, "right along this coast is where man first flew."

"How come?" asked Scuttlebutt. "I thought it was at Kitty Hawk, North Carolina—the Wright brothers."

"The time I'm talking about was a couple of thousand years ahead of the Wright brothers," said the Professor. "A guy by the name of Icarus."

"Never heard of him," said Scuttlebutt.

"It tells all about him in the early Greek mythology books," said the Professor. "Icarus and his old man were banished to this island by the Greeks. Icarus figured the only way he could get away was to make himself a pair of wings and fly away. So he got a lot of feathers and stuck them all over himself and fixed up a pair of wings covered with feathers for his arms. His old man didn't think it would work but warned him, if it did, he had to be careful about flying too high and getting near the sun. The heat of the sun might melt the wax he used to hold the feathers on. Well, when he was all set, old Icarus went up on one of those mountains right over there, flapped his wings, and off he went. He felt so good about it that he forgot about what his old man had told him. He flew up too close to the sun, melted the wax on his wings, and that was the end of him."

"Even if that was *so*—I wouldn't believe it," declared Jughaid.

They coasted along the north shore of Crete and ran in and beached themselves in the little harbor of Iraklion. We have an air strip there and keep a small detachment of men there. About the only time they have anything to do is when the marines have landing exercises on Crete; their air strip is busy then, handling marine planes and helicopters. The rest of the time it's just an emergency landing strip for planes of the Sixth Fleet.

Fatso had a couple of hundred pounds of freight for the detachment here. A station wagon came down to the beach, they loaded it up, and then Fatso and Scuttlebutt climbed in to go out to the station for a visit with their old shipmate Chief Storekeeper Corky Barnes.

They found Corky installed in a primitive little office in a Nissen hut. There were a desk, file cabinet, a cot, and a coffee urn in it and that was about all. After a big hello all around, Fatso cocked an eye around and remarked, "Sort of rugged layout you got here, Corky."

"Oh-h-h—it's okay to work in," said Corky. "I got air conditioning, it's nice and quiet, and when things get slack I can take a siesta."

"You always used to live pretty high on the hog," said Scuttlebutt. "I'm surprised you haven't got yourself fixed up better than this."

"Well, like I say," said Corky, "all I do is work here. I got things fixed up a little better where I live."

"Where is that? Here on the station," asked Scuttlebutt.

"No, I got a little place up in the hills here," said Corky. "I'd like to have you two guys come up and have chow with me there tonight."

They both agreed.

That afternoon Corky came by the ship in a station wagon driven by a young Greek and they set off up into the hills. They followed a paved road through very pretty countryside, dotted with small farms and olive groves. Then they took off up a dirt road that wound up the mountainside. The whole mountainside was under cultivation. In most places the slopes were too steep for ordinary fields, but the mountainside was terraced into small level plots with stone walls holding up the terraces.

About halfway up they came to a small shoulder looking out

over the sea, with a little olive grove on it. There was a driveway leading in through the grove with a big five-ton anchor at the entrance to it.

"Well—here we are," said Corky.

They drove through the grove and up to the edge of the cliff, where there was a little villa in the middle of a beautiful garden. On close inspection you could see that the villa was built from three Nissen huts joined together in a T with the crosspiece of the T facing the sea, and a screened porch on the front. The Nissen huts formed the framework for rock walls and a slate roof.

Inside there were a kitchen and dining room in the shank of the T, and a bedroom and living room in the crossbar. It was furnished like a modern suburban home, with leather furniture and color photographs of naval scenes on the walls, and had a large bar, a hi-fi, a ham radio station, color TV, and a big open fireplace. One wall of the living room was lined with books. Two large bay windows looked out over the sea to the north.

"Hey hey! This is a pretty plush pad you got here, Corky," said Scuttlebutt.

"It ain't bad," conceded Corky. "Let's sit out in front in the garden."

They settled down at a round table on the edge of the cliff, surrounded by an array of beautiful flowers and shrubs. In the middle of the garden and right in front of the house was a tall flagpole from which flew an American flag. An elderly Greek wearing a bartender's uniform approached and Corky said, "What will you have, boys? How about some mint juleps? I grow my own mint and Amaxagorous makes them very well."

For the next hour they sat around sipping tall mint juleps as the sun sank lower in the west, swapping info about various old shipmates.

"You remember old Sparky Wright?" asked Fatso.

"Sure. Used to run the electronics shop on the *Enterprise*," said Corky. "Used to always have a spot of gin for his real good friends in his cubbyhole whenever things got quiet—which wasn't often on that ship. What's he doing now?"

"He got out right after the war," said Fatso. "Got himself a nice job with RCA. He's a big-shot electronics expert with them now, making more dough than any of us ever thought of. I saw him last time I was in New York. He's got a big place out on Long Island with a wife, four kids, and a couple of Cadillacs. He says

that with inflation and sending his kids to college, he's just one
jump ahead of the sheriff all the time. Used to have more dough
in his pocket at the end of the month when he was in the Navy."

"You remember old Bosun Anderson?" asked Scuttlebutt.

"Sure," said Corky. "I remember he used to say that as soon as
he got his twenty years in, he was going to start walking inland
with an oar over his shoulder. When he finally got so far inland
that somebody stopped him and asked him what the hell that
thing was he had on his shoulder, that's where he was going to
settle down for the rest of his days."

"Yeah," said Scuttlebutt. "That's what he used to say—and
that's what he did. But a year of it was all he could stand. He's
back in again now, doing thirty. He's got the fo'c'sle on the
America."

And so it went for the next hour, until the sun was just about
to sink below the horizon. Then the butler came out and cast
loose the halyards on the American flag.

"Colors," announced Corky, putting down his drink and rising.
The others stood and faced the flagpole. Evening colors rang out
loud and clear over the hi-fi loudspeaker while the butler slowly
lowered the flag and the three sailors stood at attention.

Dinner that night was a spread that would have done credit to
Toots Shor. They had oysters, soup, roast beef, salad, and a flaming
dessert. They had red and white wine, champagne, and liqueurs
afterward. It was served out in the garden under the stars by an
elderly countryman dressed in elaborate local regalia. Soft music
conducted by Toscanini poured forth from the hi-fi throughout the
evening.

"That was quite a spread, Corky," remarked Fatso after dinner.

"Tell it to the cook," said Corky, and he called the waiter over
and told him to go back to the galley and get the cook.

The cook was the waiter's wife, a little old lady with tanned
face and sparkling eyes. She beamed from ear to ear as Fatso and
Scuttlebutt praised her cooking and said, "I try specially hard to
please any friends of Senor Corky. We all love him very much."

As they lingered over the liqueurs afterward, Fatso remarked,
"It's going to be tough for you to give all this up, Corky."

"Whaddya mean, give it up?" demanded Corky.

"I mean when this tour of duty is up, and you've got to start
living like the common people again."

"Well," said Corky, "I've only got another year to do on thirty.

Then I retire."

"That's what I mean," said Fatso. "It's going to be a hell of a comedown for you to settle down somewhere back in the States."

"You must think I'm nuts," said Corky. "I own this place. This is where I'm settling down when I retire. Hell, I've got everything I want here. I got five servants and only pay them thirty bucks a month, but they all think I'm wonderful. I got my shortwave radio, hi-fi, and TV with an attachment that picks up the satellite broadcasts. I got my books, and all kinds of hunting and fishing. Do you think I'd go back to the rat race we've got in the States now, with the hippies, draft-card burners, and black-power groups—to say nothing of inflation? My taxes on this place are about twenty bucks a year. No sir. I'm settling down right here where I'll be a rich man on my retired pay. Hell, at the end of the month, I'll be better off than old Sparky Wright is as vice president of RCA. I'll keep the Bureau of Personnel advised of my address, and if they need me when the next war breaks out, I'll be ready. But until then—this is where I'm staying."

Next morning LCU 1124 got underway and headed for Tel Aviv. At breakfast that morning Adams had only a glass of orange juice.

"Whatsa matter, Adams?" asked Webfoot. "You ain't eating."

"I guess I've gotta cut down some on my eating," said Adams. "I'm getting fat. I've put on about ten pounds since I've been aboard here."

"I noticed you seem to be getting kind of big around the fanny," observed the Judge.

"It's my belly," said Adams. "I've had to let my belt out three notches."

"No-o-o," said the Judge judicially. "It ain't your belly. It's your ass."

"What the hell?" said Adams. "Why should my ass get bigger?"

"Well, you see, you spend so much time on it. On a small ship like this you spend most of your time sitting down. So your ass begins to spread out, and of course it works up to your belly. We all had the same trouble when we first came on board. But you can lick it by taking exercise. Jumping rope is good for it."

That afternoon, Adams started jumping rope, and put in morning and afternoon sessions at it every day from then on. Webfoot quit shortening his belt and diddling with the scales, and pretty soon Adams was eating full meals again.

That evening after dinner the boys were sitting around the messroom when Adams lit up a rather pungent-smelling cigarette. After he had taken a few puffs on it Jughaid said, "What the hell are you smoking, Adams?"

"Pot," replied Adams. "You want some?"

"What the hell did you say?" demanded Fatso.

"Pot," said Adams. "You ever tried it?"

"Put that goddamn thing out," said Fatso.

"There's no law against smoking pot, skipper," said Adams, taking another drag on his cigarette.

Fatso got up, walked over to Adams, snatched the cigarette from his mouth, dropped it on the deck and stamped on it.

"You got no right to do that," said Adams indignantly.

"We got a ship's order on here—no pot smoking," said Fatso. "You got any more of those things?"

"Yeah—I got some more," said Adams.

"Well, hand 'em over," said Fatso.

Adams looked around the table and saw nothing but stony stares directed his way. He reached into his pocket, hauled out a pack of cigarettes, and laid them on the table.

"You got any more in your locker?" asked Fatso.

"No," said Adams.

"Open it up and let me see," said Fatso.

"No," said Adams.

"Listen, bud," said Fatso. "I'm the skipper of this ship. You don't say 'no' to me."

"Well, I just said it," said Adams.

Fatso hauled off and clouted Adams alongside the ear, knocking him backward onto the deck. "Now," said Fatso, "I don't want to get into no argument with you about this. So we'll have somebody else open your locker up. Scuttlebutt, you and Webfoot open Adams' locker."

"All right, skipper," said Adams, picking himself up off the deck. "You win. I'll open it."

Adams opened his locker and produced two cartons of marijuana cigarettes. "This is all I got," he said.

"Thrown them overboard," said Fatso.

Adams opened the door at the end of the compartment and tossed the two cartons overboard. Then he said, "You're all wet on this pot deal, skipper. Pot is no more harmful or habit forming than cigarettes. It doesn't affect you near as much as getting loaded up with liquor. Plenty of medical experts are on record about it."

"Yeah. I know," said Fatso. "The experts disagree. And, as long as they do, I'm believing the ones who say it's a habit-forming drug and opens the gate for other drugs. We're not going to have any of it on here."

"Okay, I can get along without it," said Adams. "Easier than the rest of you guys can without cigarettes."

"Have you ever tried LSD or heroin?" asked the Professor.

"Not heroin," said Adams. "But I've had a couple of trips on LSD."

"What does it do for you?" asked the Professor.

"It's hard to describe," said Adams. "But a good trip is a hell of an experience. You're just at peace with the whole world. Time slows down, colors are brighter, and music sounds better. You have beautiful hallucinations. You understand all about everything and you think of all sorts of wonderful things. You can't keep a record of them and you can't remember much about them afterwards. But they're good while they last."

"You still use the stuff?" asked the Judge.

"No. I saw three or four kids when they were off on bad trips. It was really grim. Scared the hell out of me. So I quit."

"I hear you can get pot, LSD, and even heroin on almost any college campus these days. Is that so?" asked Fatso.

"College campus? Hell, you can get them in any high school. Plenty of high-school kids are hooked on heroin now. Some of 'em put out fifty to two hundred bucks a day for it."

"Two hundred bucks a day!" said Fatso. "Where the hell does a high-school kid get that kind of dough?"

"They steal it," said Adams. "They start off stealing it at home and then work up to muggings and stickups. Once you're hooked you've got to have it and you'll do anything to get it. A lot of 'em wind up as pushers, peddling dope to the other kids to pay for what they've gotta have."

"From what I hear," said the Professor, "it's even in the grade schools now around New York and Washington. I was reading just the other day how they're finding twelve- and thirteen-year-old kids who are hooked on heroin. Twelve- and thirteen-year-olds— mainlining it. Stealing from supermarkets and snatching purses to pay for it. When their parents find out about it, they won't believe it."

"Well, what the hell?" said Fatso. "Their teachers must know about it. Can't they stop it?"

"Hah," said Adams. "In a lot of the schools now, the teachers are afraid of the kids. If a teacher says anything to a kid that's high on heroin, he's apt to get beat up. And, as a matter of fact, it was a college professor at Harvard that started this LSD business. And they had a hell of a time getting rid of him. He claimed it came under the heading of academic freedom."

"Dope is a hell of a big thing in the States these days," said the Professor. "It's a multibillion-dollar racket, and it's spreading. The pushers are going after little kids now—and getting a hell of a lot more of them than people realize. This stuff, once it gets a foothold in school, spreads like wildfire. The kids try it just for kicks, or because some friend of theirs had done it and they want to do the 'in' thing too. Before they know it, they're hooked. It's one of the biggest problems we've got in the country today."

"Well, by God," said Fatso, "I think we ought to hang any son of a bitch who peddles dope to kids. I mean it. Hang him."

"But even if you catch the peddlers," said the Professor, "They're really just little cogs in the machine. The big wheels, the ones who bring it into the country in quantities, are the Mafia. You'll have a hell of a time pinning anything on them."

"Well, there's nothing I'd rather do than help nail one of them," said Fatso.

⚓ CHAPTER NINE

En Route Tel Aviv

NEXT MORNING they backed off the beach, got underway, and headed east.

"Where are we going now, skipper?" asked Jughaid.

"Tel Aviv and Athens," said Fatso. "We got two big shipments of liquor to deliver to the embassies in Israel and in Greece."

As they ran along the coast a flock of pelicans began circling the ship and diving into the water after fish. This generated a discussion about pelicans between Fatso and Scuttlebutt, with the rest of the crew listening to the old-timers respectfully.

"I remember one time early in the war out in the South Pacific I was on a little seaplane tender called the *Half Moon*. Our skipper was a Commander Galloway and he was one hell of a guy. They sent us out with a squadron of PBY's to establish a base in a little lagoon on New Ireland. It was right under the guns of the Japs in New Guinea and we couldn't afford to risk a big ship up there. But the *Half Moon* was a little bit of a spit kit and she was expendable. We got to this lagoon and we tied up to the beach right under some big palm trees, so you couldn't see us from the air. We put out buoys for the planes around the lagoon right close to the beach, where the trees hid them. There was a lot of Jap planes flew right over the place and never saw us.

"There was a lot of pelicans in this lagoon and I guess they'd never seen an airplane before. Anyway they seemed to be quite interested in these big birds we had, and whenever a plane landed or took off they would flock around watching it and squawking to each other. Well, one day there was a bunch of aviators back on the fantail taking in the sun when this one old pelican decided to put on a show for them and demonstrate how the real experts fly. He got up at a couple of hundred feet astern of the ship and dove straight down at the water. Just before he hit he leveled off and came shooting past the ship about half a foot off the water. Then he did a steep wing-over at the bows, did a 180, dove at the water again, and came back past the stern going the other way. He put on one hell of an exhibition for the boys, and whenever he passed the stern he would look up at all the aviators who were watching him as if to say, 'How am I doing, boys?'

"After four or five passes he decided to land. So he did his wing-over and dive and then leveled out for a full-stall landing about twenty feet from the stern. He did a beautiful job of it, except there was about a fifteen-knot wind blowing that day and the old guy missed the wind by 180 degrees and landed smack downwind. Naturally he was going so fast when he hit that it up-ended him and ducked him headfirst in the water. As the old guy righted himself, paddled around into the wind and shook the water out of his eyes you could practically hear him saying to himself, 'Son of a bitch.' "

As Fatso was telling this yarn Scuttlebutt got his story-telling gleam in his eye. As soon as Fatso finished he said, "I was on a destroyer at Espiritu when we made friends with an old pelican one time. There was a lot of pelicans hanging around there and one day we noticed one old guy who just sort of paddled around and never flew. He looked kind of old and feeble. So we sent a boat out, caught him, and brought him on board. When we got him aboard we found out his pouch was split. So he couldn't eat any fish. When he caught a fish and tried to swallow it, it would pop out through the slit in his pouch. So our pharmacist's mate decided to sew him up. He got a sailmaker's needle and some surgical thread and a couple of us held the bird while the medic sewed him up. When he got through we fed him a fish and he gulped it right down. So we filled him up with fish and turned him loose. At first he still couldn't fly because he was too weak and too full of fish, I guess. But the next day, after he had digested the fish, he flew just as good as any of them, and pretty soon he was catching fish the same as the rest of them. The old guy knew our ship and was grateful to us. He used to hang around when we were in port. Whenever we got underway he would circle around and escort us out, and would meet us when we came back in again."

Fatso still hadn't finished with the saga of the *Half Moon*. "That skipper we had on the *Half Moon*," he observed reminiscently, "that Commander Galloway was a can-do guy. Nothing ever fazed him. They gave us the wrong kind of fuses for our bombs. They had a long delay element in them so when a bomb hit a Jap ship it would punch a hole clear through it, come out the bottom, and explode way the hell and gone down deep in the water, where it wouldn't do no harm. The Japs would just plug up the clean hole it had made and go on about their business. So the Captain had all our fuses sent up to his cabin and went to work on them. He took out the detonator caps, took the fuses apart, changed the delay element, put the detonators back in, and reassembled them."

"Boy! That's a tough way to make a living," observed Webfoot, who was a bomb-disposal expert and knew a lot about fuses.

"You're damn right it is," said Fatso. "You make one little mistake handling one of those detonators and it goes off right in your face."

"You're not supposed to monkey with fuses aboard ship," said Webfoot. "The book says you gotta ship them back to an ammo depot to make changes."

"Yeah," said Fatso, "but when you're hiding out in a little lagoon right under the Jap guns and the nearest ammo depot is a couple of thousand miles away you don't feel like doing that. But if anybody else on that ship had tried to monkey with a fuse, the skipper would of hung him higher than a kite. He got a letter from the Bureau of Ordnance a couple of months later telling him he could be court-martialed for it. But in the meantime we had sunk eighty thousand tons of Jap ships.

"Our skipper used to get letters from Washington, too," observed Scuttlebutt. "When he wanted to do something and he wasn't sure whether it was allowed or not he would break out the regulation book and start going through it. Finally he would come to a regulation that said something about what he wanted to do, and then he would 'interpret' it, the same way the Supreme Court interprets the Constitution. He used to always talk about the spirit of the regulations rather than the letter, and could always read a hell of a lot between the lines. Anyway, when he got through interpreting the book, it always said he could do what he wanted. About six months later he'd get a letter from Washington saying, 'What the hell. Can't you read the regulations?' But by that time it didn't matter any more."

"Our skipper used to run the *Half Moon* pretty much the way he thought it ought to be run," said Fatso, "irregardless of what the book said. He hardly ever held mast. But one time when he did he marooned a guy."

"Marooned?" said the Professor incredulously. "I didn't think anybody had been marooned since the days of sail—and only pirates did it then."

"Well, Cap'n Bill Galloway of the *Half Moon* did it," said Fatso.

"What for?" asked the Professor.

"For mutiny," said Fatso. "We had this wardroom messboy who just ran up the red flag and wouldn't do as he was told. The exec gave him a direct order and he just said, 'No, I won't do it.' So the exec had him up to mast before Cap'n Bill. Cap'n Bill said, 'How about it, Johnson? Are you going to do as you're told?' 'No, Cap'n,' said Johnson. So Cap'n Bill gave him a long fatherly lecture about how refusing to carry out orders was mutiny and mutiny in time of war is a very serious offense. When he got through he said, 'Now how about it, Johnson? You going to carry out orders?' 'No sir,' said Johnson. So Cap'n Bill said, 'O.K., we'll have to maroon you, Johnson. Lock him up,' he said to the master at arms. So the MAA took Johnson below and locked him up in the brig.

"Then they got all Johnson's stuff together and put it in a sea bag. They got another sea bag and filled it up with a lot of canned provisions. They put in a fishing rod, a shotgun and some shells, and a couple of cartons of matches. We was on our way to that little lagoon at the time, and the next day we passed a little uninhabited island with a lot of palm trees on it. Cap'n Bill stopped the ship about half a mile offshore, and they lowered a boat and put Johnson's gear into it. Then Cap'n Bill had Johnson brought up from the brig. They put him in the boat, took him ashore, and left him on the beach. The boys in the boat's crew said he expected to spend the rest of his life on that island. Everybody else on the ship throught he would too, for that matter.

"So we steamed off and left him standing on the beach watching while the ship disappeared over the horizon. But the island was only about thirty miles from the entrance of the lagoon.

Cap'n Bill knew we were only going to be there for a month and that when we came out, *if* we ever came out, we'd have to go right past that island on the way back to Nouméa.

"On the way back, we stopped and picked Johnson up. He was the happiest guy in the whole South Pacific when he saw that boat coming in. He swam out to meet it and didn't even want to go back in to the beach to pick up his gear.

"When he came back aboard the Captain met him at the gangway and said, 'How about it, Johnson—you going to do as you're told now?' 'Yes sir, Cap'n—I sure am,' said Johnson. From that time on he was the best messboy in the whole Pacific Fleet. He stayed in after the war and I hear he's now a cabin steward."

"That's right, Cap'n," said Satchmo. "I know him. Old Sam Johnson. He's flag steward for Com Air Lant now. And he runs a hell of a fine mess. And he won't stand for *no* monkey business from any of his messboys."

That evening after dinner the boys gathered around the radio for the evening news.

"Cairo: Nasser announced today that four Israeli airplanes attempting to bomb a hospital and a school have been shot down in flames by the Egyptian Air Force.

"Jerusalem: The Israelis announced today that two Egyptian planes attempting to bomb a convent were shot down by Israeli planes. The Egyptian planes were piloted by Russians."

"Hah!" said Ginsberg. "Even with Russians flying their planes they still can't do anything. Our pilots are just too good."

"Peking: The Chinese Communists announced that a Russian force invading Chinese territory at Bing Ding has been repulsed with heavy losses."

"Moscow: The Russian government announced that a Chinese force invading Russian territory at Bing Ding has been repulsed with heavy losses."

"There seems to be a slight difference of opinion as to who did what at Bing Ding," observed the Judge.

"Yeah," said the Professor. "You pays your money and you takes your choice. If things work out right, this could develop into a real big war between Russia and China."

"In that case," observed Fatso, "we should give all-out military aid to both sides."

Later that evening Fatso said to Scuttlebutt, "You know that shipment of liquor we got for the ambassador in Jerusalem?"

"Yeah," said Scuttlebutt. "It's enough to stock a waterfront barroom for a year. The ambassador will have a hell of a time drinking all that up."

"Don't worry about that," said Fatso. "That liquor is to feed junketing congressmen. It won't last more than a couple of months."

"They can lap it up all right," observed Scuttlebutt.

"Well, I notice we got six cases of Old Grand-Dad in this shipment," said Fatso. "I only want to give them five."

"Good idea, skipper," said Scuttlebutt. "I'll take care of it. Do you think the embassy will squawk about it?"

"No—I don't think so. They may never notice it. And, even if they do, they pay for this stuff out of counterpart funds. So it doesn't make a damn bit of difference to them."

"What's counterpart funds?" asked Scuttlebutt.

"Well, I can tell you what it is. But I can't explain it," said Fatso. "It's money that we get for the aid we give a country. But it can't be taken out of the country. It's got to be spent there. So the ambassador dishes it out to visiting congressmen and uses it to buy liquor for them."

"Okay, skipper," said Scuttlebutt. "I'll hold out one case of Old Grand-Dad when we deliver the ambassador's booze."

Next morning as they cruised along they met a British destroyer on opposite course which was going to pass close aboard. Fatso cast a seaman's eye around the upper works of LCU 1124 and had the boys belay a couple of Irish pennants so things would look shipshape when they passed abeam. Fatso called down on deck to the men working there: "I'm going to sound attention to starboard when we pass this guy abeam. I want all you guys to square your hats and stand at attention facing to starboard when we do. I want to let this guy know we're a real man o' war."

The ships were passing about a hundred yards abeam. When the destroyer was broad on the starboard bow, Fatso blew one long blast on a police whistle. All hands stopped work and stood at attention facing the British ship. On the destroyer there was an answering whistle blast and all her men on deck stood at attention facing LCU 1124.

Just as the ships came abeam, Fatso happened to glance up at the colors. They were at half mast. He jumped to the rail of the bridge and looked down on deck. There was Adams down there with the halyards in his hand, watching the British ship.

"What in the goddamn hell are you doing?" yelled Fatso.

"I'm dipping the colors to them, Cap'n," replied Adams.

"Two block 'em," roared Fatso.

Adams ran the colors up to the peak. "Now come up here," said Fatso.

"Just what the hell was the idea of that stunt?" demanded Fatso, when Adams got up to the bridge.

"Well, I was just dipping the colors to them," said Adams. "I thought friendly warships always dipped their colors to each other."

Fatso counted ten before replying. Then he said, "Listen, stupid. Warships never dip to each other. They return the dip when merchant ships dip to them. The only time a warship ever hauls down its colors to another is when it surrenders. That Limey destroyer probably thinks we're nuts."

"I'm sorry, skipper," said Adams. "On my old man's yacht we always dipped the colors."

"On your old man's yacht?" said Fatso. "So that's where you learned how to handle a boat, I suppose?"

"Yeah. My old man had a Chris-Craft. Seventy-five-foot cabin cruiser."

"He must of been in the chips."

"Yeah, he is. He's a vice president of General Motors."

"Well, coming from a background like that, how the hell did you become a hippie?" asked Fatso.

"I dunno. I guess the main thing was I wanted to be able to feel I was doing something worthwhile with my life."

"Well, couldn't you do that by getting a job with your old man's company?"

"Yeah. I suppose I could have worked for him if I wanted to. But we couldn't communicate. He made me go to college. But it all seemed irrelevant until I joined the SDS."

"So then what did you do?"

"Oh, I took part in demonstrations. I helped publish an underground newspaper. I was in a raid on the Dow Chemical Company's offices and I took part in a lot of other happenings."

"Well—did you accomplish any of the things you set out to do?"

"You can't tell yet," said Adams. "We got a lot of things started. But it takes time for them to eventuate. It's hard to tell where they will wind up."

"Of course, what you guys are aiming at is revolution, and if that comes, Gawd help you. You'll have to go to work."

"Oh no," said Adams. "What we're in favor of is love—share and share alike. We'll do away with poverty, with all class and race distinctions, and everybody will live the good life."

"You mean to tell me you really believe that stuff?" asked Fatso.

"Of course I do. Everybody will do his own thing, and everything will be peace, love, and prosperity."

"Listen, buddy," said Fatso. "If you get your revolution, you'll wind up with what the Russians have got. Everybody but a few party officials will have to work like hell—no union hours and no overtime."

"No, that's not the way we plan it. Everybody will do his own thing the way he wants to do it."

"Lemme tell you a story, bud, that you better start thinking about," said Fatso. "There was this commie on a soap box at Hyde Park Corner in London. He was telling the crowd about how good things would be for the common people after the revolution. While he was talking, some high-toned lords and ladies came riding down the bridle path on fancy horses. He pointed at them, called them a lot of dirty names, and said, 'Come the revolution and those dirty capitalists won't be able to ride any more. We'll take their horses away from them and you, the people, will ride in the park.' A little Limey standing in the crowd piped up and said, 'Not me, my friend—I don't *like* to ride horses.' The commie fixed his eye on him, shook his fist, and said, 'Come the revolution—you'll do as you're told.' "

That evening right after sunset Fatso, the Professor, and Satchmo were up on the bridge to get the evening fix. Fatso had a sextant, Satchmo a stop watch, and the Professor had a notebook and pencil. Fatso aimed his sextant at a bright star in the west, brought it carefully down to the horizon, and yelled, "Mark." Satchmo called out the reading of the stopwatch and the professor recorded it in his book. Fatso read the sextant and said, "Venus thirty degrees, fifteen minutes, eighteen seconds." The Professor recorded this in his book.

Soon other stars began coming out. Fatso shot Pollux Regulus, Capella and Polaris, and the Professor duly recorded the altitudes and times. The Judge was over at the pelorus noting the bearings of the stars. Then they adjourned to the charthouse, where the Professor broke out the Nautical Almanac and went to work. With the present-day almanac it took only about five minutes to work out the five sights.

Each one defined a line of position on the chart. A sight on one star never gives the navigator a fix. It gives him a line, and he can be anywhere along the line. This is because the altitude of the star at a certain instant of time will be the same for observers on a certain great circle around the earth at right angles to the bearing of the star. So to get a fix you have to shoot two stars and you are at the intersection of the two lines of position they give you. Since you can make mistakes in measuring altitudes, refraction of the horizon can vary erratically, and you can also make mistakes in arithmetic, prudent navigators like to shoot a number of stars and get a number of lines. These would all intersect in a point if everything were perfect, which it seldom is.

When the Professor got his sights worked out they all gathered around the chart to lay down the lines of position. The Professor pricked a small hole in the chart at the dead-reckoning position he had used to work out the sights. Then he laid down the bearings of the stars and drew his lines of position at right angles to them. When he got through he had five lines of position, which formed a little hexagon about three miles west of his DR position. The hexagon would fit inside a circle two miles in diameter. The Professor made a prick in the center of the hexagon and said, "Well, there you are, Cap'n—about as pretty a fix as we've had in some time."

"Yeah," said Fatso, "give or take about a mile, that's it. We ought to be off the entrance buoy about noon tomorrow."

"You know, Cap'n," said Satchmo, "what I'd like to know is how do the astronauts navigate? Do they shoot the stars too, the same way we do?"

"No," said the Professor. "This kind of navigation is only good on the earth. Each sight gives you a line around the earth that you know you're on. Out in space this is no good to you, and you can't measure altitudes anyway, because you've got no horizon. So they have inertial navigators."

"What's that?" asked Satchmo.

"It's a system that depends on gyros, accelerometers, and computers," said the Professor. "You know what a gyro is. It keeps pointing in the direction you set it, no matter what the thing it's mounted in does. Well, these astronauts have gyros that are out of this world to keep track of directions for them. Out in space you can't feel 'up' or 'down' any more, so you've got to have a gyro to keep track of it for you."

"Yeah," said Satchmo. "When you get out in space you got zero gravity, so everything just floats around inside the capsule."

"They've also got accelerometers," said the Professor. "You know what they are?"

"No," said Satchmo.

"Well," said the Professor, "you know when you're inside an elevator and it starts up or down, you can't see it move but you can tell when it starts up or down. This is on account of inertia. It's the same thing that tells you when you are turning one way or another in a car, even if you can't see the outside. These accelerometers are very, very accurate, and they measure the inertia. As long as you are going in a straight line at a constant speed, they don't register. But if your speed or heading changes the least bit, they feel it and feed it into a computer. The computer keeps figuring how fast you're going and in which direction, so it always knows where you are."

"They've got the same thing for ships and planes now, haven't they?" asked Webfoot.

"Yeah," said the Professor. "The Polaris subs were the first ones to get it. They've gotta have it because they run submerged all the time and never see the stars. They worked so well on the Polaris subs that all the big ships are getting them now—and even some of the big jet airliners."

"How accurate are they?" asked Webfoot. "Can they tell you where you are as good as these sights we just worked out?"

"Better," said the Professor. "Hell, the astronauts fly to the moon and back and splash down just two miles from the carrier that picks them up."

"And what's this I hear about a satellite navigation system we got now that's just as accurate as the inertial system?" asked Webfoot.

"Yeah," said the Professor. "We got a bunch of satellites in orbit now that go round the world going beep, beep, beep. A couple of them pass overhead or nearly so every few hours. The astronomers can predict their orbits just as accurately as they do the moon's. So you tune your radio in on the satellite and the radio feeds what it hears into a computer. You know the exact frequency of the beeps, but they don't come in at exactly that frequency on account of what they call the Doppler effect. This Doppler effect depends on just exactly where you are with reference to the satellite. The computer does some figuring on the Doppler effect and comes up with your exact latitude and longitude."

"Uh huh," someone said.

"And this thing works day or night, rain or shine. All you gotta do to get a fix off it is to hear it on the radio."

"Is that what guides the Polaris missiles to their targets?" asked Satch.

"No. Not satellites. An inertial system does that. The sub's navigation computer keeps feeding the ship's present position into the missiles. Each missile has its own computer on which the target position is set. When the missile is fired, its own accelerometers and computers take over, and put it on course to the target."

"Do you think this Polaris system is as good as we claim it is?" asked Webfoot.

"You're damn right it is," said the Professor. "There's no defense against it. Those submarines are moving around all the time, so the Russians never know where they are. They are ready to shoot on about one minute's notice at all times. Even if the Russians made a sneak attack and wiped out SAC and our Minute Man silos, Polaris would still be ready. And if they ever shoot, about 150 of Russia's biggest cities will go up in smoke."

"But aren't they working on the same sort of thing, too? What happens when they get a Polaris system, too?"

"That won't bother us much," said the Professor. "It will just be a standoff and we will both be able to wipe each other out—just as we are now, for that matter. The thing that would really upset the applecart would be if they should find some way of tracking our Polaris subs and knowing where they are, so they could knock them off in a sneak attack. But there's no sign of them getting anything like that yet."

The night before they arrived in Tel Aviv, the boys gathered around the radio for the evening news.

"Cairo: The Egyptians announced they have received modern radars, anti-aircraft missiles, and M 16 fighter planes from the Russians. Russian technicians are training the Egyptians in the use of this equipment."

"Hoo boy!" said Jughaid. "That's apt to make a big difference in this war. The Israeli airplanes won't be able to run hog wild any more."

"Jerusalem: The Israelis announced today that a commando raid yesterday across the Suez Canal surprised an Egyptian early-warning station. The station was equipped with the latest Russian radar and electronics gear. The commandos loaded ten trucks with the secret Russian equipment and brought it back to be evaluated by our experts."

"Hah!" said Ginsberg. "The Russians will find out that giving that stuff to the Egyptians is just pouring it down a rat hole."

"Washington: The President announced today that he was holding up the sale of forty Phantom jet fighters to the Israelis. He said this sale would disturb the balance of power in the Near East."

"Balls," said Ginsberg. "We're selling planes to the Arabs in Libya. There are forty million Arabs and only two and a half million Israelis. The Russians are giving the Arabs all-out help. The real reason why we won't let the Israelis have those planes is Middle East oil. We get a hell of a lot of oil from the Arabs, and none from the Israelis."

After the broadcast, Ginsberg said to Fatso, "Skipper, how would you like to get a real inside look at this country we're coming to and find out what this Arab-Israeli war is all about while we're in Tel Aviv?"

"Sure," said Fatso. "Okay by me."

"Well, I got a friend here," said Izzy. "A guy I used to go to school with back in Brooklyn. He's in the Israeli Army now and maybe he can show us around."

⚓ CHAPTER TEN

Arrive Tel Aviv

EARLY NEXT MORNING they were approaching the entrance to Tel Aviv, still about five miles offshore, when a PT boat came boiling over the horizon, circled around them, and hoisted a signal saying, "Heave to or I will fire." LCU 1124 had her colors flying and all hands were in their blue uniforms with white hats, ready for entering port.

"Son of a bitch," said Fatso. "This is the way the *Pueblo* business started. Just who the hell does he think he is? We're in international waters. Pay no attention to him."

LCU 1124 held her course and speed, and the PT circled them a couple of times at close range. An ensign on the bridge was looking them over with a pair of binoculars. Two fifty-caliber machine guns were manned and were kept pointed at LCU 1124.

"She looks like one of them five PT boats the Israelis wangled from the French," observed Fatso.

"Yeah. That's what she is all right," said Scuttlebutt. "And look at those guys pointing their machine guns at us."

"Yeah," said Fatso. "The dumb clucks can see we've got no Arabs on board. We got our colors flying and we're all in uniform."

Soon the signal light on the PT's bridge began blinking. "What ship?" came the message.

"Answer them 'USS LCU 1124,'" said Fatso to Jughaid.

Next camp a message, "Stop your ship."

"Answer that I am in international waters," said Fatso.

This reply caused a conference on the bridge of the PT boat, which had settled down now about twenty yards abeam. The signal, "Heave to or I will fire," was still flying. After the conference they hauled this signal down and ran up another one. The meaning of this one in the international signal book was "We wish to send officer on board."

"Run up the negative flag," said Fatso. "Now send him a blinker message—'We will heave to when we reach territorial waters.'"

When they reached the three-mile limit Fatso stopped his engines. The PTA boat came up alongside and a boatswain's mate armed with a .45-caliber pistol was standing by to come aboard. Fatso yelled over at the bridge, "He won't come aboard wearing that gun."

There was another conference on the bridge, after which the boatswain's mate took off the gun. When he came aboard and was escorted to the bridge, Fatso said, "What can I do for you?"

"I want to see the Captain," said the Israeli.

"That's me," said Fatso.

"I wish to know your nationality," said the Israeli.

"Well, look at our colors," said Fatso. "Look at our uniforms. We're not Arabs. We're not Russians. Have you ever heard of the *Liberty?* We're the same nationality they were."

"Thank you, sir," said the Israeli and returned to the PT boat. Soon the PT hoisted a signal "You may proceed," and hauled clear.

"The clumsy ham-fisted swabs," observed Fatso. "You'd think that after the *Liberty* thing they would be more polite to us."

"Their Navy ain't as good as their Air Force and Army," observed Ginsberg. "It's a very small outfit and they get the left-overs from the other services."

That afternoon Ginsberg went ashore to look up his friend. Tel Aviv was a busy place. It was full of people in uniform bustling about with purposeful looks in their eyes. Everyone seemed in a hurry. Ginsberg finally located his friend in an office at the Army HQ with an orderly, a couple of clerks, and a WAAC receptionist.

"Do you speak English, good-looking?" asked Izzy of the WAAC.

"Yes indeed," said the gal. "What can I do for you?"

"Tell your boss an old friend of his from Brooklyn wants to see him."

Soon Izzy was ushered into a large office where a young captain sat behind a large desk. The Captain was a sharp-looking character about Izzy's age who looked like a linebacker for the Green Bay Packers. As Izzy entered a broad grin spread across his face, he jumped up and advanced to meet him with his hand stuck out.

"Izzy Ginsberg," he exclaimed, giving Izzy a grip that made him wince. "Last time I saw you was that time the cops nailed us for swiping those two bicycles from that shop in Brooklyn. How the hell are you?"

"I'm fine," said Izzy. "I heard you were here, so I thought I'd look you up. Pretty nice layout you got here," he added, glancing around at the spacious, well-furnished office.

"Yeah," said his friend. "It's a little different from the old days in Brooklyn. I'm on the staff of the commanding general here. Been in this army five years now. I see you're in service, too."

"Yeah. I joined the Navy a couple of years ago and I'm on a little craft that came in here this morning. We're going to be here three or four days."

"Fine," said his friend. "I'd like to show you around and let you see what we got here. This is a great country—and it's going places. You might even want to join us after you see it."

"Well—I don't know about that," said Izzy. "I joined the Navy to get out of going to war, and you guys are up to your ass in war right now."

"And we're winning it hand over fist," said his friend. "I'll be glad to take a couple of days off and take you on a tour of the fronts."

"That would be fine," said Izzy. "Could I bring my skipper and maybe one other guy from the ship along?"

"Sure. The more the merrier," said his friend. "We can start off tomorrow morning and in three days I'll give you the grand tour, including Jerusalem, Suez, and the Sinai Peninsula."

"Okay," said Izzy. "We'll be here at eight tomorrow morning."

Next morning Scuttlebutt, Fatso, and Izzy were at the Captain's office at eight. "Captain Cohen," said Izzy, "this is Captain Gioninni and Machinist's Mate First Class Grogan."

"Pleased to meet you," said Cohen. "The name I go by is Benny. What do you gentlemen call yourselves?"

"I'm Fatso and he's Scuttlebutt," said Fatso.

"Now so far the only contact you've had with our people has been with the Navy, hasn't it?" asked Benny.

"That's right," said Fatso.

"Well, don't judge the rest of us from that," said Benny. "The Navy is inexperienced. They haven't had much part in this war, and they're anxious to get into it and show what they can do. They sometimes get pretty ham-fisted—like they did with the *Liberty*."

"Ummm," Fatso murmured.

"Now I'm going to show you the other side of the coin," said the Captain. "I'll take you on the grand tour and show you anything you want. We'll get to some places where the natives are unfriendly. It will take three days. Okay?"

"Okay," said Fatso. "We've heard a great deal about Israel from our friend Izzy here. We'd like to have a look at it."

So the four of them set out in an Army station wagon for Jerusalem. The country they passed through on the way was a far cry from the usual Near East countryside. There were green, well-kept, and prosperous-looking farms on all sides. The people were clean, alert, and happy looking. Highways were well paved and roadside villages, obviously only a few years old, were of modern construction and the houses were all neatly painted with bright gardens around them. Electric power and telephone lines crisscrossed the country, and every house had a TV antenna on top.

"Hell, this doesn't look much like what I thought it would," observed Fatso. "It looks almost like our country back home."

"It does now," said Benny. "But you should of seen it five or six years ago. Most of it was just about the same as it had been for the past two thousand years.

"Didn't anybody live here then?" asked Fatso.

"Yeah. The Arabs lived here," said Benny.

"What happened to them?"

"We moved 'em out," said Benny.

"Just moved 'em out? Where to?" asked Fatso.

"Across the border to Jordan," said Benny. "Later on I'll show you their camps. They were a shiftless, no-good bunch."

"So you just threw them out. Just like that?"

"Well, after all," said Izzy, "this country is ours by rights. We owned it two thousand years ago and got thrown out. Now we're just taking it back again. What's wrong with that?"

"I don't take no stock in this idea that just because a country belonged to you two thousand years ago you got a right to take it back now," said Fatso. "If you figure things that way some Indian wearing a crummy blanket is apt to come up to my house someday and say, 'Get out—this place belonged to my ancestors a couple of hundred years ago.'"

"I go along with that," said Benny. "This stuff about having title to this place two thousand years ago is just a lot of malarkey the longhairs put out because they aren't willing to face the facts of life. We're in here because we're a tough, industrious, and adventurous people. We found a desert here and we've converted it into a thriving, prosperous country. It belongs to us now because we developed it from nothing and because we are willing and able to defend it. The six-day war settled that pretty well."

"Now you're talking a language that I understand," said Fatso. "That's exactly what I say to the Indians who want to throw me out."

"This world is still run by force, whether you like it or not," continued the Captain. "Hell, even your peaceniks back in the States know that. They agitate for peace by defying the cops, heaving rocks, and setting fire to things."

"Of course, you know we've got the UN now to keep the peace," said Fatso.

"The UN! Hah!" snorted the Captain. "The UN don't amount to a fart in a piss pot. They had a peacekeeping force here for some years, but they bugged out the minute Nasser said boo to them."

"Israel is a member of the UN," said Fatso.

"Sure. But I'll be damned if I know why," said the Captain. "All these brand-new cannibal republics in Africa have one vote, the same as we do, and most of them side with the Russians now."

"You don't believe in this one-man-one-vote idea?" asked Fatso.

"Hell, no. That's the damnedest bill of goods the longhairs ever sold to a gullible world. 'All men are born equal,' they tell you with a straight face. Hell, if you think the Arabs and the Israeli are equal, just compare this country right now with what it was only twenty years ago. The only time all men are equal is when they die. And the churches will all give you an argument about even that proposition."

⚓ CHAPTER ELEVEN

Jerusalem

IN JERUSALEM they made the grand tour of the city, visiting the Wailing Wall, the Mosque of Omar, and all the holy places of the Christian religion. In the Jewish sections the city was a beehive of activity, with alert citizens bustling about with purposeful looks on their faces. One very noticeable feature of the Jerusalem scene was that everyone of military age was in uniform. The only civilians were youngsters and old people.

The Arab section of the city provided a marked contrast. The streets, patrolled by armed soldiers, were full of beggars and urchins. Many of the shops were closed, and even in those that were open sullen-looking Arabs glared at them evilly as they went by.

"Quite a contrast between the old and new sections of the city," observed Fatso.

"Yes. They're about a thousand years apart," said the Captain. "In the buildings, the people, and their outlooks on life."

"What are you going to do with these people?" asked Fatso.

"If they are willing to conform, we can absorb them. Otherwise they will have to get out."

"Where can they go?"

"That's *their* problem," said the Captain.

That afternoon they visited a fighter field just outside Jerusalem. The Captain checked in at the CO's office, where his credentials were obviously of the very best, and a young lieutenant was assigned to them as guide. The Lieutenant took them out to the line and introduced them to the pilot of one of the fighter aircraft sitting there on two minutes' notice to take off.

He was a bright-eyed young lad of about twenty, who spoke good English. He rattled off a lot of performance figures on his aircraft, described the armament, and then said, "Of course, these are planes we got from the French. They're good planes. But the Russians are now supplying the Egyptians with MIG's, which can outperform these by quite a bit. We are now negotiating with your country for forty Phantoms of more modern design."

"You guys seem to be doing pretty well with the planes you've got," said Fatso.

"That's because the Arabs are stupid," said the pilot. "Their planes are better than ours, but they don't know how to fly them. And we haven't come up against any of the late MIG's the Russians are supposed to be giving them now."

"What will you do if the Russians start flying them?"

"We'll have to knock them out on the ground," said the pilot. "And the Russians don't really want the Egyptians to win this war, anyway. They just want to keep it going."

From the line they went into the operations room. When they got there the controllers were in a huddle at the big early-warning radar scope.

An unidentified blip had just appeared on the southern edge of the scope, heading for Jerusalem.

After a quick glance at the big board showing the location of all of his own airborne planes, the senior controller said, "Okay, challenge him an IFF." After the third challenge the senior controller said, "Okay—sound the alarm—scramble four fighters." Everyone on watch immediately put out their cigarettes and settled down to business as the siren outside let out a wail, followed shortly by the roar of jet engines starting up.

The controller took station in the middle of the room facing the big vertical plotting board and put on his phones. His board was now showing a plot of a bogy approaching Jerusalem from the south about eighty miles away. It also showed two fighters orbiting over the field at forty thousand feet.

The controller called the fighters and said, "Unidentified bogy approaching from the south at forty thousand feet, eighty miles. Vector 180. Intercept and identify."

Back over the loudspeaker came a "Roger," and the plot of the orbiting aircraft became a line heading south.

A minute later the controller talking to the aircraft then scrambling from the field gave them the same orders. Then he called the pair making the intercept and said, "Bogy shows no IFF. Vector 160."

Back came a matter-of-fact "Roger."

By now the bogy was only sixty miles from Jerusalem. The four scramblers were streaking south and climbing. The two interceptors were closing rapidly. The air of the control room was tense and silent as all hands riveted their gaze on the big board. The wing commander had come in and taken station right behind the controller.

Soon the loudspeaker said, "We've got him on radar," and a moment later, "Tallyho. It's a MIG—am attacking."

On the big radar scope the blips of the bogy and the interceptors had now merged into one. The controller walked over and peered at the scope. Soon word came in from the leader of the scramblers: "Have sighted spiral of black smoke dead ahead about ten miles."

Israeli smoke is just as black as Egyptian—so for a few seconds the tense silence held. Then came a jubilant call from the interceptor, "Have shot down a MIG in flames," and a wild cheer broke out from everyone in the ops room. The voice from the air continued, "It was a late-model MIG—I put a long burst into him—he torched and blew up."

There was another wild cheer with all hands in the control room dancing up and down and slapping each other on the back.

"How the hell can your obsolete French planes knock down a late-model MIG that way?" demanded Fatso of their escort when the cheering subsided.

"Our pilots are better," said the escort simply.

When they left the ops room the Captain said, "I suppose you guys would like to spend the night on the town, but this town closes up at eight P.M."

"Why is that?" demanded Ginsberg.

"Everybody is either in uniform or is working like hell," said the Captain. "We don't have time for any night life around the town. But there's apt to be plenty on the base tonight, celebrating the victory you just saw. I suggest we spend the night here."

They had dinner in the mess hall and went around to the enlisted men's club afterward. The club was jammed and everyone was in a hilarious mood celebrating the kill. Three American sailors in uniform naturally attracted attention, and soon a group of young Israelis who spoke English had gathered at their table.

"Well, how do you like our country?" asked one of Fatso.

"Fine," said Fatso, "what I've seen of it. But it looks like defending it is the major occupation."

"That's right. It is," said the Israeli. "Another showdown with the Arabs is coming up soon. We've got to be ready for it—or we won't have any country left to defend."

"Are you worried about it?" asked Fatso.

"Not a damn bit. We've beaten them twice in the past ten years. They haven't learned a thing. We'll do it again."

"Well, yeah," said Fatso. "Maybe you can take the Arabs all right. But how about the Russians?"

"As long as all they do is supply the Arabs with arms, we'll still beat them. The Arabs are just inferior people, and the Russians will find out sooner or later that any arms they give them just go down the drain. Last week you know we captured a whole Russian radar station intact at Suez. This afternoon we shot down one of their latest MIG's."

"Well, yeah. But suppose the Russians take an active part in the war. Then what?" asked Fatso.

"We'll cross that bridge when and if we come to it. The Russians don't want to get into any all-out shooting war down here. They've got the Chinese to worry about, you know. They just want to keep this war going, and they really don't give a damn who wins it."

"They're giving the Arabs Navy ships now, and MIG's with Russian pilots," said Scuttlebutt.

"Sure. And you saw what we did to their MIG this afternoon."

"And you just watch," said Ginsberg. "Pretty soon we are going to be sending some of our Phantom jet fighters to these people. They'll knock every MIG right out of the sky."

"One thing that's quite noticeable around here," said Fatso, "is that nearly everybody of military age is in uniform."

"Yeah. We're one hundred percent mobilized. We have to be."

"Do you have any hippies, peaceniks, or conscientious objectors?" asked Fatso.

"Hell, no," said the Israeli. "I've never heard of one. But lots of people over and under draft age lie about their age to get into the service."

"Boy! That's a hell of a lot different from the way we've got it at home," observed Scuttlebutt. "Every college campus is full of beatniks, hippies, and draft-card burners. They have big parades and rallies in Washington where they haul down the American flag and hoist the Viet Cong."

"Your situation is different from ours," observed the Israeli, "in at least two important ways. First of all, your war is on the other side of the world eight thousand miles away. Ours is right here in our own front yard. That makes a hell of a difference. We're fighting for our lives."

"Well, so are we, when you come right down to it," said Scuttlebutt. "We're not fighting in Vietnam because they're friends of ours and we want to free them. That's just incidental. We're fighting to prevent the Reds from dominating the world. If they get to be top dog, we will become a slave nation like Czechoslovakia. That's the real reason why we're in Vietnam. I'd a damn sight rather fight the Reds in Vietnam than in the United States."

"Yeah," said the Israeli, "but your hippies don't look at it that way. They were born after the war and got too much too easy. There's a whole generation of them that have had everything handed to them on a silver platter. They think the world owes them a living and the only place they're willing to fight for it is in the streets. They're in favor of peace except when the cops show up. Then they yell, 'Kill the pigs.' "

"What I don't understand," said another Israeli, "is why the older people stand for it. Hell, there's ten times as many of them as there are hippies."

"The trouble is that the hippies get all the publicity," said Fatso. "The press and radio feature everything they do. Matter of fact they promote a lot of it. They set up their cameras in front of a government building and then egg the hippies on to tear down the flag."

"Sure, your press helps to promote a lot of it," said the Israeli. "But the real trouble is a lot deeper than that. There's another big difference between your country and ours."

"What's that?" asked Fatso.

"Our country is a new one. We're in the pioneer stage, where your country was two hundred years ago. Our people are willing to work, and fight if necessary. Yours is an old country—and it's getting soft."

"Whaddya mean an old one?" demanded Izzy. "We're less than two hundred years old."

"Sure. But you're really the oldest government in the world

today, except maybe for some primitive tribes that haven't heard about democracy yet. Till the end of World War II, you were a hard-working, industrious people who had to work for what you got. But your country just doesn't have the pioneer spirit any more. I think Khrushchev was right when he said he would bury you."

"Now wait a minute," said Fatso. "We're still the greatest country in the world by a wide margin."

"Sure. But not by anywhere near as wide a margin as you were only twenty-five years ago. At the end of World War II you were by far the most powerful country on earth—militarily, industrially, politically—any way you want to look at it. Since then you've fought two wars with third-rate Asiatic powers. The first one was a stalemate. You're losing the second. And you're losing it for the same reason that France lost their Indo-China war. The people back home just don't have the guts to win it."

"You can say that again," said Fatso. "We're losing the war on the home front."

"But after all you people did pretty good with your country," said the Israeli. "You brought it from a third-rate colony to the greatest country in the world in a hundred and fifty years. It has started coming apart at the seams now, but you've still got thirty or forty years to go before you become second raters like France and England."

"I wouldn't bet on that," said Fatso. Then changing the subject he said, "Your boy sure did a nice job on that MIG this afternoon."

"Yeah. That's the fifth MIG that pilot has shot down. That makes him an ace, and he'll get a big medal for it," said an Israeli.

"No. That's only number four for him. He's still got one more to go," said another lad.

"It's five by my count," said the first.

"He's got four confirmed kills, counting the one today, and one only probable. He's got to get one more sure kill for his medal," said the second.

"Did you ever hear about the Australian fighter pilot who was getting decorated during the Battle of Britain by His Majesty the King?" said Fatso.

No one had.

"Well, it seems," said Fatso, "that this young Australian fighter pilot went out one day during the Battle of Britain and he shot down five Nazi aircraft over the Channel. Five in one day. So, of course, the next time they had an honors ceremony down in London, they had this young man out to Buckingham Palace, so His Majesty could give him a medal.

"Now you may remember, King George the Sixth used to stutter a little bit. But he had been working on this handicap and had almost overcome it. At the honors ceremony this morning, he got through all the citations except the last one without a single stutter. The last one was the one for this Australian, and when he read that one he said, 'This medal is for shooting down f-f-f-four Nazi airplanes.'

"Well, of course, it wasn't four, it was five. And you know how these Australians are—they have no respect for anything or any-body, and if they think they're getting a bum deal they'll speak up and say so, no matter when nor where. And this young lad was not about to be short-changed on his citation. So he spoke up right there in the palace. And unfortunately he stuttered a little bit too.

"He said, 'Your M-majesty, there's been a m-m-mistake. It wasn't f-f-f-our Nazi airplanes. It was f-f-f-five.'

"Well, of course, everybody was flabbergasted at this gawd-awful breach of palace etiquette. But His Majesty kept his cool, and he looked back at the citation and said, 'Well—it s-says here f-f-f-four.'

"The Australian still wasn't buying it. He said, 'Your M-ma-jesty, I was there. I sh-sh-shot them down and I c-c-counted them. It wasn't f-f-f-four Nazi airplanes. It was *f-f-f-five!*'

"Well, then the King began to get a bit goaty with this whippersnapper who was lousing up a formal palace ceremony. But he kept his temper as best he could. And finally he said, 'Young man. What d-difference does it make? Even if you shot down t-t-ten Nazi airplanes—you're only going to get *one* f-f-f-fucking medal.'"

On that note the party broke up.

⚓ CHAPTER TWELVE

Suez

NEXT MORNING they set forth in the station wagon for the Dead Sea. Before starting the Captain said, "We're going to be in former Arab territory today. This is territory we captured in the six-day war, and some of the natives are hostile. I've got a .45-caliber pistol for each of you, and we've got four Thompson submachine guns in the car. I don't think we're going to need them—but we've got them just in case."

The country through which they drove was quite different from that between Tel Aviv and Jerusalem. The roads were dirt—and dusty—and they passed many more oxcarts than they did automobiles. The countryside was bare and barren except for small groves of olive trees and a few little cultivated fields. The most modern piece of farm machinery they saw was a hand scythe. The houses and villages were primitive; there were no electric power lines and no TV antennas. Most of the people were dirty, listless-looking Arabs who glowered at them.

"This is what all Israel looked like twenty-five years ago," observed the Captain. "Put our people in here and in ten years we'll make a modern, prosperous country out of it just like it is around Tel Aviv."

"Couldn't these people do it, too—if you helped them a little bit?" asked Fatso.

"No," said the Captain. "You've just got to realize that these are inferior people. There are such people in the world, you know, despite what all the long-haired liberals say about all races and peoples being equal."

At the end of the Dead Sea, they stood on the west bank of

the Wadi d'Araba and gazed across the dry river bed at a huge array of tents and shacks.

"That's Jordan over there. And those are Arab refugees," said the Captain.

"Where did they come from?" asked Ginsberg.

"These people probably came from around Tel Aviv."

"What did you do? Just kick them out?" asked Fatso.

"More or less," said the Captain. "You probably think we gave them a rough deal. But it was just the price of progress. If we had left them where they were, that area around Tel Aviv that we drove through yesterday would still be the same as this area we're driving through today. These people would be eking out a miserable existence there and the country would be worthless. We moved them out, and by the sweat of our brows we've made something out of the country. And these people really aren't any worse off here today than they would be if they were still living around Tel Aviv."

"What's that stuff growing in those fields out around the edge of town?" asked Scuttlebutt.

"Mostly opium," said the Captain. "The Arabs grow a hell of a lot of opium."

"What the hell do they do with it?" asked Scuttlebutt.

"Most of it winds up in the United States," said the Captain. "They smuggle it out in bales to the big dope rings in Marseilles and Naples. They take the raw stuff and refine it to morphine and heroin and smuggle it into your country. The Arabs get about a hundred bucks a bale for it. By the time a bale has been processed into morphine and heroin and sold in the U.S. it will probably bring a couple of million bucks."

"Those sons of bitches that are peddling dope are a bigger threat to the future of the country than the hippies or the Black Panthers," observed Fatso. "They're even selling it to high-school kids now. On nearly any high-school campus you can get any kind of dope you want, including even heroin. I think the people who supply that stuff to kids are the lowest scum of the earth. It ought to be a capital offense."

"Well, there's big money in it," said the Captain. "Real big money. And a hell of a lot of it comes from these Arab countries."

From there they cut across Israel to the Gaza Strip. The country was dotted with small farms and kibbutzim. Tractors and power-driven farm machines were visible everywhere, roads were good, and irrigation ditches crisscrossed the country.

"All this place was practically a desert just a few years back," said the Captain, as they passed a pasture with a fine big herd of beef cattle. "Give us another ten years and this will all be rich farmland. We've got plans for some big irrigation projects as soon as the war is over."

From the Gaza Strip they drove along the Mediterranean coast through desolate desert country. It was deserted except for occasional refugee camps, but the road was a busy one, with military convoys going both ways.

"Our first line of defense is now the east bank of the Suez Canal," explained the Captain. "We shoved them back about a hundred miles from where they were before the six-day war, and we've also shoved the Jordanians and the Syrians back and, as you saw, we've got all of Jerusalem now."

"You gonna keep all the territory you captured?" asked Fatso.

"You're damn right we are," said the Captain. "We've got to. Just remember there are less than three million of us against forty million Arabs."

"But suppose the big powers and the UN were willing to guarantee your old borders?" asked Fatso.

The Captain spit and said, "Hah! the UN can't even guarantee to stop a tribal war in Africa. The policy of the big powers changes with each new election. No sir. We've got to go it alone and stand on our own feet. We're perfectly willing and able to do it, too."

They drove down the east bank of the Suez Canal. It was a deserted waterway. The only ships they saw were sunk, with their upper works sticking up out of the water.

"Nothing goes through this canal except small craft now," said the Captain. "The channel is blocked by wrecks and it's filling up with sand. This gives you a good example of what kind of worthless people the Arabs are. It used to be that a hell of a lot of oil went through this canal. Now they're building pipelines to get it out of Arabia—and tankers that carry half a million tons and take it around the Cape. Even if they opened up the canal now, there wouldn't be much use for it, any more."

As they were proceeding along the shore of the canal a plane trailing black smoke behind it came out of the west, losing altitude rapidly.

"Hey. That guy's in trouble," said Fatso.

"Yeah. And he's one of ours," said the Captain. "A Mirage."

They stopped the car and watched as the plane neared the bank of the canal, coming down and smoking heavily. As it crossed the canal, by this time only one hundred feet in the air, an object shot up in the air out of the cockpit and, an instant later, a parachute opened with a man swinging below it.

The plane flew on about a quarter of a mile and then dove into the ground and exploded. The chute came down about one hundred yards from the car and the four occupants got out and started running to the spot.

As soon as the flyer saw them he flopped to the ground, whipped out a pistol, and sent a shot whistling over their heads, causing them all to flop into the sand too.

"Hey—we're friends," yelled the Captain.

After a moment the flyer yelled back, "One of you come forward with his hands up."

The Captain got up and advanced slowly, his hands in the air. The flyer made him halt about twenty feet away, looked him over carefully, and they exchanged a few words. Then the flyer put up his gun, they embraced each other, and the Captain waved the others forward.

"These are American friends of mine," he said, introducing Fatso, Scuttlebutt, and Izzy. "Are you okay?"

"Yeah—I'm all right," said the flyer. "But I just barely made it back to this side. For a while I was afraid I was going to come down in Egypt."

"What happened?" asked Ginsberg.

"One of those goddamn SAM's the Russians are giving them got me near Cairo. I saw the son of a bitch coming about ten seconds before it hit. But I couldn't dodge it."

"You're lucky you made it back to this side," said the Captain.

"You're telling *me!*" said the pilot.

The four of them helped the pilot to gather up his chute and load it into the car.

"You want to go look at the wreck?" asked the Captain.

"No indeed," said the pilot. "There isn't much to look at anyway. She torched as soon as she hit."

They got in the car and proceeded.

After a few moments the pilot said, "I didn't think the U.S. Navy was on speaking terms with the Israelis."

"What do you mean? On account of the *Liberty?*" asked Fatso.

"Yeah," said the pilot.

"You better not get me talking about the *Liberty*," said Fatso, "or we may not be friends any longer."

"You can't hurt my feelings by anything you say about the *Liberty*," said the Captain. "The Army had nothing to do with that snafu."

"Yeah," said the pilot. "It was a Navy show all the way."

"The hell you say," said Fatso. "There were a couple of Air Force planes that strafed her and shot the hell out of her."

"Yeah, I know," said the pilot. "I was there. But I didn't take any part in the shooting. My job was just to get pictures."

"Well, how the hell do you explain what happened?" asked Fatso.

"We got booby-trapped into it by the Navy," said the pilot. "The Navy had torpedo boats right there. They actually put a torpedo into the *Liberty*. You couldn't blame our pilots for opening up on her after that."

"Well, maybe not," conceded Fatso. "But how the hell do you explain your Navy going off half-cocked the way they did? They just opened up on her without even a challenge."

"Yeah, that was pretty stupid," said the flyer. "But they had no notice that you had a ship out there. They found this strange ship close to our own shores. She wasn't one of ours. She wasn't a merchant ship. You can't blame them for thinking she was working for the other side."

"Balls," said Fatso. "She was fifteen miles offshore, outside territorial waters. Your torpedo boats had her surrounded and they could make forty knots so she couldn't possibly get away from them. It was just plain murder for them to open up on her the way they did."

"It was pretty bad," said the Captain. "The real trouble was that the Navy was just too damn anxious to get a piece of the action in the war. The Air Force and the Army had been covering themselves with glory and the Navy felt left out of things. When they thought they saw a chance to make some headlines for themselves they went off half-cocked."

"That's what I've been saying ever since it happened," said Fatso.

"Well—we apologized and paid an indemnity," said the Captain.

"If you hang around the outskirts of a barroom brawl you're apt to get hurt," said the flyer.

"Humph," observed Fatso.

Soon they came to a sentry post, where they stopped, and the pilot checked in with HQ by phone and asked them to notify his home station that he had been shot down but was O.K.

They spent the night at Bohr Selim, at the north end of the Gulf of Suez, about thirty miles from the city of Suez. There was a large Army camp there, obviously a front-line outpost. The first ring of sentries was ten miles from the main camp; there were strongpoints and roadblocks every few miles along the road where they were stopped and inspected by nervously alert guards.

"We have commando raids by both sides here nearly every night," said the Captain. "We retaliate against each other, but we've lost track of who started it and which side is retaliating now."

"How do you get across to the other side?" asked Scuttlebutt.

"We've got a detachment of Navy PT boats here," said the Captain. "You remember those five boats we got from the French about a year ago? The ones that were supposed to be going to Sweden? Well, we hauled them overland to the Gulf of Aqaba and brought them up here."

After dinner that night Fatso, Scuttlebutt, and the Captain were in the operations center. The duty officer was explaining to them: "Things are quiet so far tonight. There was an Egyptian commando raid up toward the Port Said sector, which was driven back and we got ten prisoners. But nothing down this way yet. But, if you stick around about an hour, we may have some pretty good action for you up in Suez by the Navy."

"What have you got cooking?" asked the Captain.

"We've got four PT boats on the way to Suez now," said the duty officer. "They're going to make a raid into the harbor there and shoot up the waterfront. They're about halfway there now," he added, pointing to a plot on the big vertical board. "We won't hear from them until they start shooting."

"Where did you learn to speak English so good?" asked Scuttlebutt.

"In Brooklyn," said the duty officer. "I was born and raised there."

"Huh," said Scuttlebutt. "We got a guy from Brooklyn along with us. . . . Where the hell is Izzy? . . . I haven't seen him since chow."

"You mean Izzy Ginsberg?" said the DO. "Izzy and I went to school together back in Brooklyn. He was in here just before supper and we had quite a time cutting up old touches. He's gone out on one of the PT boats on the Suez raid."

"He's *what?*" demanded Fatso.

"He asked me if he could go along," said the DO, "and I told him 'sure.' Don't worry about him. It's perfectly safe."

"I ain't worried a damn bit about *him*," said Fatso. "He can get his ass shot off, if he wants to. But if something happens and he gets captured, there will be hell to pay. Nasser could make a federal case out of American sailors helping the Israelis."

"Don't worry about it. He won't get captured," said the DO.

"Hell, I hope not," said Fatso. "We got no business down here in the first place. If the Egyptians capture that guy, my ass will be in a jam."

On the No. 4 PT boat, proceeding up the Gulf of Suez, Izzy Ginsberg was at the wheel. The boats were blacked out and were making twenty knots. The skipper was explaining to Izzy.

"All you gotta do is just stay about thirty yards astern of that guy ahead of you. Just follow right in his wake. Can you see him all right,"

"Yeah. I see him," said Izzy.

"After we get in the harbor we will speed up and make one fast sweep around the shoreline. We'll catch them sound asleep, beat the hell out of them and then haul ass out of there."

"Uh huh," said Izzy.

"We're going to blast them with everything we've got so it will be pretty noisy while we are in there. But you just keep your eye on the next ahead and stay right behind him."

"I'd like to shoot one of those guns while we're in there," said Ginsberg.

"No. You steer and we'll handle the guns. Handling one of these guns in the dark is quite a trick."

Soon the lights of Suez appeared ahead. "It's lit up like a waterfront whorehouse on a Saturday night," observed Izzy.

"It won't be from now on," said the skipper.

At twenty knots they were throwing up quite a wake, so as they neared the harbor entrance they slowed down. There was no challenge at the entrance. The four boats proceeded in column at slow speed until a quarter of a mile from the west end of the waterfront.

"What the hell!" said Izzy. "Are we going to land here?"

"Just keep your shirt on," said the skipper. "We'll open up any minute now."

Suddenly there was a blast of gunfire from the leading boat and they all opened up. Each boat had two 40-mm guns and four 20-mm's, all firing explosive ammo with tracers. The bright lights of the tracers made a pretty sight as they flew converging in to the beach. The flashes of their explosions at the end of their flight danced along the waterfront, winking brightly among the other waterfront lights. For at least two minutes there was no sign of any reaction on the beach. Then lights began going out, and fires broke out along the west end of the waterfront as gunfire erupted from various points along the beach.

By this time the boats had gone up to forty knots and were leaving creamy-white wakes behind them as they swept along the beach blasting away. Much of the waterfront was in flames by now and suddenly the whole harbor was lit up with a garish light as a big oil tanker anchored near the beach blew up with a great flash.

"Holy cow," said Izzy. "It's like shooting fish in a barrel."

By then all hell had busted loose ashore. Machine guns were spitting bullets into the bay in all directions and 40-mm's were bursting all over, including on board merchant vessels anchored in the harbor. The AA batteries were filling the sky with bursting shells. There were fires and explosions all along the waterfront.

Most of the gunfire intended for the PT boats was hitting far astern. But as they neared the east end of their run along the waterfront a stray 40-mm caught the last boat smack in the engine room. All three engines stopped and the boat went dead.

The engineer leaped from the gun he was manning to the engine-room hatch as the skipper took the wheel and headed away from the beach. Izzy jumped to the gun the engineer had abandoned and got off a short burst before the skipper roared at him, "Cut that out, you crazy bastard—*cease fire*—you'll have all the guns on the beach on us."

Another crew member ducked into the engine room with a flashlight and fire extinguisher. Soon word came up through the hatch: "It looks bad, Cap'n—two engines are gone—I don't know about the third yet."

"Okay," said the skipper. "If we have to abandon ship I'll blow her up."

Meantime the other three boats had reached the end of their run along the waterfront, had ceased fire, and were headed out, leaving great white wakes behind them. The wild shooting from the beach got even wilder, and several Arab ships hit by stray bullets were blazing merrily. The whole waterfront was a mass of flames.

Soon there were a few sporadic coughs from the engine room. Then the engine began kicking over irregularly and a voice yelled up through the hatch, "I got the midship engine going, Cap'n . . . but I don't know how long it will last."

"Okay," said the skipper. "We're going out."

As they headed for the entrance at about eight knots they saw the three white plumes from the wakes of the other boats swing around and head in again.

"They've missed us," announced the skipper. "They're coming back to get us. Stand by your towline," he yelled at his crew.

The crew scrambled forward and began breaking out the towline. The skipper tried to call the other boats by radio phone but the set was dead.

They watched as the other three boats swept through the harbor again, passing about a quarter of a mile from them, and then went back out and disappeared in the west.

They limped along at eight knots, passed the harbor entrance, and squared away on a course for home. The thunder of the guns behind them continued for at least twenty minutes as the Arabs raked the harbor from all directions and filled the sky with bursting AA shells.

Meanwhile the ops room was crowded with senior officers watching the plot board and waiting for news from the raid. The radar had lost the plot on the PT boats when they were about twenty miles out. Fatso was chewing his fingernails over Izzy.

"This will be our first raid into Suez," said the station commander to the Captain. "We'll probably catch them sound asleep. The Navy has been after me to let them do this for a long time."

Presently the DO announced, "They should be entering the harbor any minute now. It seems to be going okay because they haven't been seen yet, and they're almost there now."

Suddenly the loudspeaker blared out, "Alpha Base from Night Hawk One. We are opening fire in the harbor. Complete surprise attained. Out."

A cheer went up from the assembled crowd. "Night Hawk One from Alpha Base—give 'em hell," said the DO into his phone.

For the next five minutes, broadcasts from Night Hawk One were sporadic: "All four boats in action . . . large fire has broken out near oil tanks . . . AA batteries are shooting all over the sky . . . shore batteries firing in all directions . . . have completed firing run and am standing out."

At this point word came in from watchers outside. "The sky to the north is full of AA bursts—it looks like a Chinese New Year's."

A moment later Night Hawk One came on again. "Alpha Base. One of my boats is missing. . . . I'm going back in to get him."

This threw a wet blanket over the celebration in the ops room. Five minutes later Night Hawk One came on again. "Can't find missing boat. It's getting too goddamn hot in here. Can't stay any longer. I'm coming out."

A few minutes later he came on the air again. "Alpha Base, we are back out . . . Number Four boat is missing . . . other three returning. No personnel casualties. Out."

As soon as Fatso had a chance he said to the Captain, "Ask the DO which boat Ginsberg was on."

A moment later the Captain returned with a grave look and said, "Number Four."

"Oh, my gawd," said Fatso.

An hour later the three PT boats returned to the base and the crews came up to the ops room for debriefing.

"We caught them completely by surprise," said the leader. "We were shooting for at least two minutes before they fired a shot. We shot up about six ships and the whole waterfront. We really blasted the waterfront good, and by the time we left there were a dozen fires going ashore and one of them, down by the oil tanks, was real big. I don't know what happened to Number Four. She was the last boat in column and nobody knows when she fell out. When they finally opened up on us from the beach things got pretty hot, and everybody was so busy looking out for himself we didn't have time to watch the other boats. When we got out and found Number 4 missing we went back in as far as we dared. By that time all hell was busting loose ashore. We made one quick sweep through the harbor, but nobody saw her. We called him several times by radio, but got no answer. So—they must of got in a lucky hit on him. Too bad—they were a damned good crew."

The debriefing continued with a lot of detailed questions to all members of the crews. At the end of it Fatso said, "Well—maybe she went down with all hands and the Egyptians will never find out there was an American aboard. We can just report him missing when we leave Tel Aviv and that will be that."

"Yeah," agreed Scuttlebutt. "It will go into his record as desertion. But that don't make no difference. His dependents wouldn't get nothing anyway if they knew how it really happened."

"Except that little kike will probably swim ashore and get captured by the Egyptians just as sure as hell," said Fatso.

Fatso got little sleep that night. They started back to Tel Aviv early next morning. About fifteen miles out from Alpha Base they sighted a group of five bedraggled figures walking along the road toward them. The figures deployed across the road and began waving as they approached. Soon Scuttlebutt said, "Hey—there's Izzy!"

And so it was—Izzy and the four members of the boat's crew. They picked them up, turned around, and the Captain called the base on his walkie-talkie and gave them the good news.

Izzy bubbled over with the story of their adventure. "We was the last boat in column," he said. "I was on the bridge—had the wheel as a matter of fact. It was darker than hell in the harbor, and I could just barely see the next boat ahead. But the waterfront was lit up like a whorehouse on Saturday night. When we opened up it was really something—two 40-mm's and four 20's on each boat— all shooting tracers. We blasted away at least two minutes before they fired a shot at us. But when they finally opened up, all hell busted loose. They were just blasting away without knowing what they were shooting at—even the AA batteries opened up, and it was like a Fourth of July. . . . Then we got hit—right smack in the engine room—by an explosive shell. It knocked out our radio and all three of our engines. But it was just one lucky hit. Two of our engines were gone—permanently. We got the other going after about five minutes and limped out. We could only make about six knots, and we had no radio. We could see our other boats pull-ahead, still blasting away. After about five minutes they stopped shooting and that's the last we saw of them. The Arabs kept blasting away in all directions for about fifteen minutes after we ceased fire—just wild shooting all over the harbor. They probably did as much damage to themselves as we did. Well, anyway, we finally limped out of the harbor and headed for the base. But we could soon see we weren't going to make it all the way back. Our one engine was gradually pooping out on us. So we headed for the beach on the eastern shore and we finally ran her aground there about an hour ago. So here we are."

"Izzy did a real good job for us," said the skipper of the boat. "He was just the same as a regular member of the crew. He steered real good and never batted an eye when we got hit."

By this time they had arrived back at the first sentry post. "Let's stop here," said Fatso. "We can leave the regular crew here. Then we can get the hell on our way."

"Don't you want to deliver them back to the base?" asked the Captain.

"Hell, no," said Fatso. "If we do that, it will come out officially that this clown of mine was in the boat's crew. I want to get him the hell out of here so nothing will be said about it. The base can get a car out here in ten minutes for these other guys."

"Okay," said the Captain. "I guess you're right about that."

So they dropped off the rest of the crew at the sentry post. There were fond farewells between Izzy and the others, and protestations of eternal friendship. They headed back for Tel Aviv again.

About every twenty miles or so they were stopped by armed outposts and had to identify themselves. While still about thirty miles from the Gaza Strip, they found out why this was necessary. On a stretch of road about ten miles from the nearest outpost, they ran into a roughly constructed roadblock. When they stopped at it, gunfire opened up on them from the dunes on both sides of the road about fifty yards back. They had been ambushed by a band of Arab guerrillas.

The Captain plowed through the roadblock, but when he tried to give her the gun and get away, a burst of gunfire shot away both his front tires and he went off the road. Everybody grabbed a tommy gun, scrambled out of the car, and found shelter in the ditch. As the others blasted away at the dunes with the tommy guns, the Captain called the nearest outpost on his walkie-talkie with an SOS. The reply came back, "Okay—help is on the way."

"All right, boys," said the Captain. "Keep down low, and keep shifting your position. We'll have help here in about fifteen minutes."

There were about a dozen Arabs hiding behind sand dunes and bushes back from the road. Whenever an Arab ventured into the open, he was greeted by a tommy-gun blast. They evidently did not expect such a blast of gunfire from this harmless-looking station wagon, and were taken aback by it. They kept up a heavy fire themselves, but their bullets whistled harmlessly over the ditch. Soon they began crawling forward in relays, covered by the fire of those still behind the dunes.

"Look, Captain," yelled Fatso, as the Captain directed a long burst at a moving figure. "We'll be out of ammo pretty soon at this rate. We better start shooting single aimed shots."

"Okay," said the Captain. "We can't hold out much longer."

They got several of the Arabs, but the others kept closing in and pretty soon there was a ring of them only about twenty-five yards away. "Help better get here soon, or it will be too late," declared Scuttlebutt, as he drilled an Arab between the eyes.

The Arabs shot hell out of the station wagon. But they couldn't hit the boys in the ditch. One of them heaved a hand grenade into the ditch right alongside the Captain. Fatso pounced on it and heaved it back. It exploded just about over the spot where it had been heaved from.

The Arabs kept creeping forward and the situation was getting desperate when a fighter plane came roaring down the road at tree-top height. It spotted the car in the ditch, zoomed up, and circled the spot. Then it made a couple of firing passes at the Arabs, who were in full flight by now.

A few minutes later two whirlybirds churned up and fluttered down on the road. A dozen soldiers piled out of one and deployed into the sand dunes, shooting at the fleeing Arabs. The Captain, Fatso, and the others ran up to the second whirlybird and the Captain said, "They've beat it now. They've gone back into the desert."

"Okay," said the whirlybird pilot. "Get in."

They piled in and soon were deposited at an advance base in the Gaza Strip.

Soon they were in the ops room talking to the CO. "We've had a group of guerrillas operating around here for several days now," he said. "This is the first time we've really had a shot at them. Any of you hurt?"

"No," said the Captain. "We got three or four Arabs for you. And I think the fighter plane got a couple too. That fighter got there just in the nick of time."

"What the hell are American sailors doing down here?" asked the CO.

"They're friends of mine, and I'm just showing them around," said the Captain. "They're off a ship that's in Tel Aviv."

"Okay," said the CO. "I'll put you in a whirlybird and send you back there."

Later that afternoon they got back to Tel Aviv. As they sat around the Captain's quarters sipping tall drinks the Captain said, "Well—how about it, boys? Was the trip worthwhile?"

"Well, it was an eye opener for me," said Fatso. "You people are certainly turning the desert into a productive land here. The only bums or beggars I've seen have been Arabs. And your armed forces are all big leaguers. The way they shot down that MIG, pulled off that raid on Suez, and rescued us from the Arabs, all were absolute tops. I'm beginning to think you guys have got a good chance, even against forty million Arabs."

"Hell, we got a lot more than a chance," said the Captain. "We got it made."

As they got ready to go back aboard ship, the Captain said, "Well, I enjoyed showing you guys around. And I give you a high mark for your defense against the Arab guerrillas this morning. Here's the address of some of our underground people in Naples," he said, handing Fatso a slip of paper. "Look them up when you get there. They're all stout fellas—commando types—and anything you want around Naples they can get for you."

⚓ CHAPTER THIRTEEN

Athens

NEXT MORNING LCU 1124 sailed for Athens. This is about a three-day run, the first two being in the open sea till you pick up the island of Rhodes, where the Colossus used to be. From Rhodes on it is through the Greek archipelago and you are seldom out of sight of several islands.

Shortly after they sailed, Scuttlebutt cornered Adams with fire in his eye and said, "Didn't I tell you to fill our tanks up with fresh water while we were in Tel Aviv?"

"Gee, Chief . . . I forgot," said Adams.

"You *forgot?*" said Scuttlebutt. "Well, you goddamn left-handed swab handle. What do you think we're going to do for fresh water for the next few days?"

"Well . . . um . . . can't we drink orange juice for a couple of days?" asked Adams.

"Yeah," said Scuttlebutt, "and I suppose we can cook, brush our teeth, scrub our clothes, and take showers in orange juice, too. This means we gotta ration fresh water."

When Fatso was informed of this he said, "Okay. Ration water to half a bucket a day. Put salt water in the showers. Now these atomic age sailors can find out how it used to be in the old Navy."

For sailors who have always had all the fresh water they want just by turning a spigot, water rationing is an acute pain in the neck. You can use sea water and salt-water soap for scrubbing clothes. But taking a shower in salt water is not a pleasant experience. It leaves you feeling sticky all over as if you had showered in dilute gook. It is unsatisfactory—like trying to make love wearing a winter flying suit and heavy leather mittens.

The second day out they sighted a rain squall dead ahead. "All hands on deck," yelled Fatso. "Get that big tarpaulin out and stretch it across the deck from rail to rail."

All hands stripped bare naked. Soon they had the tarpaulin stretched from one edge of the well deck to the other. It hung down in the middle, of course, and at each end of it they put an empty fifty-gallon oil drum that had been scrubbed clean. When the rain squall hit, water poured from each end of the canvas into the drums. When a drum got full, they rolled it off and dumped it into the ship's tanks, replacing it with another empty. Fatso, gauging the travel of the storm with a seaman's eye, maneuvered to keep the ship in the middle until the tanks were full.

"You know," said Scuttlebutt as they were draining the rain water into the tanks, "this reminds me of the first time I ever ran into water rationing."

"Where was that—on the Ark?" asked the Professor.

"Naw. On the *Indianapolis*," said Scuttlebutt. "She was a heavy cruiser—nine eight-inch guns—got sunk right at the end of the war. Anyways, I come aboard her right out of boot camp. She was my first ship. And they had water rationing. You got a half a bucket of fresh water per day and you had to stand in line for damn near an hour to get that."

"Well, my first day aboard I stood in this hell of a long line and finally got my half bucketful and took it down to the washroom. I had some clothes to scrub so I wanted to heat the water up. There was a one-inch steam line in the washroom with a valve in it. You could hang your bucket on a peg with the end of this pipe sticking into it, open the valve, and blow live steam into your bucket to heat it up. So I hung my bucket on the peg and opened the valve.

"But somebody in the engine room had screwed up connections that morning. That line instead of having steam in it was hooked up to the condenser and had a vacuum in it. When I opened the valve it sucked all the water out of my bucket right back into the ship's tanks.

"I never trusted nobody or nothing on that ship from then on."

Later that afternoon, a group were standing up in the bow watching schools of flying fish and porpoises disporting themselves. The flying fish would break surface in a group of twenty or thirty, swoop along a foot or so over the surface, rising and falling with the waves for about a hundred yards or so, and then plop back in the water again.

A large group of porpoises were playing follow the leader and weaving back and forth across the bow. When they reached the bow, they would leap gracefully out of the water, arch across the bow, and dive into the water on the other side. They entered and left the water without a splash. They would clear the bow by about five feet, with their big black eyes popping and broad grins on their friendly faces, chattering away like a bunch of kids.

"You know porpoises are supposed to have a language," said the Professor. "There's a guy down in the Virgin Islands who has a bunch of porpoises in a pool. He makes tape recordings of all their chattering and claims he is learning their language. He says he can play back tape recordings to them and they repeat what they were doing when the tapes were made. He's found out now how to tell them to go lie on the bottom or to come to the edge of the pool, and they'll do it. Porpoises are the smartest animal there is. They've got a brain that's almost like a human bean's."

"We had a porpoise at the UDT school when I was there," said Webfoot. "He was a real friendly guy, just like a pet dog. He used to swim back and forth between a guy on the bottom and a boat on the surface, carrying messages and bringing tools to the guy on the bottom."

"Last time I was home on leave," said Jughaid, "I told the people about porpoises, whales, and blackfish. None of that seemed to impress them, so I told 'em one about a big sea serpent about a hunnert feet long with two heads and eyes that shone in the dark like headlights. They believed every word of it. But when I tried to tell 'em about flying fish, they called me a goddamn liar."

That evening they were sitting around the messroom and Jughaid was working a crossword puzzle. He got stuck on it and finally he asked, "What's a four-letter word ending in I-T that Governor Wallace is full of?"

"That's easy—grit," said the Judge.

"That's it!" said Jughaid. "Lemme borrow your eraser."

Pretty soon the conversation got around to some of the funny skippers they had served with. "I served with Cap'n Donnerblatz on the *Antares*," said Satchmo. "He was a square-headed Dutchman who came up through the ranks. He was an ex-signalman and he was always checking up on the signal bridge and giving them hell if they didn't answer promptly. One day we was anchored in Frisco, and we were the Senior Officer Present with a lot of destroyers and they were calling in and requesting permission for this and that. The old man was on deck, and he seen a destroyer on the other side of the harbor with our call sign flying. So he yells up at the signal bridge, 'Dot ship is callink you. Viggle vaggle over und find out vat dey vant und den viggle vaggle back und tell them no!' "

"I was shipmate with old Turn To Craven," said Scuttlebutt. "He was a character. One time a kid put in for leave because his wife was going to have a baby. In his leave request he said, 'This is to attend the launching of my first child.' Old Turn To sent it back not granted. He wrote on it, 'I can see no need for you at the launching, although your presence was required at the laying of the keel.'

"Then there was another guy put in for leave for the same reason. But he got the wording of his request mixed up a little bit and in his request he said, 'My wife is about to become pregnant and I want to be there when it happens.'

"Old Turn To sent that one back granted."

Next morning LCU 1124 stood in to Piraeus and anchored. Later that morning a clerk from the embassy came aboard to pick up the Ambassador's liquor.

"How are things going in Athens now?" asked Fatso.

"Pretty good," said the clerk. "People are friendly and you can have a hell of a good time here as long as your money lasts."

"There's been a lot in the papers recently about this government of the colonels," said Fatso. "The papers claim they're making life pretty grim here now."

"That's a lot of malarkey," said the clerk. "Things are better here now than they've been for a long time. If it wasn't for the colonels the Communists would be running things here.

"The paper and radio say they've got a dictatorship, and they throw people in jail and torture them."

"Don't believe what you read in the papers," said the clerk. "As soon as the government starts laying down a few rules that the press have to follow, all our reporters start screaming about freedom of the press. Everything else the government does from that point is wrong."

"According to the papers, they've thrown all the opposition in jail."

"That just ain't so," said the clerk. "They threw a lot of hard-core Communists in jail and then had to lock up some long-haired eggheads who were stooges for the commies. Hell, they had a choice here of either the kind of government they've got now or the Communists. If it wasn't for the colonels, the commies would be running the show and all the longhairs they've got in jail would be in Siberia, along with all the other decent people of Athens."

"How does the Ambassador get along with these colonels?" asked Fatso.

"Fine. Anything the Ambassador asks for, they give it to him."

That afternoon Fatso, Scuttlebutt, and the Professor went ashore together to hit the high spots of Athens. They hired themselves a cab and told the driver to show them the sights of the city. The first place he took them to was the Acropolis.

"Athens must of been quite a place in its time," observed Fatso as they stood looking over the ruins of the ancient temple.

"Around 500 B.C. it was the capital of the world," said the Professor. "Greece ran the show then for the whole Med and all of Asia Minor."

"Well, they must of had a hell of a city here in their day, judging by these ruins," said Fatso. "What the hell happened to them?"

"They had it so good they got soft," said the Professor. "They went in for living it up. They had a damned good Army while they were getting to the top. But, after they got there, nobody wanted to be in the Army any more. All they wanted to do was to hang around Athens and get drunk. So their Army went to pot, and then the Romans came along and took over."

"The Romans didn't last either," said Fatso.

"No. But they were good while they had it, too," said the Professor. "Maybe even better than the Greeks. They took over all of Europe including England. They built roads and aqueducts, and Rome was the capital of the world then. The Roman Empire took in the whole known world at that time."

"What happened to them?" asked Scuttlebutt.

"The same thing that happened to the Greeks," said the Professor. "They got soft, too. They put on big shows in the Colosseum, threw the Christians to the lions, and then went home and put on orgies that lasted for days. They let their Army go to pot and pretty soon the barbarians came in from the east and took over."

"How the hell can that happen?" demanded Scuttlebutt. "The Roman Army was the best in the world in them days. How could a bunch of barbarians run over 'em?"

"Like I told you," said the Professor, "the country got soft, and so did the Army. Hell, there's nothing so strange about that. The same thing is happening today."

"Where do you mean—in Italy and France?" asked Scuttlebutt.

"Hell, no. I mean right in our United States," said the Professor. "Look. At the end of World War II we were the top country on this earth. We had an Army, Navy, and Air Force that could of licked the whole world in a knock-down, drag-out fight. It wouldn't even of been much of a fight, because we were the only ones who had the atom bomb. But, as soon as the war was over, we began scrapping our Army and Navy. We set up the United Nations, and that was supposed to prevent any more wars. We weren't worried about the Russians because they had taken an awful beating in the war, and were a second-rate nation anyway. So what has happened since then? We fought two wars with third-rate gook nations. The first ended in a stalemate. We don't know how the second will come out yet, but if the hippies, draft-card burners, and long-haired liberals back home have their way, we're going to lose it. Meantime, what has been happening to the Russians? They repaired their war damage, put their country back on its feet, and have taken over more than half the world. They are the barbarians in the east for us now, just like the ones that wiped out Rome."

"Yeah," said Scuttlebutt. "But I don't think they'll ever start a war with us. They know damned well we can flatten them with Polaris."

"Sure," said the Professor. "A war with us is the last thing the Russians want. They're getting everything they want now, without firing a shot. The liberals, hippies, and Black Panthers are doing their work for them. Just look what's happening all over the U.S. Riots on all the college campuses, where they set fire to the ROTC buildings. Peace marchers who tear down and burn the American flag and run up the Viet Cong flag. They're even getting into the services now. Kooks like Adams are talking about organizing unions. Look what happened on the *Pueblo*. Eighty-three Americans surrender without firing a shot to half a dozen gooks—and millions of Americans applaud them for it."

"You make things sound pretty grim," said Scuttlebutt.

"Things are grim," said the Professor. "You remember a couple of years ago Khrushchev said, 'We will bury you'? I believe him."

"Aw, hell," observed Fatso. "The older generation has been saying for years that the world is going to the dogs. I don't believe it's as bad as you say."

"Well, they said it right here in Greece and in Rome, too," said the Professor. "And you can look out here at these ruins now and see what *did* happen."

At this point a sleazy-looking character sidled up to Fatso and said, "You wanna good guide, meestaire?"

"What can you do for us?" asked Fatso.

"I can get you anything you want," said the stranger. "I can get you very good girls—best ones in Athens."

"No. We don't go with girls," said Fatso.

"I know some nice boys, too," said the stranger. "Very good boys. They do anything you want."

"Oh—you mean fairies," said Fatso. "No."

"If you like pot, I can get for you, or speed or anything else you want."

"How about LSD," asked Fatso. "Can you get that?"

"LSD?" said the stranger. "I don't know what eet ees. But I can get you anything else—very good and very cheap."

"No," said Fatso. "Beat it."

As the stranger departed, shaking his head, Fatso observed, "It's almost as easy to get dope here as it is on a college campus at home."

Later they were seated at a table in a sidewalk café on the main drag, watching the crowds go by, when a well-dressed man about Fatso's age came up and said, "Mind if I sit down with you?"

"No—pull up a chair," said Fatso.

The stranger sat down, stuck out his hand, and said, "Name is Slanski. Nice to see you guys. I used to be in the Navy."

The others introduced themselves, and Slanski shook hands all around.

"When were you in the Navy?" asked Fatso.

"During the war," said Slanski. "I enlisted the day after Pearl Harbor and got out four years later. I was a first-class yeoman when I got out."

"What ships were you in?" asked Fatso.

"The whole time in the *Hornet*," said Slanski.

"You must of seen lots of action in that bucket," observed Fatso.

"Yeah—we did," said Slanski. "I was in her when she came out here to the Med and flew Spitfires into Malta. Then later on, out in the Pacific, we flew Doolittle's boys off for the Tokyo raid."

"I'll be damned," observed Fatso. "You really got around, all right. There weren't many who got into the war in both oceans."

"What ship are you fellas from?" asked Slanski.

"LCU 1124," said Scuttlebutt.

"What kind of craft is that?" asked Slanski.

"It's a landing craft," said Scuttlebutt. "The biggest type of landing craft we've got."

"Oh—so you belong on a bigger ship?"

"Yeah—we do. But we're not on her now. Our mother ship, the *Alamo*, is in Naples."

"So what are you doing here?" asked Slanski.

"They use us to carry miscellaneous freight around the Med," said Fatso. "We can carry as much as two hundred tons and they use us to take stuff to Tel Aviv, Istanbul, Crete, and various other places."

"Who's your skipper?" asked Slanski.

"I am," said Fatso.

"Oh?" said Slanski, with interest.

"What are you doing now?" asked Fatso.

"I'm in the exporting business," said Slanski. "How about another drink?" he asked, signaling the waiter.

Slanski seemed to be quite interested in LCU 1124, and plied them with questions about where they went, what they did, and who checked up on them. After he had bought two more rounds of drinks and listened to Fatso and Scuttlebutt tell tales of their adventures in Tel Aviv he said, "Hell, you guys have practically got a private navy all your own. You write your own ticket and do as you damn please."

"Yeah—we're pretty much on our own," said Fatso.

"Look, how about having dinner with me tonight?" said

Slanski. "I'll take you to the Trocadero, we'll have a big feed, and then I'll take you out on the town afterward."

Fatso glanced at the others, got nods of approval, and said, "Sure—let's go."

Thus began a red-letter evening for Fatso and his pals.

The Trocadero was the swankiest restaurant in town. The headwaiter there knew Slanski, greeted him effusively, and escorted their party to a choice table. They ate high on the hog—châteaubriand steak with wine, champagne, and liqueurs afterward. The check came to a whole hatful of drachmas, and as Slanski peeled them off Fatso estimated it was at least 150 American dollars, including the tip.

After dinner they took in a show. It was a musical, and although they couldn't follow the dialogue in Greek, the girls were good looking and the music and dancing were very good. After the show, Slanski said, "Wait here a few minutes, boys—I'm going backstage and see what I can stir up."

Fifteen minutes later he showed up with four of the showgirls and they adjourned to a nearby night club. The girls were very friendly and everyone got along famously. When the night club closed, they moved to Slanski's palatial suite at the Grand Hotel. He had a well-appointed bar and a hi-fi record player, so there were drinking, dancing, and what-not till the wee, small hours.

The boys took the gals home and did what sailors and chorus gals usually do under such circumstances.

When it finally broke up and they were in a taxi on the way down to the dock, Scuttlebutt observed, "This guy Slanski is a real big operator. He must of put out three or four hundred bucks tonight."

"Yeah," said Fatso. "He's a fast man with a buck, all right. But he's a phony."

"Why do you say that?" asked Scuttlebutt.

"You remember when he was telling us about his time in the Navy?" asked Fatso. "Well, he said he fought the whole war in the *Hornet*. And he also said that the *Hornet* was in the Med, and flew those Spits in to Malta. That ain't so. It was the *Wasp* that flew the Spits to Malta. And she did it just two days after the *Hornet* launched the Doolittle raid. So I don't believe he was on the *Hornet*."

"Yeah—I guess you're right about that," admitted Scuttlebutt. "But he does seem to know a hell of a lot about the Navy."

"Yeah, he does," said Fatso. "And he was quite nosy about what we do and how we operate. He made a date with me to meet him tomorrow afternoon at his hotel. Said he had a proposition he wanted to discuss with me."

"I wonder what that's all about," said the Professor.

"So do I," said Fatso. "And I suspect it's something phony."

CHAPTER FOURTEEN

Slanski

NEXT AFTERNOON Fatso met Slanski at his suite in the Grand Hotel. Also present was a burly, dark-skinned individual, gaudily and expensively dressed and puffing on a long cigar. He had piercing, shifty dark eyes scowling out from under heavy eyebrows and a deep scar across the left side of his face. He had an air of arrogant authority about him, and if he had ever appeared on TV he would have been one of the bad guys.

"Fatso, meet Salvatore Salanti," said Slanski.

Salanti acknowledged the introduction with a curt nod and said nothing.

Slanski poured himself, Fatso, and Salanti generous drinks and they sat down on the balcony outside the room overlooking the city.

"Well," said Slanski, "have your boys recovered from last night yet?"

"Oh, yes," said Fatso. "They're up and around. Quite a party though."

"I could of done better for you if I'd had a little more time to arrange things," said Slanski. "I got friends in Naples I want you to meet. Real nice guys. They'll take good care of you. Get you all the gals you want—real good ones."

"Oh," said Fatso.

After a bit of chit-chat about the previous evening Slanski poured Fatso another drink and said, "Fatso—how would you like to pick up a little dough for yourself on your trip back to Naples?"

"Well," said Fatso, "that would depend on what the deal was.

I'm always glad to pick up a little extra dough. If the deal looks right."

"This would involve delivering a package to a friend of mine in Naples," said Slanski.

"Oh," said Fatso. "Something you don't want to go through customs?"

"Yeah, that's right," said Slanski.

"How big a package?" asked Fatso.

"It's a bale of stuff—weighs about a ton."

"Well, now," said Fatso, "that's a pretty big bundle to be lugging around Naples."

"You wouldn't have to lug it around Naples. A boat would meet you outside the harbor and take it off your hands," said Slanski.

"Hmm," said Fatso. "Sounds interesting. If they meet me outside the three-mile limit I'm not doing anything the Eyetalians could squawk about. . . . I might be interested. . . . How would we arrange the pickup?"

"We would take care of that for you," said Slanski. "You arrange to get to Naples just before dark. Our boat will meet you about five miles out. As soon as it gets dark our boat comes alongside. You give him the package and that's all there is to it."

"How would I know this boat of yours when I see it?" asked Fatso.

"It will be a forty-foot fishing boat. She will be flying the Greek flag and she will signal to you by blinker light X A X."

"That sounds okay," said Fatso. "But be sure he knows the transfer has to take place outside the three-mile limit."

"Don't worry about that," said Slanski, "We'll take care of it."

"And what's in this for me?" asked Fatso.

"A couple of hundred bucks," said Slanski.

"Humh," said Fatso. "That's chickenfeed for a deal like this."

"All you gotta do is just carry this thing from here to Naples. You don't have to do a thing to it while you've got it aboard. Sounds like a pretty good deal to me. . . . How much do you want?"

"Two grand," said Fatso.

"Now wait a minute, my friend," said Slanski. "That's way out of line for just hauling a package from here to Naples."

"Well, let's put all the cards on the table," said Fatso. "What's in this package?"

"It's—er—raw material. Stuff you can't get in Italy but we need it for a product we make."

"What kind of raw material?" asked Fatso.

"Vegetable matter."

"Let's quit beating around the bush," said Fatso. "That bale of stuff is opium. . . . A ton of opium is worth well over a million bucks. I want two thousand."

"All right—it's opium," conceded Slanski. "But a ton of raw opium isn't worth that much until it's processed and delivered in the States. Two grand is way out of line."

"Take it or leave it," said Fatso.

"Well—I might go as high as one thousand," said Slanski.

"Look," said Fatso. "I've got almost thirty years in this Navy. I'm about ready to retire. It all goes down the drain if I get caught at this."

"How about fifteen hundred?" asked Slanski.

"No. Two grand is my price," said Fatso.

"Give it to him," growled Salanti.

"Okay, boss—if you say so," said Slanski.

"How do we get it aboard here?" asked Fatso.

"You said you sail the day after tomorrow. Tomorrow night at midnight a boat will deliver it on board."

"I want to be paid in advance," said Fatso.

"We usually pay on delivery," said Slanski. "The boat that picks it up in Naples will pay you."

"Look," said Fatso. "This isn't just a one-shot operation. We are running back and forth between here and Naples all the time. This could get to be a regular business. But I want my money in advance or it's no go."

"There's a lot of things could go wrong on this deal," said Slanski. "We can't afford to pay till the stuff is delivered."

"There's damned little can go wrong in this case," said Fatso. "The stuff comes in in a Navy ship. There's no customs to contend with. I guarantee to put it on your boat in Naples. What happens after that is up to you."

"Well, now . . . " began Slanski.

"Give it to him now," growled Salanti.

"Okay, boss," said Slanski. He went into his room and came back with a handful of crisp new hundred-dollar bills. He counted out twenty of them and handed them to Fatso.

"Okay," said Fatso. "We will be expecting a boat to deliver the bale to us here tomorrow at midnight."

"That's right," said Slanski.

"All right. I'll take care of it," said Fatso as he got up to go.

"Just a minute," said Slanski. "Let me give you the name of a friend of ours in Naples. You can look him up later. He'll show you a real good time and he's got a big stable of good gals."

Slanski wrote a name and address on a sheet of paper and gave it to Fatso. As Fatso was about to leave Salanti stomped out the butt of his cigar and said, "Look, sailor. This is the big time you're getting into. You do a good job for us and there's plenty more where this comes from. . . . Just one thing I want to warn you about—if you ever get involved with the cops, *keep your mouth shut.* We've got top-level connections everywhere and we can bail you out and fix any rap. But remember—you never seen or heard of me."

"Okay," said Fatso.

"The one thing we can't stand is a squealer," said Salanti with a dark scowl. "We treat them pretty rough."

"Okay, chief. I understand," said Fatso. And he shoved off.

Fatso went direct from the hotel to the American embassy, where he looked up his friend the clerk to whom he had delivered the ambassador's liquor. "I've got to see the Ambassador," he told him.

"The Ambassador?" said the clerk. "He's a busy man. It's pretty hard to get to him."

"Well, this is very important and I've got to see him," said Fatso.

"Okay," said the clerk, dubiously. "I'll see what I can do."

Pretty soon the clerk returned and said, "The Ambassador's administrative assistant will see you."

The administrative assistant was a sharp young State Department type whose major mission in life was keeping track of the Ambassador's social engagements and preventing unwanted visitors from bothering the boss.

"Yes sir, Mr. Gioninni," he said. "What can I do for you?"

"I want to see the Ambassador," said Fatso.

"The Ambassador has a very full schedule," said the young man. "Is there anything I can do?"

"This is an important matter which should be handled by the Ambassador," said Fatso.

"Perhaps if you tell me what it is I can help you," persisted the young man.

"I need the help of the local police," said Fatso, "on a matter that has to be handled very carefully at the top level."

"Well, I can put you in touch with the police here," said the aide.

"No. It's got to be the Ambassador," said Fatso.

"Well—unless you tell me more about it, I'm afraid you can't see the Ambassador," said the young man.

"All right," said Fatso. "It's about a plot to assassinate the Ambassador."

"Oh—well . . . um . . . in that case, just wait a minute. I'll see if I can get you in."

A few moments later the young man returned and said, "His excellency will see you now."

Fatso was ushered into the Ambassador's plush office, where the diplomat was seated behind his large mahogany desk. "Well, what's this, young man?" he asked. "You say there's a plot to assassinate me?"

"That's what I told your flunky, sir, in order to get to see you," said Fatso. "But that's a lot of malarky. It's really about something else."

"Oh?" said the Ambassador. "Well, what is it?"

"It's about a dope-smuggling plot that I'm mixed up in, and I want the help of the local police." Fatso then related the story of his deal with Slanski to deliver a bale of opium to Naples.

"Smuggling opium from Greece to Naples," said the diplomat. "Just how does this concern the American embassy?"

"In several ways," said Fatso. "First of all, Slanski is an American. The American Navy is mixed up in it, and this stuff, after it's refined, will wind up in the United States."

"Yes. You're probably right," said the Ambassador. "We know there is a great deal of opium smuggled out of the Near East and into the U.S. This stuff is undoubtedly headed for the U.S. Eventually. But we have a hell of a time catching any of these smugglers red-handed."

"Well, we'll have a fine chance to do it tomorrow night, sir," said Fatso. "If the local police will cooperate they can come aboard my ship tomorrow afternoon and lay in wait for the people who deliver the stuff. That will give them the evidence to hang Slanski. But Slanski is just a middleman in this deal. His boss is a guy by the name of Salanti. He's the one who really made the deal with me. Get him and you'll have one of the real big shots in this dope racket."

The Ambassador thought it over for a moment and then said, "I agree." He buzzed for his secretary and said, "Get me Colonel Zagistos on the phone."

"The Greek government is usually very cooperative in anything I ask of them," he said to Fatso. "I think they'll go along with this."

Soon he had the Colonel on the phone and said, "This is Ambassador Johnson. Could you come over to the embassy right away?"

"He'll be right over," said the Ambassador when he hung up. "Are you sure this Slanski is an American?"

"Well, I'm not sure," said Fatso. "But he speaks like an American, and he claims he served in the Navy."

"I doubt if Slanski will take part in the delivery," said the Ambassador. "But I'd sure like to get him. This dope smuggling is one of our main concerns right now."

In about five minutes, Colonel Zagistos was announced.

"Colonel, this is Boatswain's Mate Gioninni," said the Ambassador. "He's skipper of a small Navy ship we have in the harbor. Gioninni, this is Colonel Zagistos, the Chief of Police of Athens."

"And what can I do for you, sir?" said the Colonel.

So Fatso again ran through the story of his deal with Slanski. Then he said, "What I would like to do is to have some of your men come aboard my ship quietly tomorrow afternoon. Then when the delivery is made at midnight, you capture the guys who make the delivery."

The Colonel's eyes had lighted up while Fatso was talking. When he finished the Colonel said, "No trouble at all. We will do it exactly the way you say. This may result in a real big killing. Of course, all we'll get at your ship will be a couple of Arab boatmen and a bale of opium. But your testimony and the evidence we get will tie Slanski in. We'll pick him up at his hotel right after midnight. We have suspected him for some time, but have never been able to pin anything on him. He's one of the middlemen in this dope ring. If we can make him talk, we'll get some of the real big ones."

"One of the big shots was there while I was making the deal with Slanski," said Fatso. "A guy by the name of Salanti. Slanski takes his orders from him."

"That's fine. We know him and have been trying for a long time to get something on him," said the Colonel. "Your testimony will put the finger on him, too."

"But I won't be here to be a witness against him when he comes to trial," said Fatso.

"Don't worry about that," said the Colonel. "We'll take a deposition from you. And I don't think we'll have too much trouble persuading him to talk. We're pretty good at that. And he'll be facing a long stretch in prison if he doesn't talk. This is going to break things open clean up to the top."

"What do I do with this two thousand bucks that Slanski gave me?" asked Fatso of the Ambassador.

"So far as I'm concerned you can keep it," said the Ambassador. "If I took it it would have to go into our counterpart funds, and I've got more money there now than I know what to do with."

"You better let me have some of my experts take a look at that money," said the Colonel. "It may be counterfeit."

"Okay," said Fatso. Reaching into his pocket he hauled out twenty hundred-dollar bills and handed them over to the Colonel.

The Colonel inspected them and said, "They look pretty good. But some very good American counterfeit is in circulation here now. I'll have my experts look it over. If it's real you can keep it. If it's phony, we've got another charge against your friend Slanski."

"Okay," said Fatso. "I'll expect your people tomorrow afternoon."

"Right," said the Colonel.

Next morning Fatso went ashore and had a secret rendezvous with the Colonel and his prosecuting attorney. There Fatso swore out an affidavit with the whole story of his dealings with Slanski and Salanti. When he got through, the prosecutor said, "This, plus the bale of opium we'll get tonight, will be enough to send Mr. Slanski and Salanti up for a number of years."

"And, when they talk, as I'm sure they will," said the Colonel, "we'll also have a number of other real big fish for you."

"Be careful," said the prosecutor. "The foreign press is raising hell about torturing prisoners. So don't put any marks on them."

That afternoon six husky plain-clothes cops came aboard at

various times and settled down to spend the evening. They agreed that, when the boat came alongside at midnight, Fatso and two of his men would accept the bale and hoist it aboard. As soon as it was on deck, the cops would move in and take over.

The cops all spoke English after a fashion. They spent the afternoon learning to play acey-deucy and regaling the boys with tales about the Communists and how about ten years back the U.S. had helped Greece to throw them out. Fatso had a movie on the well deck for them after dinner.

Shortly after midnight a small boat approached their stern and there was a guarded hail from it. Fatso hailed back and motioned it to come alongside. The motorboat eased up to the stern and threw aboard a bow and a stern line, which were promptly secured to cleats on deck. Then Fatso swung the stern crane out over the boat and lowered the hook. The people in the boat hooked on a bulky object the size of a bale of cotton, and Fatso heaved around on the winch and hoisted it up on deck.

As soon as the bale touched the deck Fatso switched on the floodlights; the six cops appeared and jumped into the boat. After a brief struggle, they subdued and handcuffed the three crew members. They were an evil-looking trio of Arabs, but obviously were just small spuds in the dope-smuggling ring.

One of the cops cut away a piece of the burlap covering on the bale and dug into the contents with his knife. "It's opium," he reported.

Another cop called a police launch alongside on a walkie-talkie radio, they loaded the bale into it, and the launch departed with the motorboat in tow and three very unhappy Arabs handcuffed together.

At the same time, Colonel Zagistos and a party of cops raided Slanski's suite at the Grand Hotel. They got Slanski and Salanti and quite a bundle of hundred-dollar American bills. The two gangsters tried to brazen it out. They demanded that various political figures be notified as well as their attorneys and made dire threats as to what would happen to the arresting officers. But the cops had trouble locating the politicians they mentioned and their attorneys.

While they were looking for them they questioned the two gangsters rather sharply—and separately. They used various tricks which they had learned from the Communists to encourage them to talk. They also used a few devices of their own, which they had found to be quite effective in dealing with reluctant culprits. Neither gangster was very successful in resisting the cops' urging. By morning both were singing like canary birds, each one trying to pin the whole rap on the other.

With a little extra urging Salanti remembered the names of some other big wheels. They were promptly picked up and subjected to similar questioning. By morning the cops had an iron-clad case against the biggest dope ring in Greece, plus four of the top Mafia men, plus Slanski and the Arab boatmen, and a bale of opium.

Next morning, just before LCU 1124 got underway, Colonel Zagistos came out in the police launch to see Fatso. "A very successful operation indeed," he said. "We got Slanski, Salanti, and two of the real big wheels. It's the biggest haul we've made in years, and dope is going to be harder to get in the U.S. for some time. We thank you very much for your cooperation, Captain, which made this possible."

"Okay," said Fatso. "I'm glad to do anything I can to help break up the dope racket. How about that money I gave you?"

"A very high grade of counterfeit," said the Colonel.

"That dirty, double-crossing son of a bitch," observed Fatso.

⚓ CHAPTER FIFTEEN

The Russian Boarder

FROM PIRAEUS they headed south. As Piraeus was dropping out of sight astern, Scuttlebutt was on the bridge discussing future operations with Fatso.

"What's the schedule now, skipper?" asked Scuttlebutt.

"Well, we go back to Naples now," said Fatso. "But there's no hurry about getting there. I think I'll stop in at the Gulf of Laconia tomorrow and see what's going on there."

"What's at the Gulf of Laconia?" asked Scuttlebutt.

"The Russians have a sort of a half-assed fleet base there," said Fatso. "They anchor out about three miles offshore, where they are in international waters, and they refuel their ships there and make minor repairs. I think I'll spend a couple of days in there and see what they're doing."

In the radio news that evening there was a lot of stuff about the Egyptian gunboat. The Israelis had demanded that we have the Sixth Fleet intercept it, and when we refused, they stated that they themselves would intercept it and make sure it never got to Alexandria. This had called forth a statement from the Russians that they intended to intercept the ship and escort it in to Alexandria. Not a word had been heard from the ship itself since she sailed from Portsmouth.

The Gulf of Laconia is a large arm of the sea at the south end of Greece about forty miles long and thirty miles wide. Cape Maléa is on the eastern end and Cape Matapan on the western. As they passed Cape Matapan, all hands were on the bridge listening to Fatso hold forth about the Battle of Cape Matapan. "The British Fleet beat the hell out of the Eyetalians here," he

said. "They never could get the Eyetalian Fleet to stand up
and fight. They had a running fight with them here and beat
the Wops so bad they never would fight again. The British had to
go in their harbors and get 'em, like they did at Taranto."

"What did they do there, Cap'n?" asked Jughaid.

"The British sent torpedo planes in from one of their carriers
and sank three or four of the Eyetalian battleships at anchor
right there in the harbor. Just like the Japs did to us at Pearl
Harbor. The Eyetalians raised them and fixed them up again, but
they kept them out of gun range of the British for the rest of the
war. The only big ship they lost in the whole war was the *Roma*.
She was a fine battleship. But she was sunk by a German air
attack when she was trying to surrender to us."

"The Wops have no guts," observed Ginsberg. "Gangsters is
all they're good for."

"Just a minute," said Fatso. "The Eyetalian subs did a good
job. And their frogmen did a hell of a job. Their big ships
wouldn't fight, but their frogmen were terrific, and gave the
Limeys a bad time."

"I never heard of them. What did they do?" demanded Ginsberg.

"Well, you saw the *York* that they sank in Suda Bay the other
day. And they snuck in to Alexandria and sank two British battleships there with limpet mines that they stuck on their bottom.
The Eyetalian frogmen were just as good as anybody's," said
Fatso.

"I hear the Russians are going in for this frogman business in
a big way too," observed Webfoot.

"Yeah," said Fatso. "And they're pretty damn good at it, too."

Presently the Russian Fleet came in sight, anchored well up
the bay about three miles offshore. There were two heavy
cruisers, a helicopter carrier, a dozen destroyers, a couple of submarines, and various supply ships, oilers, and tenders.

Fatso said to Ginsberg, "Get your cameras and get pictures of
these guys. I'm going to cruise through their fleet close aboard."

As they approached closer, Fatso observed, "I must admit
they're pretty trim and businesslike looking. Look at that cruiser.
She's a smart-looking craft."

"Yeah, she does look pretty good," said Scuttlebutt. "What are
those things forward and aft where the turrets ought to be?"

"Those are missile launchers. They got guided rockets they can shoot at planes. That's what they used to knock down that guy of ours that we picked up the other day."

"And hey . . . look at that carrier," said the Judge. "I didn't know those guys had any aircraft carriers."

"That just a whirlybird carrier," said Fatso, "like the ones we have in the amphibious force. They don't have any regular carriers."

They cruised slowly through the fleet, taking pictures as they went. The American colors were plainly flying at the main truck. As they passed the flagship they spotted the Admiral on deck with a group of officers looking them over with binoculars.

"They're giving us a real good once-over," observed Fatso. "This is probably the first time anybody has come into their private anchorage."

After getting pictures of all the ships, Fatso let go his anchor about half a mile from the Russian ships. "We'll just hang around here a day or so," he observed, "and see what goes on."

Shortly after they anchored a couple of Russian boats began patrolling around them. After about an hour, a boat with a Lieutenant in it came alongside and the Lieutenant came on board.

"What do you wish to do here?" asked the Lieutenant.

"We thought we'd anchor here for a couple of days and fish," said Fatso.

"We are having exercises here, and you will be in the way," said the Lieutenant. "You better go somewhere else to fish."

"We are in international waters here. I think we'll try it here for a while," said Fatso.

"You are in a dangerous position," said the Lieutenant. "My Admiral advises you to move." With that he saluted and shoved off.

Shortly after he left a big Russian submarine stood in to the anchorage and passed them close aboard.

"Hey, you guys," said Fatso to Izzy and the Professor, who were on deck with their cameras, "get pictures of this guy. This is one of their missile subs and we don't know too much about them."

As the giant sub passed within heaving-line distance they got dozens of photos showing the missile wells in the deck.

"She looks just like our Polaris subs," observed Izzy.

"She is a lot like them," said Fatso, "only not quite as good—

yet. We think their missiles have only got about half the range
of Polaris. But they're getting better all the time. Those pictures you just got will tell our ONI people a lot about them."

"How come?" asked Izzy. "There's no missiles in the pictures."

"No. But the tops of the launching tubes are. We'll be able to
tell a lot about the range of the missiles from the diameter of
the tubes.

About half an hour later the Russian Lieutenant was back
again. "The Admiral says you have to move," he reported.

"Did he say where he wants me to go?" asked Fatso.

"No. He just wants you to go away."

"We're on the high seas here. I think I'll stay," said Fatso.

"Well, I'm just telling you what the Admiral says," said the
Lieutenant. "We are holding underwater gunnery exercises here,
and it's dangerous for you to be near."

"Okay," said Fatso, "I'll think about it."

After the Russian left Adams said to Fatso, "I think we ought
to get the hell out of here."

"Balls," said Fatso. "We have as much right to be here as they
have."

"You know what happened to the *Pueblo*," said Adams, "and
she had a right to be where she was."

Next morning about breakfast time the boat which had been
patrolling around LCU 1124 all night was relieved by another
one. Soon a skindiver towing a good-sized limpet mine slipped
over the side and took off under water toward the American ship.

About fifteen minutes later, while the boys were at breakfast
LCU 1124 was suddenly shaken by a tremendous explosion. All
hands picked themselves up off the deck and scrambled outside.
They got there just in time to see a great column of white water
collapsing about one hundred yards away on the port side.

"Son of a bitch," observed Scuttlebutt. "I think that was
meant for us."

"It sure as hell was," said Fatso. "Let's get the hell out of here.
Heave up the anchor. Start the engines."

In half a minute they had their anchor up and were headed for
the open sea at fifteen knots. There were numerous people on
deck on the Russian ships, watching them as they went out.

"Those sons of a bitches would have blown us up the same

way they shot down that airplane of ours," observed Scuttlebutt.

"They play rough all right," said the Professor. "I wonder what the hell that thing was that blew up?"

"I dunno," said Webfoot. "I think it was meant for us but went off prematurely. Lucky for us."

"Those bastards are getting cockier all the time," observed Fatso. "They're building a hell of a big fleet and pretty soon they'll have as many ships in the Med as we have."

"I think we were just asking for it, steaming through their fleet and taking pictures the way we did," said Adams.

"What the hell do you mean?" demanded Fatso. "They were in international waters. We got just as much right to be there as they have. They've got a tin can that hangs around the Sixth Fleet taking pictures all the time."

"Yeah. But it's foolish to try to do it with a little spit kit like this," said Adams.

"Okay," said Fatso. "So we found that out . . . and damn near got our names in the newspapers doing it."

As the Russian fleet was disappearing astern half an hour later, a slightly built figure in a frogman's black skin-tight suit climbed over the bow gate and made its way up to the bridge."

"Just who in the hell are you?" demanded Fatso in amazement.

"I am Russian frogman, sir," said the figure, in a girlish voice.

"And how in hell did you get aboard," demanded Fatso.

"I hang on to your bow gate ever since mine blow up. I want to join your Navy."

"Well, I'll be gah damn," observed Fatso.

"They sent me out to put limpet mine on your ship. I made it explode too far away to do any damage and swam under water to your ship. I hang on to your bow for the past half hour."

"Well, it was mighty white of you to blow that mine up where you did, instead of attaching it to us," said Fatso.

"You will let me stay on board?" asked the Russian.

"Well, I sure as hell ain't going to take you back there," declared Fatso. "Yeah. You can stay aboard. Come on down below and we'll get you some dry clothes."

Down in the messroom the Russian removed the foot fins and oxygen bottle while all hands crowded around in amazement.

"Now," said Fatso, "tell us some more about yourself. Just who are you?"

"My name is Ivan Ivanovich," said the Russian. "I am seaman in Russian Navy. I want to join your Navy."

"Well, we can give you a place to eat and sleep until we get to port," said Fatso. "But then we'll have to turn you in, and I don't know what they'll do with you. Where did you learn to speak English so good?"

"At Moscow University," said the Russian. "I am language specialist. I speak English, French, Spanish, and some German. What port you go to?"

"Naples," said Fatso.

"Okay," said the Russian. "Naples is good. Where do I sleep?"

"Right there in the upper bunk at the end," said Fatso. "Why don't you go take a shower and we'll get you some clothes to wear. . . . Izzy, you show him where the shower is. . . . Jughaid, you go down to the storeroom and get him a couple of suits of underwear and a set of dungarees and shoes."

When the Russian withdrew Scuttlebutt said, "This guy claims he went to the university. I wonder how come he's just a seaman?"

"Maybe he's not a party member," said the Professor. "But it does seem funny for him to wind up being a frogman."

"Yeah," said the Judge. "Maybe he's an NKVD man, and they're trying to plant a double agent on us."

"No-o-o," said Fatso. "This thing was cooked up too suddenly for that. I think he was sent out to blow us up, all right."

"Maybe so," said the Judge. "But there's something funny about the guy. He's sort of frail looking. I'm not sure what it is. But he doesn't look like a frogman to me."

"I dunno," said Webfoot. "He doesn't look like a frogman. He's built too slight. But we have all kinds of them. Some are big, some are small, some look real tough, and some look almost like girls."

"I think you better tell Sixth Fleet we got a Russian on board who wants to defect to our side, and ask for instructions," said Adams.

"Why the hell should I do that?" demanded Fatso. "I'm certainly not going back in there to return this guy to the Russians. They would probably shoot him if I did. I'll take him to Naples and then dump him in Sixth Fleet's lap."

"I think you better ask Sixth Fleet for instructions," persisted Adams. "Otherwise you'll get yourself involved in an international incident."

"Nuts to that," said Fatso. "I'm skipper of this craft and this is one of those things a skipper has to decide on his own hook. If I'm wrong they can sack me and get another skipper."

At this point Ginsberg came back into the messroom with his eyes as big as golf balls and said, "Hey. I got news for you guys. This Russian is a she."

"What do you mean?" demanded Fatso.

"I mean that Russian is a woman," said Izzy.

"How do you know?" demanded Fatso.

"I seen her under the shower," said Ginsberg.

"Well, I'll be gah damn," said Fatso. "What the hell are we going to do with her?"

"We can fix her a bunk up forward on the well deck," said Scuttlebutt.

"Yeah," said Fatso. "I guess we can put up with her till we get to Naples. Matter of fact we've *got* to put up with her."

Presently the Russian came back to the messroom dressed in U.S. Navy dungarees with the skindiver's equipment under her arm. All hands present gave her a careful once-over. With her short hair, she could pass for a slightly built man with a fanny a little bigger than normal.

As she put her frogman gear down on the table, Fatso said "Um . . . er . . . say—I understand you're a woman."

The Russian shrugged, looked up at Fatso, and said, "Yes—I am. I didn't want to tell you at first because I was afraid you would put me off."

"What the hell?" said Fatso. "Do they have women on Russian Navy ships?"

"Yes. Some. In the intelligence department. Interpreters and code specialists."

"Then how come you're a frogman?" asked the Professor.

"The Captain didn't like me," said the Russian. "He knows I am good swimmer so he gives me dirty job of blowing you up."

"Why didn't the Captain like you?" asked the Professor.

"He wants me to sleep with him, and I won't do it. I tell heem to go pees up a rope. He is a goddamn motherfucking son of a bitch."

All eyes popped at that statement and after a moment the Professor said, "Where did you say you learned to speak English?"

"At Moscow University."

"Did you learn those words there?"

"No. I was assigned to make friends with American marine on duty at the embassy. He teach them to me."

"Oh," said several. "*That* explains it."

"Why? Did I say something wrong?" asked the Russian.

"Well—what you said wasn't exactly ladylike," said Fatso.

"I'm sorry. My marine friend say things like that all the time," said the Russian.

"Yeah—a marine would," said Fatso. "But you shouldn't. Now, what's your right name?"

"Tania Ivanovich," said the Russian.

"Okay, Tania," said Fatso. "We'll fix you a bunk up forward on the well deck. You can hang out here if you want to, and eat here. But you'll have a place all to yourself to sleep."

"I don't mind sleeping here," said Tania. "I'm used to sleeping with men."

"Well, maybe you are—but we're not," said Fatso. "We'll fix your bunk up forward. Now tell us some more about yourself."

"I was in intelligence. I am radio operator and code expert. I am interpreter. And I am also a good frogman. I get along all right with everyone on board except the Captain. If we didn't have Admiral on board I would have to sleep with him."

"And why do you want to desert? On account of him?" asked Fatso.

"No. Because my marine in Moscow tells me all about life in United States. How everybody has everything they want. How you can do anything you want, go anywhere you want, and say what you think."

"Can't you do that in Russia?" asked Fatso.

"Hah!" said Tania. "Every time you turn around you must get permission. We don't have automobiles and TV like you do in the States. If you are not a party member you are nobody. If the party don't like what you say or do, the NKVD comes to your door in the middle of the night and they send you to Siberia. I much rather live in United States."

"Well, we'll take you to Naples," said Fatso, "and turn you over to our Naval Intelligence there. If you know anything about codes and ciphers, the chances are they'll send you to Washington. . . . Do you think any of your people saw you hanging on to our bow when we were leaving the anchorage?"

"I don't know. Maybe."

"I think there's a damn good chance some of them did," said Scuttlebutt. "After all, we passed close aboard some of their ships coming out while she was hanging there. There were lots of people on deck looking at us."

"Well—okay, Tania," said Fatso. "Your bunk will be up forward. Make yourself at home here until we get to Naples."

Soon after this a hail come down from the bridge: "There's two ships overhauling us from astern—coming up fast." All hands went up to the bridge.

Coming up from astern with great bones in their teeth were two Russian destroyers heading right at them.

"I don't like the looks of this," said Fatso to Scuttlebutt.

"What do you think is cooking, Cap'n?" asked Scuttlebutt.

"I think those guys know we've got Tania and they want her back."

Soon a bright light started blinking on one of the destroyers: "S-T-O-P."

"Pay no attention to that. Don't answer them," said Fatso.

In a few minutes the two destroyers overhauled LCU 1124 and took station about two hundred yards abeam on each side. A flag signal went up to the yardarm of one of them. Jughaid looked it up in the international signal book.

"He says for us to stop, Cap'n," he reported.

"Okay. Pay no attention to it. Don't answer. Steady as you go," said Fatso to the helmsman.

Soon one destroyer began closing in and cut directly across their bow close aboard. Then he zigzagged back and forth, repeating this maneuver several times. Fatso paid no attention to him and continued on his course west at fifteen knots.

Fatso said to the Professor, "Get out a priority dispatch to Com Sixth Fleet. Give him our position, course, and speed, and tell him we are being harassed by two Russian destroyers. . . . Tania, you go below with him and see if the Russians do any transmitting."

"Aye aye, Cap'n. I'll get it right off," said the Professor, as he and Tania ducked down off the bridge to the radio shack.

In a few minutes another signal went up on the Russian destroyer, "Stop or I will fire on you."

"Sixth Fleet acknowledges our dispatch," reported the Professor over the voice tube.

"Get out another," yelled Fatso. "Urgent priority on this one —Russians have ordered me to stop or they will fire. I will not comply."

After this signal had been flying about five minutes the light on the destroyer started blinking again: "You—have—one—of—our —sailors—on—board.—We—want—him—back."

"Pay no attention to it," said Fatso.

A minute later word came up from the radio shack: "Sixth Fleet has our second message. Tania says the Russians have radioed their Admiral asking for instructions."

"All right now," said Fatso. "These guys may be thinking of trying to board us. I want everybody to get a tommy gun and five clips of ammunition. Then take station around the top side with the weapons in plain view."

"You're not going to try to fight against these two guys, are you?" demanded Adams.

"I sure as hell am," said Fatso.

"You must be crazy," said Adams. "It would be murder."

"Listen, bud," said Fatso. "There comes a time when you've got to stand up and fight no matter what the odds. This may be our time. . . . You take the wheel, Adams, where I can keep an eye on you. The rest of you guys go get the guns . . . and, Jughaid, bring one up for me."

For the next fifteen minutes the ships plodded west at fifteen knots. One of the Russians eased in to about twenty yards abeam for a few minutes and had a good look at the armed men on deck.

"Cap'n," said Adams, "the odds against us are much larger than they were against the *Pueblo*. I think you're a fool to fight these guys."

"Don't talk *Pueblo* to me," said Fatso. "This is a different Navy from the one they were in. . . . Sure, these guys can take us if they want to. But it will cost them a couple of dozen Russkies to do it. . . . Webfoot!" he shouted. "I want you to get demolition charges ready so we can scuttle this bucket if we have to."

"Aye aye, sir," said Webfoot, and disappeared below.

Word came up from the radio room, "The Russian Admiral has told them to fire a shot across our bows."

In a minute the bow gun on one of the tin cans swung out,

there was a loud BOOM, and a four-inch shell whistled across
ahead of LCU 1124 and hit the water about two hundred yards
beyond. "Steady as you go," said Fatso to Adams at the wheel.

"Tell Sixth Fleet," yelled Fatso down the tube, "they have
fired a shot across my bow. I am proceeding on course."

"Aye aye," replied the Professor. "The Russian is telling his
Admiral he fired a shot and we didn't stop."

Meanwhile Fatso's report of being harassed was taken in by
the *Milwaukee*, flagship of the Sixth Fleet. The young staff duty
officer did not consider this report urgent enough to interrupt a
high level staff conference then being held by the Admiral. He
put it on the dispatch board to be brought to the Admiral's
attention as soon as the conference broke up.

However, this dispatch was also taken in by the *America*, at
sea just east of Sicily. It was brought to the Admiral's attention
in flag plot immediately.

"How far away is that position he gives?" demanded the Admiral of the operations officer.

The ops officer made a quick plot on the chart and said, "Two
hundred miles, sir."

"Okay," said the Admiral. "We've got a six-plane CAP over the
ship, fully armed. They can get there in 20 minutes. Tell them
to proceed there and render any assistance necessary to LCU
1124. . . . Get them going right away and then launch another
CAP to replace them over the ship."

"Aye aye, sir," said the ops officer, and passed the word down
to CIC over the squawk box.

Half a minute later the six fighters which had been orbiting
over the ship at forty thousand feet nosed down, poured on the
coal, and headed east at Mach 1.5.

About five minutes later, Fatso's second dispatch, about
"Heave to or I will fire," was received in the *Milwaukee*. This
one was immediately brought to the Admiral's attention.

"What the hell have we got here? Another *Pueblo?*" demanded
the Admiral.

The Admiral looked at his watch and at the time group on the
message. "This first message was written just fifteen minutes
ago," he said. "*America* is only a couple of hundred miles from
her and can have planes overhead in half an hour. . . . Pass
these messages to *America* and tell her 'assist as necessary.'"

As the staff duty officer hurried off to send this message the Chief of Staff asked, "Do you want to cut Washington in on this? We can get through to them with a 'critical' message in a couple of minutes."

"Not yet," said the Admiral. "If the whiz kids get in on this act God knows what they'll tell us to do. When the thing is all over and we know how it comes out, I'll tell 'em."

A few minutes later the staff duty officer bustled back with a message from *America*. "Six VF sent to assist LCU 1124 fifteen minutes ago on receipt of first message. Have also sent two destroyers."

"Good old Joe," observed the Admiral. "He didn't even wait for us to tell him. Well, this scenario reads a little different from the *Pueblo*, so far anyway."

"What else do you want to do, Admiral?" asked the COS.

"Nothing. We'll be getting further word on this in fifteen minutes. We'll play it by ear then. I think the Russians will back down when our planes get there."

There was a wait of about fifteen minutes after the Russian got off his message about firing the shot. One of the destroyers eased in close aboard LCU 1124 with an armed party on deck and three jacob's ladders over the side. She stayed there for a minute with her skipper looking over the LCU, which had her armed men conspicuously deployed on deck. Then she eased out again to about two hundred yards.

"He's got to get the go-ahead from his Admiral," observed Fatso. "If he closes us again, he'll mean business."

"They can overwhelm us easy, Cap'n," said Adams. "They must have two hundred men on that ship."

"Well, they won't have two hundred by the time they get through taking us," said Fatso. "I think he's bluffing anyway. Tania ain't that important to them."

As the Russian began moving in again, Fatso yelled to the boys on deck, "Take cover, you guys. Load and lock. Keep your guns ready, and if anybody starts down those jacob's ladders—let 'em have it."

While all hands were watching apprehensively from behind the bulwarks, six small specks began taking shape in the sky to the west and suddenly a section of six Phantoms roared over at masthead height and began circling. The lead plane fired a burst from his machine guns into the water about four hundred yards ahead of the Russian ships. The Russians immediately stopped closing in and then hauled out again to a position about three hundred yards abeam.

Presently word came up from the radio shack, "Russian is reporting arrival of planes and requesting instructions." A few minutes later the Professor called up, "Russians are getting orders to return to base." A minute later the two Russians reversed course and steamed off to the east.

The fighter planes continued to circle LCU 1124 till the Russians were well beyond the horizon. Then they came down low, flew past Fatso close aboard, waggled their wings in a friendly manner, and disappeared to the west.

⚓ CHAPTER SIXTEEN

Russian Merchantman

LATER, IN THE MESSROOM, all hands were rehashing the day's events.

"I don't mind telling you I thought our number was up," said Jughaid.

"Yeah. I thought so too," said Webfoot. "It sure was a beautiful sight when those planes showed up."

"We were just lucky as hell," said Adams. "If those planes had come fifteen minutes later we'd all be dead by now. I think we should have surrendered like the *Pueblo* did."

"Listen, bub," said Fatso. "In the Navy I grew up in there's no such word as 'surrender.' You hold out and they can get help to you, like they did to us today—and like they might have to the *Pueblo* if she had fought. You can find out how to do most anything you want in the regulations book except how to surrender. There ain't a word in the book about how to do that. You just don't surrender."

"The *Pueblo* did," said Adams.

"All right. So the *Pueblo* did," said Fatso. "And those guys have got to live with that from now on. That ain't something that you can brag to your grandchildren about."

"It's better than being dead," said Adams.

"That depends on how you're built," said Fatso. "You can't live forever. I dunno of any really nice way to die. But there are lots of ways worse than to do it fighting for your country."

"Aw, that's just a lot of the old story-book stuff," said Adams. "It's not relevant any more."

"When enough guys get to feeling like you do," observed the

Judge, "the Russians will move in on us and take over. Then all the constitutional rights and freedoms that you hippies keep screaming about will go down the drain. You'll be free to do as you're damn well told or else to wind up in the salt mines.

"How do you feel about this thing, Tania?" asked Fatso.

"Well," said Tania, "I'm very glad you didn't let them come aboard. It would have been too bad for me if you had."

"Do you think they really intended to come aboard?"

"Yes. Until the planes came, I think they did."

"They saw our people on deck with guns," said Fatso.

"Yes. But they didn't believe you will really fight. They think you will surrender like *Pueblo* did."

"Your people know about the *Pueblo*, do they?" asked Fatso.

"Yes indeed. The whole story was in *Pravda* and on the radio. The political commissars on all ships told us all about it. We thought it was a sign that you were getting soft and were a paper tiger. The commissar said this showed you would only fight when you were sure to win."

"Did your people believe this?"

"Well—yes. You had eighty-three men on the *Pueblo*. There were only six Koreans in the boarding party that captured her. You could easily have killed them. Then with only six Koreans on board you allowed them to take the ship into harbor. No Russian crew would have done that. They would have fought. And if they saw they were losing they would have blown up their ship and sunk it."

"They didn't have explosive charges to do that," said Fatso. "And they were taken by surprise. They were on the high seas, and taking a ship on the high seas is piracy. Until the *Pueblo*, the last case of piracy on the high seas had been over a hundred years ago."

"But *Pueblo* was not on high seas—she was inside Korean territorial waters."

"Oh, no she wasn't. She was seventeen miles offshore."

"But your country signed a note admitting they were in Korean territorial waters and apologizing for it."

"Well, yes. We did," conceded Fatso. "But we disavowed that as soon as the men were released and said this was not so."

"They didn't tell us anything about that," said Tania. "All we heard about was that you signed an official note admitting you were in their waters and apologizing for it."

"Well—there's no use talking about that," said Fatso. "And anyway, the *Pueblo* was a special case. I don't think it will ever happen again. And it sure as hell won't happen to this ship."

About an hour later the upper works of a big ship began coming up over the horizon astern of them to the east. Whenever a big stranger appears, all hands gather on deck to have a look at her. This one came up fast, making about twenty-five knots. She was a twenty-thousand-ton cargo ship flying the Russian flag. She was a new spick-and-span smart-looking craft, with the latest type of deck winches, booms, and cranes. She passed about a mile abeam to port.

"That's a real smart-looking ship," said Fatso to Tania.

"Yes," said Tania. "We are building lots of them now. Pretty soon we have the biggest merchant marine in the world."

"I guess maybe you will," said Fatso. "At least so far as we are concerned, you will. At the rate we're going now, we won't have any merchant marine at all pretty soon, except for some old World War cargo ships."

"What happened?" asked Tania. "At the end of the war you had the biggest merchant marine in the world. You had shipyards that could turn out ships the way you build automobiles. You have to have ships for your foreign trade. But now you hardly ever see a ship with the American flag."

"It's a long story, Tania," said the Professor. "All the American ships are registered under foreign flags now, because under our laws we have to pay the crews so much the ships lose money. Our shipyards are all closed because it costs twice as much to build a ship in the U.S. as it does in Japan, for instance."

"Well, don't you do anything about this?" asked Tania.

"Not a damn thing," said the Professor. "Our unions won't let us."

"I do not understand your country," said Tania. "How can you expect to be a great country if you don't have cargo ships and tankers?"

"I dunno," said the Professor. "But we seem to be doing pretty good without them."

Then Tania said to Fatso, "Captain, I like to use your radio."

"What for?" asked Fatso.

"I want to see if I can play trick on that ship that just passed us."

"What do you wanta do?" asked Fatso.

"I know that ship's call sign," said Tania. "I want to call him using the call sign of Russian Admiral and tell him, 'Return to Odessa.' "

"Hunh," said Fatso. "Do you think he will?"

"Yes. He will turn right around and go back."

"Okay," said Fatso. "Go ahead and try it."

Tania got a piece of paper and wrote out a short message in Russian. She showed it to Fatso and said, "This is from Admiral Commanding Mediterranean Fleet to the *Borich*. Urgent. It says, 'Return to Odessa.' "

"Do you think he'll believe it when you don't give any reason?" asked Fatso.

"The Russians never give reasons. They just issue orders," said Tania.

"All right. Go ahead and send it," said Fatso.

Tania sat down in front of the radio transmitter and began looking it over. "I'll set it up for you," said the Professor. "What frequency do you want?"

Tania motioned him away. "You don't have to help me," she said, twiddling the dials. "I know how to use this set." She finally got it adjusted to the frequency she wanted and then started calling the Russian at very low power. As she tapped out the call letters on the key, the Professor observed, "She's a pro, all right. You can tell that from her fist on the key." She continued calling, gradually increasing power, and after a few minutes an answering call came back from the Russian.

"Hah!" said Tania. "He answers me."

Then she sent her message and the Russian receipted for it. "Now," she said, "We go up and watch. Pretty soon you see him come back."

All hands adjourned to the bridge, from which the masts of the Russian were just visible over the horizon to the west. Jughaid put his big telescope on them and in a few minutes he shouted, "She's changing course, coming back this way!"

Soon her upper works and hull came over the horizon and she passed LCU 1124 a mile abeam to port, heading east.

"It's a wonder the Russian flagship didn't hear your transmission and cancel it," observed Fatso.

"That's why I used very low power," said Tania, "just enough to go a little beyond the horizon. Russian flagship was too far away to hear it."

"This gal knows all the angles, all right," observed the Professor.

"You know," said Fatso, with a gleam in his eye, "this business of being able to issue orders to the Russians may come in handy sometime."

Later, in the messroom, the boys were discussing Tania.

"She knows her stuff on that radio set . . . and she handles a key as well as I do," said the Professor.

"She must be a pretty good frogman, too," observed Webfoot. "She had to swim about half a mile under water with that mine, set it to go off so she'd be some distance from it, and then get over and hang on to our bow for twenty minutes or so."

"She don't look like much in that dungaree outfit," said Izzy. "But if you dressed her up and put some makeup on her she might be a pretty good-looking dish."

"I wonder what she'd be like in bed," said Adams.

"Aw, hell, they're all alike in bed," said Ginsberg. "After you get their pants off language don't make no difference."

"Yeah," said the Judge. "But they ain't all the same. I had a dame in Naples last time that was just as cold as a block of concrete till we got in bed. Then she turned into a fireball."

"Well, this Tania dame looks like a pretty cool customer to me," observed the Professor. "If any of you have got any ideas about her, I think you'll just be wasting your time."

"I'll betcha I can make her," said Adams.

"What makes you think you're such a Don Juan?" demanded the Professor.

"Hell, give me a week to work on them and I can make any dame in this world," said Adams.

"Okay, Romeo. You wanta bet?" asked the Professor.

"Sure," said Adams. "I'll betcha ten bucks I can make her before we get to Naples."

"It's a bet," said the Professor.

All the others wanted a piece of this action too, and soon there was fifty bucks in the pot—covered with fifty more by Adams.

CHAPTER SEVENTEEN

Board Egyptian

IN THE NEXT DAY or so, things settled down to normal again and the boys were getting used to the idea of having a Russian girl living with them. For a while it had cramped their style on their language a little bit. But by now they had found out that Tania knew all the words they did, plus some real robust Russian words too. So she was accepted and treated as one of the crew, the same as anybody else.

They had heard on the radio news about the Israeli protest on the sale of the ship to Egypt and about our decision to stop it. This had almost been forgotten when the ship burst into the news again with the phony sale to Ecuador and her departure from the U.S. with an Ecuadorian crew, presumably bound for Cairo.

"Those dirty bastards," said Izzy, when this news broke. "We oughta have the Sixth Fleet intercept that bucket and take it away from the Spigs."

"Yeah, you're right about that," agreed Fatso. "But this is exactly the same stunt the Israelis pulled on the French a year ago. Remember?"

"Well, what the hell," said Izzy. "They took their chances that the French would stop them, but the French didn't. That doesn't mean that we can't stop these guys."

"You know it was Russians who bought this ship, don't you?" asked Tania.

"No. How do you know that?" asked Fatso.

"I read the dispatches from Moscow to our Admiral about it. The Russians gave the money to buy the ship to Ecuador.

Moscow told us about it so we would be alert for it when it got to the eastern Mediterranean. We were supposed to meet it, put a commissar on board, and take it in to Alexandria. She was going to stay close to the North African coast after passing Gibraltar, and the Russians were going to meet her off Benghazi. I had to write a message to be ready to send to him when he got near Benghazi telling him that a Russian would come on board and take charge."

For about the next fifteen minutes while the radio news continued, Fatso had a faraway look in his eye and sat there taking no part in the comments on the news. When the news signed off he said to Tania, "Would you know how to call those Spigs on the radio?"

"Sure," she said. "I remember his call sign. I can get him on radio."

"That's good," said Fatso. "I've got an idea I want to think about a bit. I'll tell you more about it tomorrow morning."

"Oh oh!" said Scuttlebutt, as Fatso withdrew to his cabin. "We'd all better brace ourselves for heavy weather. Whenever he starts talking like that, things start to happen—and gawd knows what they'll lead to."

At breakfast next morning Fatso said, "Tania, you said last night you know how to call that Egyptian ship on the radio."

"Yes," said Tania, "I know how to call him."

"Suppose you called him," said Fatso, "and told him to meet us at sea. Do you think he would do it?"

"Of course," said Tania. "He is expecting a call from the Russians before he gets to Alexandria, telling him where to meet them to pick up the commissar. If I use Russian call signs when I send the message he will believe it."

"Okay," said Fatso. "Suppose we send him a message telling him to meet us off Cape Bon. That's six hundred miles west of Benghazi, where the Russians were going to meet him."

"What are we going to do then?" asked Webfoot eagerly. "Board and capture him?"

"Just keep your shirt on for a while," said Fatso, "and you'll find out.

"So okay," he continued. "We meet him off Cape Bon. Then you and I go aboard. You tell them you're the Russian commissar. I'm your assistant. We tell them there has been a change of plans and we've got to go in to Naples first. Do you think they will believe it?"

Tania's eyes lighted up. "But of course," she said. "They are South American mercenaries. They don't know who is supposed to come aboard. I can easily convince them that I am Russian commissar."

"Yeah," said the Professor. "But if you bring that packet into Naples and dump it in the Navy's lap there, you'll be handing them a keg of dynamite. You'll be as popular with the Sixth Fleet as a dose of clap."

"You're jumping to conclusions," said Fatso. "Sixth Fleet won't have anything to do with this. I'll dump it in the lap of the Israeli underground there. Our pal Benny back in Tel Aviv gave me the name of their top man. Remember?"

"Yeah. But it will be a hell of an international incident just the same, and Sixth Fleet will be in it up to their ass."

"Not if it works out the way I want it to," said Fatso. "We bring her in to the amphibious base after working hours, when all the big wheels are up at the officers' club having a drink. We tell the signal station at the entrance that we're a mine sweep. She looks like one, and mine sweeps are coming in and out of the amphib base all the time. They probably won't even report it to the OOD, and he won't think anything of it if they do."

"And how does the Israeli underground get into the act?" asked the Professor.

"I'm coming to that," said Fatso. "As soon as we tie up, I beat it ashore and get in touch with this friend of Benny's. He whips up a group of eight or ten huskies and they come down to the amphib base, go aboard, get her underway, and take her to Tel Aviv. This all happens during the night, and next morning the chances are the big wheels at the base don't even know she was in there."

"Isn't there going to be a hell of a fight on board when this Israeli crew tries to take over?" asked Scuttlebutt.

"I don't think so," said Fatso. "For one thing, they will be taken by surprise. And maybe, if we work it right, there won't be any fight at all."

Everyone pondered over this for a few moments and then the Judge said, "Well, if it comes off the way you say, everything will be fine. I think the U.S. government would be glad to see the Israelis get the ship. But they sure as hell wouldn't want to have any hand in the job. You would never be able to keep it quiet. It would get out eventually."

"I don't think so," said Fatso. "She'll only be at the amphib base for a few hours. If things go right, hardly anybody will know she was ever in there. Mine sweeps are coming in and out all the time, and no one pays any attention to them. After they get her to Tel Aviv, the Israelis can announce that they boarded and captured her at sea."

"I don't think you can get away with it," said the Judge.

"What do you think, Scuttlebutt?" asked Fatso.

"Well, skipper," said Scuttlebutt, "I dunno. If it was anybody but you doing this job, I'd say no. But with your luck we may be able to swing it. And, if we get caught at it, a hell of a lot of people in the States will be on our side."

"Okay," said Fatso. "I'm going to have a shot at it. Tania— you get busy on the radio and see if you can raise those guys."

"Da," said Tania. "I call them right away."

"Meantime," said Fatso, "I want to rig this craft to look like a Russian ship. I want to paint out our numbers and put a Russian name in their place. Tania—you think up a Russian name for us. We gotta make up a set of Russian colors to fly. And I want to make up Russian insignia for our uniforms. Tania can give us the dope on that."

Later Adams said to Satchmo, "This skipper of ours is a madman."

"Yeah," said Satch. "But he's crazy like a fox."

"He'll never get away with this," said Adams. "This thing could get blown up into a hell of an international incident. The Russians could make a big thing out of this."

"Well, you just let Cap'n Fatso worry about that," said Satch. "I been in some tight places with Cap'n Fatso, and he always lands on his feet."

That evening they were sitting around the table with shears, needle, and thread, making up various Russian insignia. They had completed a Russian flag and were working on Soviet rating badges to wear on their arms. Adams was seated next to Tania, who was cutting the insignia out. He dropped his hand under the table, slid it up to her thigh, and gave it a squeeze.

"Stop that," said Tania.

Adams slid his hand a little higher, said, "I could really go for you, kid," and gave another squeeze.

"You son of a bitch. Quit pinching my ass," said Tania out of the corner of her mouth.

Adams slid his hand a little further up, winked at her, and squeezed again. Tania put down the shears and suddenly uncorked a right jab that caught Adams square in the eye and knocked him off the bench backward and onto the deck. All hands stopped work and looked at Tania in open-mouthed amazement.

"He was pinching my ass," announced Tania. "In Rawshain Navy we do not allow ass pinching on board ship."

"We got the same rule in the American Navy," said Fatso. "The regulations are very strict about it . . . and I don't think you'll have any more trouble," he observed as Adams picked himself up off the deck.

"Not from me she won't," observed Adams, ruefully fingering his eye, which was already beginning to swell shut.

For the next couple of days LCU 1124 cruised back and forth between Cape Bon and Sicily. Tania kept calling the Egyptian by radio, but got no answer. The third evening the newscast announced the Egyptian had been sighted passing Gibraltar. This was followed by a lot of speculation that the Israelis would try to intercept her and that the Russians would meet and escort her. A confrontation on the high seas between the Israelis and Russians seemed to be in the making.

"One good thing about this job we're going to do," observed Scuttlebutt, after listening to the radio experts' speculations, "is that it's too improbable for anyone to think of it."

"Yeah. That's right," observed Fatso. "Now there's one item we've got to take care of before we meet these guys. We gotta organize a boarding party."

"Oh, boy," said Jughaid. "That's my meat. Put me down for it, Cap'n."

"Now let's see," said Fatso. "There's nine of us on board here. Tania and I go aboard the Egyptian, so that leaves seven. We need one guy on the wheel and one on deck to handle lines. So that only leaves five for the boarding party. I want Adams at the wheel and Satchmo on deck. The rest of you will be in the boarding party, armed with tommy guns and .45's."

"But I thought we were going to bamboozle them into this thing, rather than take 'em by force," objected the Professor.

"We are," said Fatso. "We'll go alongside them and tie up. Then Tania and I go aboard and the boarding party lies low, out of sight, in the messroom. Tania gives them the pitch that we are Russians and are in charge from then on. We'll soon find out whether they buy it or not. If they do, everything is lovely and we don't need the boarding party. If they suspect something is phony and try to make trouble, you guys swarm aboard and release us."

"What do we do then? Take over the ship?" asked the Professor.

"No," said Fatso. "Unless they fall for our pitch, the jig is up. We get the hell off, go on about our business, and forget the whole thing."

Next day Tania raised the Egyptian ship and sent them the message, ostensibly from the Russian Admiral, directing them to rendezvous with a Russian ship off Cape Bon and receive a commissar with further instructions for them. At the end of the message they got back a routine receipted and understood sign from the Egyptian.

"So far, so good," said Fatso. "Now we go down and hang around Cape Bon waiting for them."

This was a rather uncertain business, because they weren't too sure what she looked like. They knew she was a two hundred-footer of about four hundred tons and that was all. They ran up the Russian flag and hove to off Cape Bon, waiting.

They had several false alarms. One was over a little French gunboat and the other over a Tunisian mine sweeper. The mine sweep, flying no colors, hove to and let them come alongside. When they discovered the crew were all black and spoke no Spanish, they hauled clear and let her proceed.

Each night on the radio there was speculation as to what was going to happen to the Egyptian gunboat, but no word as to her whereabouts. Finally one morning a speck began taking shape on the western horizon. All hands were on deck with binoculars, and as it drew closer, Fatso said, "I think this is her. Give her a call on your light, Jughaid, and remember to use the Russian call."

The stranger answered promptly—and it was the Egyptian. She drew closer, hove to, and LCU 1124 went alongside. Fatso and Tania were on deck wearing caps with hammer and sickle prominently displayed and Russian insignia on their sleeves. The boarding party was in the messroom armed to the teeth and raring to go.

As they came alongside Satchmo threw them a line and the

Egyptian lowered a jacob's ladder over the side. Tania climbed aboard first, closely followed by Fatso. They were greeted on deck by a middle-aged Spaniard.

"I am Commander Voznik, Soviet Navy," announced Tania in Spanish.

The Spaniard saluted and bowed. "I am Captain Romero de Silveo. Welcome aboard. What do you want us to do?" he asked.

"I have special instructions from my Admiral about you," said Tania. "I will take charge from here on."

"Sí," said the Spaniard.

"We have to go to Naples first," said Tania. "All arrangements have been made. My ship will accompany us."

"Sí," said the Spaniard, with a shrug. "Whatever you say."

Fatso leaned over the rail and said to Satchmo, "So far everything looks okay." Satchmo passed his sea bag and Tania's up to him and cast off, and LCU 1124 hauled clear.

They adjourned to the charthouse, where Tania indicated she wanted a course to Naples around Sicily to the north. The Spaniard agreed. Fatso sent a blinker message to LCU 1124 and they squared away on a course for the Egadi Islands just west of Sicily.

Then Tania said, "I'm sorry to disturb you, Captain, but you'll have to move out of the cabin. My assistant and I will occupy it."

The Spaniard was not pleased about this, but agreed to it.

There was a crew of eight aboard the Egyptian. The engines were controlled from the bridge, so they only had one man on watch at a time, the helmsman, the same as on LCU 1124. The rest of the crew spent most of their time in their bunks or sleeping on deck, except at mealtimes. They all accepted Tania and Fatso without question.

At dinner in the mess hall that evening the skipper asked Tania, "How long do we stay in Naples?"

"Just one night," replied Tania in Spanish. "We have to pick up another Russian there. Then we will get an escort of two Russian destroyers and go to Cairo."

"Bueno," said the skipper. "We want to deliver the ship and go home as soon as possible."

"You can go home the day after we get to Alexandria," said Tania.

"Who is going to pay us?" asked the skipper.

"Don't worry about that," said Tania. "It's all arranged. You'll be paid in Alexandria."

"But there has been a revolution in my country since we sailed," said the skipper. "The new government won't pay us."

"Nichevo!" said Tania. "The Russians will pay you."

"We are supposed to get ten thousand dollars American money for this job," said the skipper.

"Okay—you'll get it," said Tania.

All hands looked relieved at this news.

"You pay it to me and I'll pay my crew," said the skipper.

"Okay," said Tania.

The faces of the crew grew noticeably longer at this development and there was some ominous muttering around the table.

Next morning they got a radio call from the Russians. Tania went down to the radio shack to take care of it. It was a message telling them to rendezvous off Benghazi with two Russian destroyers, the message which Tania herself had written up before she deserted. She answered the message with a "will comply" signal.

She showed the message to the Spanish skipper and explained, "We proceed from Naples to Benghazi and pick up our escort there. Then we go to Alexandria."

"Sí," said the skipper.

Next afternoon Tania informed the skipper, "We send my ship on ahead to make arrangements in Naples so we can get out next morning."

The skipper agreed. Fatso sent a blinker message to LCU 1124: "Proceed Naples. Arrive about 6 P.M. Get berth at amphibious base near entrance. We will arrive about 7 P.M. Have car on dock for me. Everything going fine here so far."

The Egyptian slowed down and LCU 1124 disappeared over the horizon toward Naples.

On the bridge that afternoon Fatso said to Tania, "It looks to me like they believe every word we've told them so far."

"That's right. They do," said Tania. "The only thing they are worried about is who is going to pay them and I've told them the Russians will."

"When we come into Naples tomorrow," said Fatso, "I want to do it with no colors flying. When the signal station at the entrance challenges us I'm going to give them the call sign of a U.S. mine sweep. We look like a mine sweep and they never pay much attention to them."

"Korosho! That's fine," said Tania.

⚓ CHAPTER EIGHTEEN

Capture

LATE NEXT AFTERNOON, LCU 1124 entered the harbor at Naples
and tied up to a berth just inside the entrance to the amphibious
base. An hour later the Egyptian appeared off the entrance with
the call flags of U.S. Mine Sweep 232 flying at her yardarm and
requested clearance to the amphibious base. A signal came back in
due course, "Permission granted. Proceed."

The Egyptian entered the base and tied up outboard of LCU
1124 about 7 P.M. It was after sunset, so no U.S. colors were flying
at the base. There was little activity ashore, and nothing to tell the
Spaniards that they were not tying up to a normal Naples waterfront dock. As they were securing the lines, Fatso said to Tania,
"I'm going ashore now and get a gang of Israelis to take over. You
invite the crew over to our ship to see the movies, beginning at
eight-thirty. We may be able to sneak the Israelis aboard, cast off,
and get clear without the Spigs ever knowing about it."

"Korosho! Will do," said Tania.

Back on his own ship Fatso was immediately surrounded in the
messroom by all hands, eagerly demanding info on how things
were going.

"So far, it's perfect," said Fatso. "They think we're Russian and
that they will leave for Alexandria tomorrow morning. Now, Scuttlebutt, I want you to set up movies in the messroom tonight.
Tania is inviting the Spigs to come over at eight-thirty. She can
translate the sound track for them. You guys are all supposed to be
Russians, so don't talk any English to these guys. I expect to be
back here about nine-thirty with a gang of Israelis. We will try to
sneak aboard during the movie without the Spigs knowing it. If

things work out right, we'll cast her off and they can take her out without the Spigs knowing a damn thing about it till the movie is over. There's eight of them in their crew, so if anything goes wrong we may have a little trouble restraining them. But I don't want any shooting. If necessary, we'll just have to strongarm them. Any questions?"

When a proposition like this is suddenly dropped in your lap it's hard to know what questions to ask. There were none.

"Now how about the car, Scuttlebutt?" asked Fatso. "You got it ready?"

"Waiting on the dock, skipper," said Scuttlebutt.

"Okay," said Fatso. "Satchmo, I want you to drive it."

So Fatso and Satchmo got in the car and away they went. Fifteen minutes later they pulled up in front of a small, shabby-looking house on a side street. Fatso knocked and waited for some time. Then a peephole in the door opened and a pair of eyes examined him skeptically.

"Does Aaron Goldberg live here?" asked Fatso.

"What do you want?" demanded a voice from within.

"I want to see Aaron Goldberg," said Fatso. "It's important."

"About what?" demanded the voice.

"I can't tell you," said Fatso. "I've got to see Goldberg."

"Wait," said the voice, and the peephole closed.

A minute later it opened again and Fatso got another searching examination by a pair of eyes. Then a new voice said, "What do you want?"

"Are you Goldberg?" asked Fatso.

"What's your business?" asked the voice.

"I'm a friend of Benny Cohen in Tel Aviv. I was with him there a couple of weeks ago and he told me to look you up when I got to Naples."

"Oh," said the voice. "Are you Fatso?"

"Yeah. That's me," said Fatso.

A bolt was slid back, the door opened, and Fatso was greeted by a young, tough-looking Israeli of heavy-set build who looked like a paratrooper.

"Come in," he said, sticking his hand out and giving Fatso's a grip that made him wince. "I had a letter from Benny last week. He told me you might look me up. Come on upstairs."

Goldberg led the way upstairs and into a large clubroom, where there were half a dozen hard-looking young huskies sitting around reading and playing cards.

"Here is the friend that Benny wrote us about," he announced. "Captain Fatso."

Everyone raised a hand in a friendly greeting.

"Have a cup of coffee?" asked Goldberg, as they seated themselves at a table.

"Yeah, thanks—I will," said Fatso.

Goldberg held up two fingers to a lad at the coffee urn and said, "Benny told us in his letter about how you saved his life. Those goddamn Arabs almost got you in that ambush. So anything we can do for you—just let us know. We are at your service."

"I got a big job for you," said Fatso. Then, glancing around the room, he said, "I suppose you can rely on all these people to keep their mouths shut?"

"Yes indeed," said Goldberg. "We are all in the Special Forces Unit. I can vouch for every one of these people. You can speak freely."

"Okay," said Fatso. "You know that Egyptian gunboat that sailed from Hampton Roads a couple of weeks ago? The one your country protested about and the Ecuadorians bought it?"

"Yes indeed. We know all about it—except where it is. It passed Gibraltar several days ago. Our Navy and Air Forces are on the lookout for it and will intercept it—if it isn't escorted by the Russians."

"Well, that ship is tied up at the U.S. Navy amphibious base right here in Naples right now," said Fatso.

All activity in the room stopped. Everybody laid down his cards and books and looked at Fatso quizzically.

"What happened?" asked Goldberg. "Did you people intercept her and bring her in here?"

"In a way, yes," said Fatso. "But the U.S. Navy doesn't know a thing about it officially—doesn't even know she's in here."

"How do you mean?" asked Goldberg.

So Fatso explained how they had sent the phony radio message, met the ship at sea, gone aboard posing as Russians, and had taken over. He explained that the Spigs expected to sail for Alexandria next morning.

"But your Navy won't let them do it. Will they?" asked Goldberg.

"So far our Navy doesn't know a damn thing about it, and I don't think they want to get mixed up in it at all," said Fatso. "In fact they wouldn't want to touch it with a ten-foot fending-off pole. But if you guys are ready to act fast, you can get down there tonight, take possession of her, and take her to Tel Aviv—sailing tonight."

Everybody got up and crowded around Fatso and Goldberg, eager to hear every word Fatso had to say.

"It sounds great," said Goldberg. "How do we do it?"

"Just get together a crowd of about ten husky men," said Fatso, "and come with me down to the amphibious base. I'll get you through the gate. All the Spigs will be over on my ship watching the movies, except the gangway watch. The movies are inside, so you can sneak across my ship without being seen. You may have to overpower one guy as gangway watch. Then you cast off, start up the engines, and away you go to Haifa. Very few people at the amphibious base will know that the ship was even in there next morning."

The whole crowd looked at Goldberg, with eager anticipation on all faces.

"It sounds too good to be true," said Goldberg.

"But it is true—just like I told it to you," said Fatso. "All you need is a couple of guys who know how to run diesel engines and somebody who can navigate. You take her out of here tonight and you go through the Straits of Messina tomorrow night. Take her between Crete and Greece along the coast of Anatolia north of Cyprus and then run down the west coast of Syria coming down from the north. The Russians will be looking for her coming along the north coast of Africa. You just steam right into Haifa with her and surprise everybody."

There was an excited chorus of approval from the crowd.

"Boy, oh boy!" said Goldberg. "They'll declare a national holiday in Israel about this. We'll probably all get promoted."

"Well, get your crew organized then," said Fatso. "About an hour and a half from now you should be going aboard. You'll be underway five minutes later and out of the harbor in twenty minutes."

Goldberg counted noses of those present. There were seven. "Okay," he said, "get Abraham, Joseph, and Aaron. That will make ten. Also get John—I want him in charge of this place till we get back. Can any of you guys run a diesel engine?"

There were four who professed to be experts on diesels.

"Herman," he said to a bright-looking lad, "you're a lieutenant in the naval reserve. You ought to know how to get us out of the harbor and how to lay the courses and navigate for us."

"Yes indeed," said Herman. "Don't worry about that. I'll take care of it."

He picked out the two biggest in the crowd and said, "You two go aboard right behind Fatso and overpower the gangway watch."

"We've got to do that very quietly," said Fatso. "No shooting, or anything like that."

"It will be done very quietly," said one of the pair confidently. "We won't make a sound."

"Are you coming with us to Tel Aviv?" asked Goldberg of Fatso.

"No," said Fatso. "As soon as you are in possession, I'll get off."

"Too bad," said Goldberg. "You'd get a big welcome in Tel Aviv."

"I can't afford to be mixed up in this thing at all," said Fatso. "You gotta keep my name out of it. You can tell your bosses the true story, but the official story they release has got to be that she was captured at sea by the Israeli Navy. It's very important that you keep the U.S. Navy out of it."

"Okay," said Goldberg. "We can handle that all right. What happens on your ship when the Spigs who have been watching the movies find out their ship is gone?"

"Well," said Fatso, "we may have a little excitement for a while when they find out their ship has disappeared. But I'll handle that. We'll need another car to take all your people down to the amphib base. And I'll want a driver to stay with the car who knows the way to the Russian embassy here in town. I think I'll take the Spigs there and dump them."

"Okay," said Goldberg. "We'll take care of that."

An hour and a half later, two cars crowded with men pulled up at the gate of the amphibious base. Fatso showed his ID card to the sentry and said, "These people are friends of mine. I'm taking them down to my ship."

The sentry waved them on. The two cars pulled up at the dock alongside LCU 1124. Fatso got out and looked the situation over carefully. No one was in sight on either ship. The sound track of the movie in the messroom was clearly audible. Fatso motioned to the others to get out, and they all slipped quietly aboard LCU 1124. They gathered in the darkness of the well deck alongside the jacob's ladder leading up and over the side of the Egyptian.

Fatso went up the ladder first, followed a few seconds later by the two designated to take care of the gangway watch. The watch was seated inboard under a light, reading a book. The Spaniard got up and turned to put his book down on a hatch nearby. He never knew what hit him. While his back was turned, the two Israelis were on him and knocked him cold with a couple of karate blows. Soon he was securely gagged and bound and shoved into a dark corner. The rest of the party then climbed quickly aboard and each one went to his designated station. Fatso showed them the two mooring lines that had to be cast off. He showed the diesel experts the way to the engine room and then hurried up to the bridge where Goldberg and the Navy Lieutenant were. The Lieutenant took a quick look around the harbor, saw that all was clear, and took his station at the wheel with his hand on the engine throttles. In a minute the ship began to tremble as they felt the engines start. Soon word came up on the voice tube from the engine room, "All ready to get underway."

Fatso shook hands quickly with the Lieutenant and Goldberg and said, "Good luck to you."

"May Jehovah be good to you, Fatso," said Goldberg, as Fatso scrambled overthe side and slipped down onto the well deck of LCU 1124.

He signaled to the men standing by the mooring lines and they threw them off. The Egyptian began slowly backing clear. She eased silently astern until her bow was about even with LCU 1124's stern, then kicked ahead, put her rudder over, and squared away on a course for the entrance. In a few minutes she was swallowed up in the darkness.

As she passed the signal station on the way out she flashed the call letters of U.S. mine sweep 232, and got a belated acknowledgment from the sleepy signal watch there.

Fatso then tiptoed into the messroom and took a seat in the back to watch the rest of the movie. He sat down alongside Scuttlebutt, gave him a nudge, held his fist out with thumb up, and made a circle with his thumb and forefinger.

When the movie was over, the Spanish captain made a little speech to Tania, thanking her. She invited them all to stay for a cup of coffee. While they were having their coffee, one of the Spaniards went out on deck and soon burst back into the messroom, his eyes as big as golf balls, and announced that the ship was gone. The others rushed out on deck and gazed in open-mouth amazement at the empty spot where their ship had been. Fatso, Tania, and the rest of the boys put on an act of being amazed too.

"Where is my ship?" demanded the Spaniard of Tania.

"I don't know," said Tania. "Someone has taken her away."

"What do we do now?" said the skipper, wringing his hands as an excited jabbering broke out among his crew.

"I don't know," said Tania. "I must report this immediately to the Russian ambassador. . . . You and your men must come with me."

When a skipper's ship suddenly disappears, leaving him and his whole crew ashore, he's apt to be a bit bewildered and open to suggestions as to what to do. He agreed immediately to notifying the Russian authorities. He and his whole jabbering crew piled into the cars on the dock and made their way to the gate. Fatso again showed his ID card and said, "I'm taking my friends home again now."

The gate sentry did not notice that this was a different bunch of friends from the ones he had brought in an hour before.

In town they made their way to the home of the Russian consul. It was a large house with the Russian coat of arms over the entrance gate. Here they all got out of the cars and Fatso rang the bell at the gate. Then, before the Spaniards realized what was happening, Fatso and Tania popped back into the cars and away they went and left them standing there.

Back at the Israeli HQ Fatso, Tania, and John gathered around the bar to have a drink.

"This is the biggest thing since the six-day war," said John, as he measured out the bourbon and water. "There will be a wild celebration in Tel Aviv about this and all our people will be heroes."

"It sure went off slick," said Fatso. "I'll never forget the look on that Spig captain's face when he realized his ship was gone. And all of our boys put on a hell of a good act about being surprised, too. That Spig still thought we were on his side till we ran off and left him at the consulate. I wonder what the hell the Russian consul will do with those guys?"

"He'll have a hell of a time," said Tania. "There's nothing in his book to tell him what to do. He'll have to request instructions from Moscow. The Russians don't like to look stupid to the rest of the world, so this will put them on the spot. They will understand this perfectly because this is the way they work. But I think they'll just try to hush it up."

"They'll have a hell of a time doing that," said John. "When the ship gets in to Tel Aviv the Israelis will tell the whole world about it."

First thing next morning LCU 1124 got underway and nosed up to the stern gate of her mother ship, the USS *Alamo*, which was moored in another part of the base. The *Alamo* lowered her stern gate, admitted LCU 1124 to her roomy well deck, and closed the gate. Thus, for all practical purposes, LCU 1124 simply disappeared off the face of the earth, or at least off the waterfront of the amphibious base.

Later that morning the Russian consul came down to the amphib base with the Spanish skipper and drove along the entire waterfront. They saw no trace of LCU 1124. The consul had spent a hectic night with the seven excitable Spaniards on his hands and wanted no further part of them. When they couldn't find LCU 1124, he loaded the skipper and his crew aboard a Russian ship that was sailing for Alexandria and sent a dispatch to Moscow telling their whole improbable story. He then went back to his regular business of trying to stir up trouble among the members of the Italian Communist party.

⚓ CHAPTER NINETEEN

Tania Leaves

As soon as LCU 1124 was securely moored in the well deck, Fatso went up to the cabin to report to the Captain. The Captain had known Fatso a long time and had implicit confidence in him, except in matters involving the MP's, which he considered to be more or less Fatso's private business. He regarded Fatso as one of the *Alamo's* senior citizens.

He was seated at his mess table having coffee when Fatso came in, and waved him to a chair at the table. He buzzed for the messboy to bring him a cup of coffee and said, "Well, Gioninni— glad to see you back. How did things go this trip?"

"Oh—about the same as usual, Cap'n," said Fatso.

"Where did you go this time?" asked the Captain.

"Malta, Iraklion, Tel Aviv, and Athens," said Fatso.

"Did any of your boys get in trouble ashore?" asked the skipper.

"No sir. No trouble at all. We also stopped in at the Gulf of Laconia, where the Russian fleet bases sometimes."

"What were you doing there?" asked the skipper.

"I was just curious to have a look at their ships," said Fatso. "I thought we might get some good pictures of them. But we didn't have much chance to look at them."

"Oh?" said the skipper. "Why not?"

"They tried to blow us up," said Fatso. "So I decided to get the hell out of there."

"A smart move, I would say," observed the skipper. "Just how did they try to blow you up?"

"They sent a swimmer to put a limpet mine on us," said Fatso. "But this guy detonated the mine about one hundred yards from us. It went off with a hell of an explosion and shook us up pretty bad. When we got underway to get the hell out, we found this frogman hanging on to our stem. We hauled him aboard and he told us he had purposely fired the mine a safe distance from us and that he wanted to defect from the Russians and come over to our side."

"Well, I'll be gah damn," said the skipper.

"So we took him aboard—and we've still got him," said Fatso.

"Hmmm," said the skipper. "Our ONI people should talk to him. Do you think he can be of any use to us?"

"Yes. I think he can help us plenty. He's one of their CIA types and a radio operator. He knows a lot about their communications, codes, and ciphers."

"Well," said the skipper, "we better hang on to him. . . . Lemme see, now . . . I think I'd better take this up with Com Sixth Fleet right away. His flagship is in port now. I think you better come along with me."

"Oh, and one more thing, Cap'n," said Fatso. "This deserter is a she."

"Whaddaya mean? A *female?*" asked the Captain incredulously.

"Yeah. That's right," said Fatso. "We didn't find it out till she had been aboard awhile."

"Well—I don't see that that changes things much," said the skipper. "Okay. Let's go see the Admiral."

A half hour later the Captain and Fatso got in the Captain's gig and headed for the *Milwaukee*, anchored out in the harbor. The *Milwaukee* was a sleek, businesslike-looking heavy cruiser, and was shined up like a yacht. As they neared the starboard gangway, four side boys and a boatswain's mate took station at the head of the gangway while the young OOD, a spyglass under his arm, stood on the upper platform looking down as the bow hook grappled the guest warp. As the Captain started up the gangway followed by Fatso, the OOD stepped inboard. When the Captain's head appeared above the deck coaming all side boys cracked up to a salute and held it while the boatswain's mate started a long blast on his pipe. At the head of the gangway the Captain faced aft, saluted the colors, and then stepped aboard, saluted the OOD, and said, "Permission to come aboard, sir." As he stepped aboard, the boatswain's mate finished his piping and the side boys cracked down with their salute.

Fatso, right behind him, repeated the salute to the colors as he came over the side and tipped a broad wink to the boatswain's mate as he passed him.

"I want to see the Admiral," said the Captain.

"Messenger," barked the OOD, "show this officer down to the Admiral's cabin."

A messenger wearing white leggings and a duty belt led the way aft along the spotless quarterdeck, resplendent with shiny brightwork and fancy doodads. A small piece of marlin adrift on that quarterdeck would have been as conspicuous as an ashcan on the White House steps.

As they were ushered into the cabin the staff was just finishing the Admiral's morning briefing on the global situation. They took station at the rear until it was over.

The Operations Officer was saying, "That Egyptian gunboat that shipped out of Hampton Roads and was sighted at Gibraltar a few days ago is still unaccounted for. The *America*'s planes are searching for her along the North African coast."

"The *America* understands, don't they, that if they find her they are to take no action except to shadow her?" asked the Admiral.

"Yes sir. They understand that," said the ops officer.

"When we find her we'll pass the information along to the Israelis. What they do with it is their business," said the Admiral.

"The new Ecuadorian government has proclaimed the ship to be an outlaw," continued the commander, "and disclaims all responsibility for her."

"Yes. I know," said the Admiral. "She may be an outlaw so far as the Ecuadorians are concerned, but there was a legal sale of the ship to either Egypt or Russia. Washington would like very much to have her fall into the hands of the Israelis. But they are scared stiff of taking any action that would antagonize the Arabs any more than we already have. So we take no action to molest her."

"Yes sir. That's thoroughly understood by everybody," said the ops officer.

As the briefing broke up the Captain came forward and introduced himself to the Admiral. "Captain Jenks, sir—USS *Alamo*."

"Glad to meet you, Jenks," said the Admiral. "Have a cup of coffee? What can I do for you?"

"Admiral," said the Captain, "a rather unusual situation has come up which I think your office will want to handle. I've got a deserter from the Russian Navy who wants to defect to our side."

"Well, that's interesting," said the Admiral. "What are the circumstances?"

"It's a very unusual tale. I've got one of my men here who can tell you all about it," said the Captain, motioning to Fatso to come forward.

When the Admiral saw Fatso his face lit up, he stuck out his hand, and said, "Fatso! How the hell are you? Long time no see."

"Oh—you already know Gioninni?" asked the Captain.

"Know him? Hell, I've known this scoundrel for twenty-five years or more," said the Admiral. "When the *Lexington* got sunk at the Battle of the Coral Sea, he saved my life—swam around holding me up for about an hour."

"Well, he's in my ship now," said the Captain. "He's skipper of my LCU and he's been off with her on independent duty for the last month. Tell the Admiral what happened, Gioninni."

Fatso related the story of their visit to the Gulf of Laconia, of the Russian attempt to blow them up, and of Tania's coming aboard.

"Those commie sons of bitches," said the Admiral. "They shoot down our planes if we fly over them and now they try to blow up our ships."

"They would of got us, too," said Fatso, "except that this frogman deliberately set the mine off about a hundred yards away from us. It shook the hell out of us but didn't do any real damage."

"And what does this fellow want to do now?" asked the Admiral.

"He wants to come over to our side and work for us," said Fatso. "He's a radio operator and knows a lot about their codes and ciphers. He's also a language specialist and thinks he could be useful to CIA."

The Admiral considered for a moment and then said, "All right. We'll send him back to the States and let CIA figure out what to do with him."

"Oh—and one other thing," said Fatso, "which complicates things a little bit . . . he's a she."

"Hunh? What do you mean?" demanded the Admiral.

"This defector is a woman," said Fatso. "But you'd never know it. We didn't find out till she's been aboard awhile."

"Well, I'll be damned," said the Admiral. "But I don't see that this makes any difference. We'll ship her back to the States and let them worry about that. . . . Get her out here today and I'll

arrange to have her flown back to the States with an escort. . . .
Now what else have you been up to, Fatso? You're usually just
about one jump ahead of the MP's wherever you go. What else
have you been doing since I saw you last?"

"Well—nothin', sir," said Fatso piously. "We've just been going
about our business, delivering freight to various places around the
Med."

"Uh huh," said the Admiral. "Of course even if that was so, I
wouldn't believe it."

"There was nothing else, sir—at least nothing else that you'd
want to hear about, Admiral," said Fatso.

"Okay," said the Admiral. "Captain, we'll get that Russian gal
off your hands today and send her to the States. . . . Glad to
have seen you again, Fatso. . . . Drop in and see me any time
you're aboard."

Going back in the boat the Captain said to Fatso, "I didn't know
you were so palsy-walsy with the Admiral."

"We've known each other quite a while," said Fatso. "Almost
twenty-five years."

"What's this about saving his life?" asked the Captain.

"He was an ensign aviator on the *Lexington* when we got sunk
at the Battle of the Coral Sea. I swam around holding him up
for about an hour after the ship went down. Admiral Halsey gave
me a medal for it. Old Admiral Bull Halsey just loved to hand out
medals."

"Pretty nice to have an in like that with Com Sixth Fleet," remarked the skipper. "The Admiral says he wants to see that Russian today. So let me know as soon as she's ready and I'll send
her out."

"Aye aye, sir," said Fatso. "She'll be ready a half hour after we
get back."

When Fatso got back to the ship Tania was in the messroom
playing acey-deucy. "Pack up your stuff," said Fatso. "You're
going to the States . . . leaving in about half an hour."

"I have nothing to pack but my skindiver's outfit. This is all I
have," she said, indicating the suit of dungarees she was wearing.
"So I have time to finish this game. This will be the first game of
acey-deucy I ever win."

"Okay. Finish your game," said Fatso. "We'll get you a suit of blues and dress you up like a regular sailor. They're going to turn you over to the CIA when you get to the States, and they'll decide what to do with you."

"Korosho!" said Tania. "I've always wanted to see United States."

"They will ask you a lot of stuff about the Russian Navy," said Fatso, "and about codes, ciphers, and communications."

"Okay. I tell them everything I know," said Tania.

"But don't tell them anything about the Egyptian ship," said Fatso. "It's very important to keep that quiet and there's no reason why they should know anything about it. So don't volunteer any information about it. Not a word. You understand?"

"Okay," said Tania. "I do what you say, Captain."

A half hour later a boat came alongside the *Alamo*'s gangway with an intelligence officer in it. Tania was on deck dressed up in a new apprentice seaman's uniform, and all hands from LCU 1124 were on hand to see her off. She shook hands with each of them, and told Adams she was sorry about his black eye. When she got to Fatso she said, "Captain, I'll luff you as long as I live." She then planted a kiss smack on Fatso's mouth, got in the boat, and shoved off, leaving Fatso completely flabbergasted for the first time in many years.

CHAPTER TWENTY

Smythe

THAT AFTERNOON Adams went ashore on liberty. The first thing he did was to stop at a bar and get himself a couple of stiff snorts. After they had taken effect he proceeded uptown to the office of the *Time* Magazine representative, an alert young reporter whose name was Smythe and whose main job was keeping track of the activities of the Sixth Fleet.

"What can I do for you, sailor?" asked Smythe, when Adams was shown into his office by his stenog.

Adams waited till the girl withdrew and then said, "Mr. Smythe, I've got a hell of a story for you—a scoop that will make you famous."

"Well, that's fine," said Smythe. "Always glad to get a good story. What is it?"

"You know that gunboat we built for the Egyptians at Portsmouth?" said Adams. "Then a fake Ecuadorian company bought it and it sailed for the Med and everybody is wondering what the hell became of it?"

"Yes indeed," said Smythe. "I know all about it—except where it is now."

"Well, I've got a hell of an exclusive for you about it," said Adams.

"Okay. Let's have it," said Smythe, getting out a notebook and pencil.

"We've got a little business to settle first," said Adams.

"How do you mean?" asked Smythe.

"How much are you going to pay me for it?" said Adams. "This is the scoop of the year. It might win you a Pulitzer prize. I ain't giving it to you for nothing."

"How much do you want?" asked Smythe.

"Ten grand," said Adams.

"Now wait a minute," said Smythe. "Ten grand! You must be nuts. You're way out of line with a price like that."

"I don't think so," said Adams. "This will be the feature story on the front pages all over the world when it breaks. It will be the cover story for *Life* and *Look*. If you don't want it, either *Newsweek* or the AP will gobble it up."

"Well, you gotta give me some sort of an idea what the story is all about before we talk that kind of money," said Smythe.

"All right. I'll tell you this much," said Adams. "The Israelis have intercepted that craft and they're taking her in to Haifa. That's a pretty good scoop for you right there. But there's a hell of a lot more to it than that. Real sensational stuff that will stir up an international hassle."

"Okay," said Smythe. "You give me the rest of it, and if *Time* uses it—as a feature—I'll pay you a thousand bucks."

"Look," said Adams. "Make it two thousand and it's a deal. That's just for the news story. *Life* and *Look* will both want my personal story on this and that ain't included in this deal."

"Okay," said Smythe. "Two thousand. Now let's have it."

"And first of all I want fifty bucks cash money right now," said Adams. "And a memo from you on *Time* stationery about the rest of it."

Smythe did a little mental figuring. After all, the whereabouts of the Egyptian gunboat was the big mystery in all the world's newsrooms at the present moment. If the Israelis really had captured her, this was indeed a scoop that would make him famous. If the story turned out to be a dud, he could probably slip the fifty bucks in on his swindle sheet and get away with it.

"Okay," he said. He picked up his pen and wrote on an office memo pad, "*Time* Magazine hereby promises to pay Seaman Adams $1,950.00 for exclusive story on Egyptian gunboat if the story checks out." Then he signed it, took fifty dollars out of his wallet, handed the memo and the money to Adams, and said, "All right. Let's have the story now."

So Adams related the whole story to Smythe, including Tania's part in it. He told how a U.S. Navy ship had impersonated a Russian, had boarded the Egyptian at sea and brought her in to Naples. He told how the Israelis had sneaked aboard and captured it right there in the amphibious base at Naples the night before, and were now on their way to Haifa with her. By the time he got to the end, Smythe was in a dither of excitement. "Gawd almighty, Adams," he said, "this is a hell of a story. This will blow the roof off the State Department, Pentagon, and White House. There will be hell to pay about this. But I've got to have something more than just your word for it."

"Well, all the fellas on the ship are ashore this afternoon and won't be back until late tonight," said Adams. "You come down to the *Alamo* first thing in the morning and you can check it with all the other guys in the crew. But that has nothing to do with the deal between you and me for the story."

"Okay," said Smythe. "I'll be aboard first thing in the morning. Meantime, I'll check with Commander in Chief Allied Forces Southern Europe."

"I doubt if he'll know anything at all about it," said Adams.

"Well, he can check the Sixth Fleet and find out," said Smythe.

"I don't think Sixth Fleet knows anything about it either," said Adams. "And neither one of them would admit it even if they knew all about it."

"Well, I'll check with them anyway," said Smythe. "And I'll be aboard the *Alamo* at nine o'clock tomorrow morning. Meantime, keep your mouth shut about this. You tell anybody else about it and our deal is off."

On that note Adams adjourned to the nearest bar and Smythe got a cab to the HQ of Commander in Chief Allied Forces Southern Europe.

C in C Allied Forces Southern Europe is one of the major NATO commands in Europe. It is a joint command consisting of allied armies, navies, and air forces and staffed by high-ranking officers from all the countries of western Europe. The C in C was a four-star U.S. Navy Admiral, who among the many forces available to him counted the Sixth Fleet. The Admiral knew Smythe well and cordially detested him as he did nearly all members of the press. But he knew which side his bread was buttered on, so he handled them all with fur-lined silk gloves.

Arriving at the Admiral's HQ in a palatial villa on the outskirts of town, Smythe went first to the public relations officer, Captain Twiggers.

"Hello, Smythe," said Twiggers. "What can we do for you today?"

"I'm trying to check out a hell of a story," said Smythe.

"Okay," said Twiggers. "We'll be glad to help you in any way we can within the limits of security. What do you want to know?"

"This is a matter on which I'll want to see the Admiral," said Smythe.

"Umm," said Twiggers. "Well, can you give me some idea what it is all about? The Admiral is pretty busy, and he's hard to get to."

"It's about the Egyptian gunboat that slipped out of Hampton Roads and was sighted passing through Gib the other day," said Smythe. "I'll give the full details to the Admiral."

Captain Twiggers pricked up his ears right away. That Egyptian gunboat had been the hottest potato on their situation board ever since she sailed from Hampton Roads.

"Just what do you want to know about her?" asked Twiggers.

"I've got all the dope I want on *her*," said Smythe. "I want to check on what the Sixth Fleet has been doing about her."

"I can tell you that," said Twiggers. "It hasn't done a damned thing. We don't know where it is. Sixth Fleet has had air searchers out looking for it for the past week, but we haven't seen hide nor hair of it."

"I have reason to believe otherwise," said Smythe. "And I want to talk to the Admiral about it."

"Don't you believe what I'm telling you?" bristled Twiggers.

"You may not know about this yet," said Smythe. "This is top-level stuff that would be held very closely. I want to see the Admiral about it."

"All right," said Twiggers. "I'll see if he can fit you in. Wait here. I'll be back in a few minutes."

In the anteroom of the Admiral's office there were several WAVES, a chief yeoman, and a marine orderly, presided over by a sharp-looking young lieutenant in immaculate uniform with gold aiguillettes on his shoulders. When Twiggers said he wanted to see the Admiral, the Flag Lieutenant flipped aside the cover to a small peephole in the wall alongside his desk and peeked in at the Admiral. The old gentleman was seated at his large mahogany desk puffing on a cigar and poring over a document with a pencil in his hand. The aide flipped a switch on the squawk box and announced, "Captain Twiggers to see you, sir."

"Okay, send him in," said the Admiral, shoving the crossword puzzle on which he was working into his top drawer.

The orderly opened the door to the inner sanctum and Twiggers went in.

"Admiral," he said, "Smythe of *Time* Magazine would like to see you."

"That nosy little son of a bitch again?" asked the Admiral. "What the hell does he want?"

"It's about that Egyptian gunboat from Hampton Roads," said Twiggers. "He claims he has a hot story on her."

"Humph," said the Admiral. "I doubt if he knows a damned thing about her. He's probably just fishing for information and fixing to write a nasty piece about the Sixth Fleet for not intercepting her. All right. Bring him in."

Smythe came right to the point. "Admiral," he said, "I've got a story on that Egyptian gunboat that everybody is wondering about. I want to check it with you."

"Well, what's the story?" asked the Admiral guardedly.

"The story is that she has been intercepted by the Israelis. They have taken her over and she's on her way to Haifa now," said Smythe.

"Well—that's good news, if it's true," said the Admiral. "Where did you get this story from?"

"From one of your sailors, sir," said Smythe. "He claims his ship had a lot to do with it. Actually captured it and turned it over to the Israelis."

"Ridiculous," said the Admiral. "If you believe all the stories you hear from sailors you won't be working for *Time* Magazine much longer."

"Well, this lad told a fantastic story, all right," said Smythe, "but somehow or other I believe it." He then related the whole story about how a ship of the Sixth Fleet had posed as a Russian, intercepted the Egyptian, and persuaded her to let them take over. They had brought her in to the U.S. Navy amphibious base in Naples, where she was taken over by a crew of Israelis, and she was now on her way to Haifa.

As he was talking a look of incredulous disdain came across the Admiral's face. When he finished the Admiral sniffed scornfully and said, "That's the most fantastic yarn I've heard in a long time. It's absurd. I don't think even *Time* will fall for a fairy story like that one."

"This just happened at the amphibious base last night," said Smythe. "Maybe word about it hasn't got up the line to you yet. How about checking with Com Sixth Fleet about it?"

"Sixth Fleet would have informed me instantly about this," said the Admiral. "But if it will make you feel any better I'll check with him, although it's just a waste of time." He buzzed for his aide and said, "Get me Com Sixth Fleet on the scrambler phone."

A minute later the red phone on the Admiral's desk rang and a voice said, "Good afternoon, sir. Admiral Hughes here."

"Joe," said the Admiral, "I've got a *Time* reporter sitting here in my office now with a fantastic story about a small ship in your fleet intercepting that Egyptian gunboat, boarding and capturing her, and turning her over to the Israelis."

"Wait a minute," said Hughes. "There seems to be something wrong with this phone. Now . . . would you mind saying that again?"

The Admiral repeated.

"Yeah. That's what it sounded like the first time," said Hughes. "There isn't a word of truth in it. I've got the *America* scouring the African coast for that craft, and we haven't seen hide nor hair of her."

"This *Time* man claims she was brought into the amphibious base here by your people," said the Admiral. "He says they turned her over to the Israelis and the Israelis sailed with her for Haifa last night."

"He's nuts," said Hughes. "Why don't you let him go ahead with his story. It will make him and his goddamn magazine look foolish."

"Okay, Jim. Over and out," said the Admiral, hanging up.

"Sixth Fleet knows nothing whatever about this," he said to Smythe. "So there you've got it, right from the top. What you do with it now is your own business. But of course, even if it were true, you shouldn't publish it."

"Why not?" asked Smythe in blank amazement.

"It would cause all sorts of high-level international complications," said the Admiral. "It would be very embarrassing to the United States. The only ones who would benefit from it would be the Arabs—and the Russians."

"But it's a hell of a scoop. It might even win a Pulitzer prize."

"Well, yes," admitted the Admiral. "You and your magazine would also benefit from it. You'd make a hell of a splurge with it, but it would be against the interests of the United States."

"Well, I can't be concerned about that," said Smythe. "My job is simply to find out what is happening and report it."

"Regardless of what effect it has on our national interests?" asked the Admiral.

"You gotta take a long-range view of things, Admiral," said Smythe. "Freedom of the press is the cornerstone of all our freedoms. An informed public is necessary for the welfare of the country. We've got to report everything of interest, regardless of whose ox gets gored."

"Balls," observed the Admiral. "But anyway, in this case you've got the word right from the top now—not a word of truth in the story."

"Well, you gotta remember, Admiral," said Smythe, "that in the My Lai incident, the top Army brass didn't know anything about it for a long time. And even when they did know they kept quiet about it. They almost succeeded in sweeping it under the rug until an enterprising reporter broke the story."

"And gave Ho Chi Minh the biggest propaganda windfall he'd had in years," observed the Admiral. "Exposing that thing did nothing but harm for our side. But of course about half of you reporters are working for the other side anyway."

"Well—okay, Admiral," said Smythe, getting up. "Thank you for your time. I'm going to do some more checking on this before I drop it."

Back in Twiggers' office, Smythe said, "Look. There's a signal station at the harbor entrance that keeps track of all ships entering and leaving. How about checking with them on what ships came in yesterday afternoon?"

"Okay," said Twiggers. He called the signal station and was informed that the only ships that came in yesterday were LCU 1124 and three U.S. mine sweeps.

He then checked with the OOD at the amphib base. The OOD knew nothing whatever about any Egyptian gunboat.

Smythe used Twiggers' phone to call the Israeli consulate. The consul professed no knowledge of the Egyptian gunboat.

He tried to get the Russian consul. But the Russian refused to talk to him.

"Well—okay, Captain," said Smythe. "Thank you for your time. I'm going aboard that sailor's ship tomorrow morning and talk to the people on it. I still think there is something to this story."

⚓ CHAPTER TWENTY-ONE

Finale

AFTER MAKING his deal with Smythe, Adams proceeded to the nearest bar and got himself well crocked. He returned to the ship about 7:30 P.M. and found only Scuttlebutt and Fatso aboard, playing acey-deucy.

Adams seated himself across the table from them with a silly smirk on his face. "We're all going to be famous," he said. "We'll be ce-leb-rities."

Fatso and Scuttlebutt regarded him disdainfully and went on with their game.

"We'll all be better known than the astronauts," said Adams.

"What the hell have you been drinking, anyway?" asked Scuttlebutt.

"They'll probably have our pictures on the cover of the next issue of *Time*," declared Adams. "And personal interviews with everybody."

"I think he's high on pot," said Fatso. "You better go to bed, kid, and sleep it off. You'll feel better in the morning."

"Cap'n," said Adams, "it's going to make you another John Paul Jones."

"What the hell are you talking about anyway?" asked Fatso.

"You're going to be in *Time* Magazine next week, skipper," said Adams. "The whole damn story about the Egyptian gunboat."

"You must be nuts. What makes you think so?" asked Fatso.

Adams reached into his jumper pocket, fished out the memo of his deal with Smythe and flipped it across the table to Fatso. "Read that," he said.

Fatso's eyes popped when he read it. "Why you lowdown son of a bitch," he exclaimed. "You mean to say you spilled that story to *Time?*"

"I sure do," said Adams. "And I'm getting two grand for it—and that's nothing to what I'll get from *Life* or *Look* for my personal eyewitness story."

"Well, god damn you!" said Fatso. "You've sure put my ass in a bight—and maybe some other high-level asses, too."

"That just squares us up for that haircut you gave me, skipper," said Adams. "My friend Smythe will be aboard first thing in the morning to talk to all the boys and check up on this story. . . . You want a drink, skipper?" he asked, unwrapping a bottle of whiskey he had brought aboard.

"No," said Fatso. Scuttlebutt shook his head, too.

Adams took a long pull from the bottle. "That *Time* Magazine guy is all excited about this story," he said. "Thinks it's going to be the story of the year. . . . Well . . . I gotta be up bright-eyed and bushy-tailed to meet him when he comes aboard in the morning."

So saying he took another long swig from the bottle, got up from the table, staggered over to his bunk, collapsed in it clothes and all, and passed out.

"That son of a bitch," said Scuttlebutt.

"Gawd almighty," said Fatso. "There will be brass-bound hell to pay about this. This will stir up a high-level international rhubarb and before it's over we'll be ground up to hamburger. I'll probably get ten years in Portsmouth for it . . . and maybe the Admiral will, too."

"Yeah," said Scuttlebutt. "You may go to Portsmouth. But not the Admiral. The worst they would do to him would be to retire him on three-quarters pay."

"We gotta figure some way to kill that story," said Fatso.

"You'll have a hell of a time killing it now that Adams has spilled it to this *Time* guy," said Scuttlebutt. "They'll print it come hell or high water."

"Well, so far they've only got Adams' word for it," said Fatso. "None of our other guys will talk. If we could get Adams out of here the reporter wouldn't be able to back up his story."

"Well, he's out like a light now," said Scuttlebutt, indicating the prostrate figure on the bunk. "Maybe we could stick him in the brig for a couple of days and hide him."

"That's no good," said Fatso. "We gotta make the son of a

bitch disappear. Get rid of him."

"You mean bump him off, Cap'n?" asked Scuttlebutt respectfully.

"No. Not exactly," said Fatso. "But we gotta get him a long ways away from here—and fast. . . . By gawd, if I could get to the Admiral I think I could swing it."

"Well, the *Milwaukee* ain't showing any absentee lights, so the Admiral's aboard," said Scuttlebutt.

"By gawd, I'm going out and see the old guy right now," said Fatso. "I'll change clothes and get a boat from the OOD. Meantime, you keep an eye on that guy," he said, indicating Adams, "and make sure he doesn't get ashore again."

"He won't come to until morning," said Scuttlebutt.

"Well, if he does, give him a couple of husky shots out of that bottle and pass him out again," said Fatso. "And by the way—did we turn in Adams' record and pay accounts to the *Alamo* today?"

"No," said Scuttlebutt, "I was going to take them up to the exec's office tomorrow morning."

"That's good," said Fatso. "The *Alamo* has never heard of this guy Adams. If things work out right they never will. Keep those records and pay accounts handy in case we need them tonight. . . . I ought to be back in about an hour."

Fatso shifted to dress blues, got a boat from the OOD, and soon was aboard the *Milwaukee*.

Sailors don't just go aboard the flagship at odd hours of the day or night and get to see the Admiral. The Admiral is protected by a large staff whose job it is to see that only those people with problems of prime importance get in to see the Admiral.

The first underling to interview Fatso was the staff duty officer, a young Lieutenant. "And what do you wish to see the Admiral about?" he asked skeptically.

"It's a private matter that I can only discuss with the Admiral," said Fatso.

"Well, I gotta know more about it than that," said the Lieutenant.

"It's about that Russian defector that you got this morning," said Fatso.

"Okay. I'll let you talk to our intelligence officer about that," said the Lieutenant.

"I want to talk to the Admiral about that Russian defector that you picked up today," said Fatso when he was ushered into the intelligence office.

"Oh? What about her?" asked the Lieutenant Commander.

"I have some more information on her that the Admiral ought to know about," said Fatso.

"Okay," said the Lieutenant Commander. "I'll be glad to listen to it."

"I've gotta tell it to the Admiral," said Fatso.

"Humph," said the Lieutenant Commander. "Well, you gotta tell me more than that before I bother the Admiral with it at this time of night."

"How about the Chief of Staff? Can I see him?" asked Fatso.

"Not until you tell me what this is all about," said the Lieutenant Commander. "We shipped that Russian off to the States this afternoon, so there's nothing more we can do about the case now, anyway."

"Okay, sir," said Fatso. "Thank you."

Fatso made his way up to the Admiral's country and presented himself to the marine orderly on duty outside the cabin door. "Boatswain's Mate Gioninni to see the Admiral," he announced.

"What about?" demanded the marine.

"I dunno," said Fatso. "He sent for me."

"Oh," said the marine. "What's your name again?"

"Gioninni," said Fatso.

"Okay. Wait here," said the marine, and disappeared into the cabin. He reappeared a moment later, said, "Follow me," and led the way in.

The Admiral was seated at his desk in a lounging robe reading a book. "Well well, Fatso," he said. "Back again so soon? What can I do for you?"

"I got trouble, sir," said Fatso.

"That's nothing new to you. You ought to be used to it by this time. Have a seat," said the Admiral. "What is it this time? The Italian cops or the MP's?"

"It may be more than that, sir. This is high-level international stuff," said Fatso.

"Okay. I'm listening," said the Admiral.

"You remember that Russian defector we talked about this morning?" said Fatso.

"Yes indeed," said the Admiral. "I had a talk with her. She's quite a gal and may be very useful to us. We shipped her out to the States this afternoon."

"And you know that Egyptian gunboat that everybody is looking for?"

"Yes. Sure. The *America* has a big air search out looking for her," said the Admiral.

"Well, Admiral—we intercepted that ship off Cape Bon about four days ago. We was flying Russian colors. Tania and I went aboard and persuaded the Spigs that we were Russians sent to take charge of them."

The Admiral blinked and shook his head like a fighter who has just stopped a haymaker with his jaw. He stomped out his cigarette and leaned forward intently.

"Then we brought her in here to Naples," continued Fatso. "I got in touch with the Israeli underground here and they snuck aboard last night while the Spigs were on my ship watching the movies, and took her out. She should get in to Haifa in about four days."

"Good God," said the Admiral.

"There was no rough stuff involved at all, Admiral," said Fatso. "Except we did have to knock out the gangway watch. But we left him on board. We took the rest of the crew out to the Russian consulate, dumped them there, and left 'em."

"God almighty!" said the Admiral. "That story that Com South called me about this afternoon was true—every word of it. And I told him it was an out-and-out fairy story."

"Yes sir," said Fatso. "A new guy on my ship gave the whole story to *Time* Magazine here this afternoon. I just found out about it."

"Boy oh boy!" said the Admiral. "This will precipitate an international crisis that will shake the E-Ring of the Pentagon. It will mean back to the farm for me. . . . But I've had it pretty good for forty years and I'm about due to retire anyway," he added.

"Well, Admiral, this story hasn't broken yet—and maybe we can stop it," said Fatso.

"I'd sure like to know how," said the Admiral.

"Well, so far the only dope this *Time* guy has on this thing is from this lad of mine. He's coming down to my ship first thing in the morning to check the story. If we could get rid of this one guy, I guarantee you he'll get nothing out of the rest of my guys."

"Uh huh," said the Admiral.

"This guy is back aboard ship drunk now. He's passed out. We can move him around like a sack of rags. How about transferring him tonight to some out-of-the-way place like, say, Port Lyauty?"

"Hmmm," said the Admiral. "Maybe. . . . If this *Time* guy comes aboard tomorrow morning and all your people deny the story, and if his source of information has disappeared, he would probably be pretty leery of using it—just on the say-so of one sailor that he couldn't produce."

"That's right, Admiral," agreed Fatso. "And the *Alamo* knows nothing about this guy Adams. He hasn't been taken up on their books yet. So far as they know, there is no such guy. And all of my guys will deny knowing anything about him."

"That's good," said the Admiral. "How about Tania? What does the *Alamo* know about her?"

"Nobody knows nothing, sir—except the skipper, and he wouldn't give a newspaper reporter the time of day."

"Okay," said the Admiral. "So the only other sources of info that the *Time* guy might have would be the Spig crew or the Russian consul—and I don't think any of them will want to talk to him—the story would make them look foolish."

"That's right," said Fatso. "So, like you said, the only thing he will have to go by is the say-so of a sailor he never saw before and who has disappeared. He won't dare use the story."

"Okay," said the Admiral, buzzing for the orderly. "Tell the Chief of Staff I want to see him," he told the marine.

"Joe," said the Admiral, when the Chief of Staff came into the cabin, "Gioninni here has just told me a very interesting story. Maybe someday later I'll tell it to you. But right now we have an urgent matter which requires immediate attention."

"Yes sir," said the Chief of Staff.

"There is a man attached to Gioninni's ship now. He is on board drunk. Passed out. It is urgent that he be transferred to Naval HQ, Vietnam. I want him on his way tonight with an armed escort who is to stay with him till they put him on the plane in Honolulu. You can use my plane tonight to fly him to Rota."

"Aye aye, sir," said the Chief of Staff, as if the Admiral had just told him to have his barge called away. "I'll take care of it."

"Here's his name, rate, and serial number, sir," said Fatso, handing the Chief of Staff a slip of paper. "If you'll send a car to the after gangway of the *Alamo*, we'll have him and his records ready."

"Okay," said the COS. "We'll have a car on the dock alongside your ship in a little over an hour. . . . Anything else, sir?"

"That's all," said the Admiral.

An operation of this kind takes a bit of doing. Orders have to be written up, an escort provided, a car sent to the dock, the plane's crew have to be rounded up and briefed, and confidential dispatches have to be sent to various commands along the line, alerting them to the fact that this is a special case. But when Com Sixth Fleet issues a sweeping directive to his COS, as the Admiral just had, a large and efficient organization springs into action and these things all happen.

An hour and a half later a station wagon pulled up alongside the after gangway of the *Alamo*. Adams, dead to the world, was lugged down the gangway and loaded into the station wagon with the contents of his locker in a sea bag. His records were turned over to the escort, and he was whisked out to the airfield and loaded aboard the Admiral's plane. Three hours later the plane landed at the naval base, Rota, Spain; and Adams, still dead to the world, was loaded into a MATS plane bound for Maguire Air Force Base, New Jersey. He came to halfway across the Atlantic in a rather confused state, and the escort confused it some more by feeding him liquor until he passed out again. Next time he came to, he was halfway across the Pacific to Honolulu. Forty-eight hours after hehad passed out on LCU 1124 in Naples, he staggered down the gangway of the big jet transport at the Saigon airport. There he was put aboard a whirlybird, which landed him on board the USS *Suwanee* in the Mekong River, where he was assigned to duty peeling spuds in the galley.

This all happened so smoothly and so fast, and his state of sobriety was so sketchy, that Adams remembered very little of it when he finally sobered up. However, this experience did teach him that there is no use in a little guy like him trying to buck the Establishment. He gave up his old hippie ideas, shaved off his beard, and became an exemplary U.S. Navy sailor—more or less.

Meantime, back in Naples, Smythe showed up on the *Alamo* promptly at 0900 next morning and was shown aboard LCU 1124.

"I'm Smythe of *Time* Magazine," he announced to Fatso.

"Oh?" said Fatso. "What can we do for you, Mr. Smith?"

"I've come aboard to see one of your crew by the name of Adams."

"Adams?" said Fatso. "We have no one on board by that name."

"He told me his name was Adams, and that he was on this

boat," said Smythe.

"Well, maybe he gave you a phony name," said Fatso. "What sort of a looking guy was he?"

"He was a young guy, with a billiard-ball haircut and a heavy black beard," said Smythe.

"We got nobody aboard who looks like that," said Fatso.

"Well, maybe you can answer some questions for me," said Smythe.

"I'll be glad to if I can," said Fatso.

"First of all, what do you know about that Egyptian gunboat that disappeared from Hampton Roads about two weeks ago?"

"Nothin' except what we've heard on the radio," said Fatso. "I think she was sighted passing through Gib four or five days ago."

"Well, I met a sailor yesterday who told me his name was Adams and he belonged on this ship. He said you guys had intercepted this Egyptian gunboat, put an Israeli crew on board, and she was now on her way to Haifa."

"Well, that's a hell of a yarn, all right," said Fatso. "All I can say is this guy took you for a hell of a sleigh ride. He musta been drunk."

"Of course, even if the story is true," said Smythe, "you would probably have orders from Sixth Fleet to deny it."

"Well, you can talk to anybody you want to in my crew about it. You can check with personnel on the *Alamo* and find out we got no Adams on board. I think some young sailor just got himself a skinful and decided to tell you a good story," said Fatso.

"I'd like to talk to some of the other sailors in your crew," said Smythe.

"Okay," said Fatso. "If you don't believe me, Mr. Smith, talk to as many of them as you like. But if you believe all the wild tales they tell you you'll be in trouble."

Smythe talked to all the rest of the crew but got nothing about the Egyptian out of them. They all claimed that all they knew about it was what they had heard on the radio. They all claimed they had never heard of Adams and looked blank when he mentioned the Russian defector. He checked with the personnel office of the *Alamo* and found they had no one by the name of Adams aboard. He made inquiries along the waterfront and at the OOD's office of the amphib base. No one knew anything about any Egyptian gunboat.

Smythe went back to his office and made out a voucher for fifty dollars entertainment expenses to send in on his next expense account. Then he got busy trying to sniff out other exclusive stories of global interest for his magazine.

The day after the Egyptian sailed from Naples, naval HQ, Tel Aviv, got a secret dispatch from their underground HQ Naples giving them the dope on what was happening. The Israeli Navy had been in bad odor since the *Liberty* incident, so this was manna from heaven for them. They sent out three gunboats to meet the Egyptian just north of Cyprus and escort her in to Haifa, and their public-relations people pulled out all the stops on the story.

The night before she arrived, Jerusalem announced that the Israeli Navy had intercepted, boarded, and captured the ship off the Libyan coast and was bringing her in by a round-about route from the north. This, of course, was front-page stuff all over the world because by this time the whereabouts of the missing Egyptian was the number-one mystery in the world press. A large delegation of press, radio, and TV assembled in Haifa to meet her.

Her arrival in Haifa was a triumph. All ships in the harbor were full dressed and the city was bedecked with flags. A huge crowd assembled on the waterfront and bands played while the mayor and high local officials gathered on the dock to greet the conquering heroes as the ship tied up. There was a parade up the main drag and out to the airport, where they were loaded into a whirlybird and whisked up to Jerusalem for the biggest celebration since the six-day war.

When Goldberg and his crew came back from Jerusalem they threw a big party at the underground HQ for Fatso and his boys.

"Boy, they really rolled out the red carpet for us in Jerusalem," said Goldberg. "The kind of a welcome you guys give the astronauts."

"Did you see Benny there?" asked Fatso.

"Yeah. We saw him, and told him the whole story. He said to tell you guys you may have prevented a world war from breaking out because our Navy had ships off Benghazi to intercept that craft. And if it had come to a showdown, there was going to be shooting between them and the Russians."

"That's too bad," said Fatso. "I'm beginning to think you guys might even take the Russians. . . . What did you do with that gangway watch that we knocked out and left aboard?"

"Oh, he came over to our side," said Goldberg. "He's in the Israeli Army now."

A few days later C in C Southern Europe and Com Sixth Fleet were seated in the officers club having a drink.

"Well," said the C in C, pointing to the latest issue of *Time* lying on the table with a feature story about the Egyptian gunboat in it, "there *was* a grain of truth in that *Time* man's story after all."

"Ummm," said Com Sixth Fleet.

"The Israeli Navy did quite a job snatching that ship without us ever knowing about it."

"Ummm," observed Com Sixth Fleet.

"Actually, I'm glad we had nothing whatever to do with it," said the C in C. "If we had found her for them and told them where she was, it could have stirred up a hell of a hassle with Nasser and the Russians."

"Ummm," said Com Sixth Fleet. "I'm glad it turned out the way it did."